GALAXY'S EDGE

EDITED BY MIKE RESNICK

I0554551

ISSUE 35: November 2018

Mike Resnick, Editor
Taylor Morris, Copyeditor
Shahid Mahmud, Publisher

Published by Arc Manor/Phoenix Pick
P.O. Box 10339
Rockville, MD 20849-0339

Galaxy's Edge is published in January, March, May, July, September, and November.

Please check our website for submission guidelines.

ISBN: 978-1-61242-438-5

SUBSCRIPTION INFORMATION:
Paper and digital subscriptions are available (including via Amazon.com) . Please visit our home page: www.GalaxysEdge.com

ADVERTISING:
Advertising is available in all editions of the magazine. Please contact advert@GalaxysEdge.com.

FOREIGN LANGUAGE RIGHTS:
Please refer all inquiries pertaining to foreign language rights to Shahid Mahmud, Arc Manor, P.O. Box 10339, Rockville, MD 20849-0339. Tel: 1-240-645-2214. Fax 1-310-388-8440. Email admin@ArcManor.com.

CONTENTS

TROPE-ING THE LIGHT
FANTASTIC
THE SCIENCE BEHIND THE FICTION

EDWARD M. LERNER

THE EDITOR'S WORD

by Mike Resnick

Welcome to the thirty-fifth issue of *Galaxy's Edge*. We've got some fine new stories for you by new and newer writers Brian K. Lowe, Susan Taitel, Eleanor R. Wood, Marc A. Criley, Larry Hodges, Dantzel Cherry, and David L. Hebert, plus old friends Harry Turtledove, Mercedes Lackey, Nancy Kress, and Robert Silverberg. Our science columnist, Gregory Benford, chose to write a short story for this issue, so we prevailed upon his frequent collaborator, superstar Larry Niven, for an article to replace the column for this one issue. And, of course, we've got our Recommended Books column by Jody Lynn Nye and Bill Fawcett, our literary column by Robert J. Sawyer, and our Joy Ward Interview (which this month is with Hugo and Nebula winner and Worldcon Guest of Honor Michael Swanwick). And to round off the issue we're running part two of our serialization of Charles Sheffield's novel, *Tomorrow and Tomorrow*.

We hope you enjoy it.

I've been hearing a lot of heart-felt complaints from writers lately that the markets are drying up, that they're being faced with two unhappy alternatives: self-publishing, or not getting into print at all.

It's true that the field's been in the doldrums of late, but it's not quite facing the apocalypse. So let me make some suggestions:

- Find new sources of science fiction book income. They're out there, not in quantity, but there—relatively new publishers, small presses that are getting larger, old houses that are willing to experiment with science fiction.

- While we're on the subject of small presses, it's true that a lot of them don't pay front money. But more and more of them do. Hunt them down and see what you can sell them.

- Remember that novels aren't the only thing you can sell. If you're having problems with mass market publishers, you're certainly not going to sell them collections either, but the small presses have been the best home for collections for more than half a century, and they're still buying from established authors.

- There's a lot of work-for-hire going on these days: franchises, shared worlds, sharecrops, novelizations, adaptations. You probably won't get rich on the royalties since in most cases you'll be getting much less than for a book to which you own the copyright, but the advances are usually better than beginners or even lower midlist writers get.

- It won't pay all your bills, but there's money to be made selling short fiction to professional markets—and by SFWA's current definition, a professional market pays a minimum of a nickel a word (and usually more). There are new publications—and newly-professional publications—out there that are paying as much as the traditional ones, and there are non-science-fiction magazines that have no problem buying the occasional science fiction story.

- There are related fields to explore: horror, dark fantasy, and the burgeoning new realm of romantic fantasy.

- There's still a market, thanks to Tom Clancy, for well-written, high-tech thrillers.

- Don't overlook the audio market, which is getting larger all the time and paying very decent money for what are essentially reprint projects.

- Be creative. And while I generally hate using personal examples, I'll use some here. In the past few years, in addition to novels and short story collections, I've sold a book composed of fifty-five of my fanzine articles; a book composed of sixty-one of my professional articles dating back to the late 1960s; a book of first and final drafts of stories (a "how-to" book on revising and polishing); and a book of all my travel diaries and a few travel articles I'd sold previously. When you consider the subject matter of each, I'd almost have been willing to bet that none of them (except maybe the last one) could possibly sell, yet they all did. Like I say, be creative.

- Diversify. Every science-fiction writer has some subject of expertise other than science fiction. The late Josepha Sherman sold books on folklore. Jack Nimersheim sells computer books. Barbara Hambly sells mystery novels. Ralph Roberts sells collectors' guides and computer books. Rudy Rucker sells books on math. Karen Taylor sells erotica. Catherine Asaro sells romances. Kristine Kathryn Rusch sells mystery and romance novels. I've sold mystery novels, edited books on Africa, and often sell articles on horse racing.

You simply have to make the effort to find new sources of income—sometimes in wildly unlikely places—that can replace the temporarily closed spigots of your mass market publishers. The work—and the money—is there for the aggressive writer who goes looking for it. As an established writer, it's probably a little less than you want or are used to… but if you're one of the hundred or more disenfranchised souls I spoke to at cons during the past few years, it's more than you're getting, and it can help pay your bills until the science-fiction market comes back to healthy and vigorous life.

Brian K. Lowe has published a number of novels. His short fiction has appeared in Factor Four, *the* Timeshift *anthology, and elsewhere. This is his second appearance in* Galaxy's Edge.

RELATIVE FORTUNE

by Brian K. Lowe

When I was seventeen, class president, and a year from the Space Force Academy, Dad fell into an antique gun rack at work, dead from a stroke before he hit the floor.

I had been helping him in the pawn shop after school, partly to make some tuition money and partly because it looked good on my Academy application. After he died it was either take over the shop, or let Mom work it and my brother Rey raise himself while I ran off to the Academy. I opened up two hours after the funeral.

Every night, I'd sweep the floors, dust the shelves, double-lock the front door, and walk upstairs after a twelve-hour day of trading in things that people had once thought they couldn't live without, but now couldn't live without selling.

But while I was scratching out a living buying and selling second-hand guitars, the real money was in things that had gone Out There. Tools, spacesuits, uniform patches… And when it came to *interstellar* travel, stuff that had been to another star… Years before I was born, the first guys to come back from Proxima Centauri had gotten rich selling their underwear. The best part was that, thanks to time dilation, they were still young. They'd been able to retire in their thirties.

It hadn't taken long to come up with the Great Idea: Fly to Sirius B or Delta Pavonis with first editions, autographs, and rare coins carefully packed in your gear. When you return thirty years later, you sell your mint-condition treasures to the Earthbound and retire, a millionaire before you're forty.

Once everybody figured out space travel was the key to the good life, they all wanted in. Admission to Space Force Academy had never been easy, but it got tougher. Still, as soon as I could read, I knew that was what I wanted, and I worked every day to make myself good enough.

I ran until I threw up, did chin-ups until my arms cramped, and studied until my head hit the desk.

My little brother Rey used to tag along with me all the time, trying to keep up with my squats and sprints, pestering me with questions about my homework until I had to call Mom to get rid of him. It made me laugh, but I had to admit that he never quit until he was ready to fall over. Then he'd lie there with this weird look in his eye, and he'd say, "Next time, Tommy. Next time I'll beat you." He never beat me, but he never stopped trying, either.

Still, nobody I knew was smarter, faster, or tougher than me. I worked my ass off until I was a lock for the Academy. It was all waiting: adventure, fame, and riches available only to the best of the best.

Until my dad died.

Three years after I quit school, the Academy accepted Rey's application. The fact that he'd "helped his mother support the family after his father passed away" was a big contributing factor.

I missed his high school graduation because I had to work. I missed his Academy graduation because I *said* I had to work.

I missed his launch for Wolf 359 because I closed the store early and got drunk in the back room.

I hadn't gotten around to washing the shop windows lately, which made the afternoon light slanting through all streaky, when the door chime peeped. At first all I could see was the uniform, and I let my shoulders slump in resignation. I had been having The Conversation more and more lately, and I hated it. But it came with the territory. Nobody visited a pawnbroker unless he had no other options, not even astronauts. And nobody came to my shop unless he had hit bottom.

Then he came close enough that I could see his face. I knew it instantly, of course; it wasn't like it had changed in the past twenty years. I felt the old resentment rise up, but at the same time I felt an odd momentary sense of relief: At least he wasn't here to have *that* Conversation.

"Hello, Tommy."

"Hello, Rey. How are you?" Young, that's how he was. Aged two years for my twenty. By all rights our positions should have been reversed. I thought I'd gotten over it by now.

"Good, good. I just got back from Wolf 359." *Yeah, I kind of figured that out.* "You've still got the shop." Next he'd start talking about the weather.

"Yeah, well, where else am I going to go?" I asked with a shrug and a sheepish grin as if it actually was a rhetorical question, and not the elephant in the room. "I got married a few years ago." I didn't really want to get into it with him, but if I didn't mention Marilyn it would feel like I was ashamed of her. "You missed the wedding."

"Sorry. I…didn't get the invitation. I was out of town."

He looked around at the shelves like he was reacquainting himself with everything.

"I'm going to have a son," I added. Another thing I didn't have to hide. "You'll be an uncle."

His eyes came back to me, and his smile seemed real. "Hey, that's great."

"Yeah," I said slowly, reaching out to straighten a commemorative plate that didn't need straightening. "When you get to our age, you start thinking about your legacy, you know?" I looked him in the eye. "Oh, wait, you wouldn't know."

"Shit." Rey turned away, his hands half-raised in a gesture of frustration. "I *knew* this was a mistake. I knew you wouldn't be able to keep yourself from lording it over me."

I blinked. "Wait—what? You were the one who went to the Space Academy! You're the one who just came back from Wolf 359! You're the astronaut with the fame and the— Oh, shit…"

I finally looked at my brother, really looked at him, at his bloodshot eyes, sunken and haunted. How could I have missed that? He looked like he had spent the last twenty years on Earth, aging as I had, and not travelling at eighty percent of the speed of light.

I closed my eyes, and I promised God anything if He would just keep me from having to have The Conversation this one time.

Yes, men and women were retiring at the end of a subjective three-or five-year voyage at relativistic speeds, living easy lives with their student loans covered by their back pay and their futures greased by what they'd taken with them, collectibles removed from Time itself.

But not every investment paid off. Not every old book or musical chip became valuable. Not every famous person became a legend. Some travelers came back to find their gamble hadn't scored as big as they hoped, and that their investments were worth barely enough support them in a world whose technology was twenty or fifty years out of their grasp. But even they had something to cash out with. Some guys returned to find their "treasures" worthless and themselves broke, unemployed, and unemployable. Then they came to me, and we had the Conversation.

"Show me what you brought back, Rey."

He carefully produced a small leather case, opened it, and unwrapped a book. I didn't recognize it, but the dust cover was pristine.

"You've got to give me something! This is a first edition, signed by the author. He was a bestseller! And only five hundred copies were put to paper. This one's immaculate."

I entered the title into my database with no hope. The only astronauts who came down here had already exhausted the auction houses and the private collectors. If Rey's book were worth real money, he wouldn't have brought it to someone like me. I scanned the results slowly to make sure I didn't miss anything, then I named a figure.

"It's got to be worth more than that."

Actually, it was worth about half that, but he was my brother.

"I'm sorry, Rey, but after you left, the tourist trade started up. The guy who wrote this book, he took off for Cygnus Xi five years ago, and he took every copy of his book he could find with him. Until he gets back, they're a drug on the market."

I had never seen my brother with tears in his eyes.

"Look, Tommy, I'm sorry. I'm sorry it was me who went out there instead of you. But it's not my fault Dad died."

"Of course not," I said reasonably. "Just like it's not your fault you took off into space first chance you got instead of taking over here so I could go to the Academy too."

"Was that what I was supposed to do? Come back here to push a broom around in the dust so you could go back to school? It was six years since they accepted you! You think they just leave those spots open so anybody can waltz in whenever he wants?"

"That was my dream! I was supposed to explore space! I was supposed to be the one getting rich and famous…" My voice trailed off.

"Yeah, because that worked out so well for me! Do you know what it's like out there? They tell you it's great and beautiful and heroic—it's crap! Two years of living in a tin can with no windows and the same fifty people and there's nowhere to go to get away from them!" He leaned into me. "And you want to talk about getting rich? Do you know why I bought this book and took off and left you in this store? Because I was gonna come back here someday and *rescue you*! I was gonna sell it and split the money with you so that we would both have a chance to live better than Mom and Dad did, above a goddamned pawnshop! Sorry, that didn't work out, so now we're both screwed! At least you've got a job and wife and a kid—what have I got?"

I choked on my reply, my mouth hanging open. Had I gone to the Space Academy, and to Wolf 359, I would have done the same as Rey did, and I would've been standing there with him offering me twice what my merchandise was worth…

"This has nothing to do with us," I said, trying to control my breathing. "Or who left and who stayed. It's just the way things are."

"So that's it, then?" Rey gave an exaggerated shrug. "That's just how it is? The universe doesn't care about us? Nothin' we do makes a difference? Then what am I gonna do, Tommy?" Rey's voice was breaking again. "I left here when I was eighteen. I hadn't had time to build up any bank accounts or buy any stocks. My back pay's barely covering my loans. *This* was supposed to make the difference."

All of a sudden I was fighting back tears myself.

"Look. I can give you a job here. It won't pay much, but it's a start. Marilyn and I can set up a room for you upstairs, at least until you know what you're going to do next."

Rey shook his head. "No. You've got a baby coming. You're going to need that room." Suddenly he had that weird light in his eye again, that "Next time I'll beat you" look. "I know what I'm gonna do," he said, pointing his book at me. "I've still got skills. And I've got experience. I'm gonna get re-trained, and I'm gonna get me a job on one of those tourist ships you were talking about. I'm going to sail as far and as long as I can, and I'm gonna take more shit with me, and when I come back here in fifty or sixty years, I'll have something that's *worth* something."

He tucked the little volume back into the felt-covered case where it had sat protected for twenty of my years, and stood up. We looked at each other, hugged awkwardly, and broke free quickly.

"Goodbye," he said. I wondered how many more times I'd see him. He'd have to work two jobs even to make enough to finance his loans, and space training was intense. I knew I'd drop everything to see him when he took off again, but by the time he got back, I'd probably be dead.

"Rey, wait!" I pulled a comic book, carefully sealed in archival plastic, out from its niche behind my counter. "Here. This is a first issue of *The Stellar Gang*. It came out after you left, so it's not very old, but they're talking about making a movie." I shrugged.

Rey gave me a sad smile. "Save it for your son."

As I watched him walk out, I thought about how many people were heading starward every year, every one of them carrying something in his luggage that he hoped would appreciate over time. The odds against them were getting longer. Rey would never give up, but that didn't mean he'd ever win.

For a long time, I had envied him. He manned a starship; I manned a pawn shop. He was looking to succeed while he was young; I was trying to make it before I was old. But I had a wife, and a baby on the way, and he had an old book by an author whose name would probably be forgotten before either of them returned. I laughed to myself: then they'd both be broke. At least I had my shop.

Rey's voice echoed in my head. "'That's just how it is? The universe doesn't care about us? Nothin' we do makes a difference?'"

No. I could make a difference. I had already started. Marilyn and I had opened small account for the baby, ten bucks a week, rain or shine. I e-mailed my bank, opened another account, this one in Rey's name. I put ten bucks in it. I could do the same every month. Marilyn wouldn't begrudge Rey ten bucks a month. Our gift to the future. Rey's future.

Because if we don't look out for each other, the universe wins.

Copyright © 2018 by Brian K. Lowe

Eleanor R. Wood, who resides in England, has been published in Flash Fiction Online, Daily Science Fiction, Deep Magic, *and various anthologies. This is her first appearance in* Galaxy's Edge.

THE CONVINCER

by Eleanor R. Wood

A creature limited to the physical plane is a primitive animal. The Dispenser of Justice transmitted for all to comprehend, but I knew her thoughts were directed largely at me. A dozen spectators and three lesser Dispensers floated in the ether, awaiting her judgement.

The cool, dark space of the non-corporeal planes usually relaxed me. There was comfort in their sensory deprivation, in groups of minds interacting without physical distraction. But today I was tense. I longed for solid ground beneath me.

You have made a reasonable case for these animals' intelligence, Convincer Vla, but even if I accept it, mere intelligence is not enough to put them on a par with us. They are incapable of comprehending our lives. They will never be our equals. What you propose would place on them a burden of responsibility they cannot even recognize. Our basic right to freedom of movement, for instance, is irrelevant to a species that can only move on one plane of existence.

We can at least grant them freedom of movement within that plane! My protest fell into nothing as her transmittance interceptor caught and blocked it. No further thoughts could be transmitted from my quarter; my arguments were made, and I already knew I'd lost.

Their present existence contributes vastly to our knowledge and wellbeing. If they are as intellectual as you propose, they must have the capacity to realize the greater good they serve. And need I remind the chamber of the damage these creatures have historically caused? Their subjugation secures their future as well as our own. It could be argued that to free them would be a cruelty far outweighing the perceived injustice of keeping them held. I therefore cannot condone your argument for greater rights for these animals, Convincer Vla. They shall remain, as ever, under our domain.

She emitted a pulse of light, signifying the end of the proceedings. There were mindwaves of cheer from the spectators. I flipped myself into the physical and cursed vehemently.

☼

There was no use in delaying my visit to those I'd represented. I exported myself to the building in which they were being held and took their form as I entered. It limited my senses, but made it easier on them to see me like this, and I felt more able to imagine how they experienced the world when my body looked and moved as theirs did. I extended the long, ungainly limbs and moved forward on them. Bipeds were such odd creatures to emulate. It had taken me weeks of using limbs shaped like theirs before I felt I could move without making a fool of myself. The hands were the strangest of all. Hands! Primates had such comical features. But I knew their primitive appearance belied their intelligent minds.

I arrived at their complex and took minor satisfaction in the small victory I'd achieved in having them moved here. Their barren, former cells had offered them no mental stimulation and hardly any room to move. Primates needed opportunities to utilize those ungainly limbs. They were also highly social creatures that languished when kept alone.

The four of them looked up as I entered. I'd demanded simulations of trees and grass for them, despite the Handlers' assurances that they couldn't possibly miss what they'd never had. The Handlers were wrong. The looks of wonder and joy on their expressive faces had told me as much as if they'd had the ability to transmit.

I'm sorry, I told them, knowing they couldn't reply but as certain as ever that they could make sense of my thoughts.

The largest of them, a male with sandy head-hair and sharp eyes, turned away from me and placed his face in his hands. The two females made awful whimpering cries, and all three began excreting moisture from their facial orifices. It was a behavior I had come to recognize as great sadness, and my own grief and frustration rose with theirs.

The fourth was another male, older than his companions. He shook his head from side to side at me and emitted what felt like a cynical grunt. He glared at me for a moment, forelimbs crossed before him, and went to sit in a corner on his own. The other three were communicating in their crude sound-based language. I'd never learned to understand more than a handful of sounds, although I knew one or two of the most experienced Handlers could make out much of it. I privately doubted some of their interpretations, but at least they acknowledged these beings possessed language. I wished I could have said the same of the rest of my species.

I hear I'm still in a job, Tij, one of the Handlers transmitted, importing himself beside me. He exuded the contempt I'd begun to expect from him. At first, he'd championed my cause, sharing my belief that the sentients deserved better from us. But when he realized I wasn't campaigning for better conditions, but for the freedoms they'd had before we arrived, his attitude changed. Handlers had transmitted organized objections across all planes ever since my case was announced. There were plenty of other Doers who supported me, but the voice of continued oppression was greater.

For now, I replied. But I knew I'd exhausted all avenues. The Dispenser of Justice had spoken.

☼

After my defeat, I needed a rest from the wet, green planet and its dimensionally-challenged occupants. More than that, I needed a rest from my own kind. Doers' arrogance had long disgusted me, and it was stronger now than ever. We had exported from our planetary dimension to this one simply because we could. We sought new forms to emulate and new elements with which to adapt our bodies' molecular structures. Second nature to us was incomprehensible to these beings. But our capabilities did not make us superior, only different.

I was so tired of making that argument. Even some of my fellow campaigners were starting to concede to the Dispenser's "wisdom." Questioning another Doer's expertise was akin to proclaiming yourself their peer. And that was career suicide. Why specialize in one area only to later claim yourself specialist in another?

I receded to a private interdimensional pocket that I used for refreshing and centring myself. Alone in my own mind, I hibernated there, my body's needs suspended.

The New World had completed an entire solar revolution before I returned.

☼

I entered the Convincers' plane desperate to sink myself into a new case. The sentients' freedom had been denied, but I would revamp my campaign for better conditions. The moment I exported from hibernation, I was seized by another's thoughts.

Convincer Vla! You have returned at last.

Convincer Ahn, I acknowledged my colleague.

An event has transpired in your absence. A biped approached the Center for Terrestrial Lifeform Study of its own accord.

A domestic one?

No. Wild.

This was unheard of. Wild sentients avoided the Center at all cost.

What happened to it? A sense of dread began to creep in. Wild capture was frowned upon, but it still happened, especially if a sentient was foolish enough to present itself.

They took it, of course. The capture was unlike any I've ever witnessed. The biped went with the Handlers almost as if it trusted them.

Are you sure it wasn't domesticated? Wild sentients refused to approach Doers even when we took their form.

It had all the marks of wildlife. Fabric-draped, proud stature, carrying tools. We believe it emerged from one of their underground sanctuaries.

What have they done with it? I tried unsuccessfully to keep the outrage from my transmission.

They began a course of study, naturally. But what they found astounded us all.

Ahn paused and I felt him anticipating my reaction.

It transmitted thought to them.

I exported myself to the Center for Terrestrial Lifeform Study as if Ahn's last thought had propelled me there itself.

☼

Studier Pha met me outside her laboratory. She had the form of a diminutive female with tint-ed skin and glossy black head-hair. She looked askance at me.

It really is best if you take their form.

In my haste, I'd maintained my amorphous state. *Apologies. I forgot I hadn't.*

Shifting into the tall, female, biped form I usually adopted, I followed her inside. My gait was unsteady as I adjusted to the body's new balance; it had been more than a solar cycle since I'd last conformed to their shape. My skin felt tight.

I know you won't approve, but we've kept this one isolated, Pha transmitted as we walked through a corridor. *We allowed her to keep her tools. She spends long hours utilising them.*

What sort of tools?

Mostly transcribing implements. She makes endless marks on paper.

Do you concede yet that those marks have meaning? I tried not to sound snide, but it had long aggravated me that the sentients' propensity for inscribing symbols was attributed to some poorly-understood instinct. At least the Studiers had stopped referring to it as a "reflex."

Pha paused. *I am inclined to believe so. But this one is poised to change everything we believe about these creatures. The mark-making is but one aspect.*

She transmitted nothing else until we reached the chamber.

We imported ourselves inside. Sitting cross-legged on the floor was a dark-skinned female. She'd been allowed her fabric coverings, which encased her lower limbs and torso. Her head-hair was neatly arranged upon her skull in tight rows tied loosely at her neck. She regarded me with an astounding gaze, her dark eyes seeming to scrutinize me in a way the domestic sentients never had.

Nadia, this is Convincer Vla. Pha's thoughts were transmitted widely enough for both of us.

Nadia? I asked of Pha alone.

It is the name she gives herself. It seems fitting to use it.

I barely concealed my astonishment. A name, given to herself. *And she transmitted this to you?* My transmission was for the biped as well this time.

I DID.

The thought slammed into me with all the subtlety of a juvenile learning to transmit. Only worse. It had an artificial edge, as if originating from a non-organic source. The sentient gave voice at the same instant, her crude language presumably mirroring the transmission.

How did she do that? I sent in shock to Pha.

We don't know for certain. But she has an artificial device implanted in her brain. We are unable to study it without risking her life, but she tells us it enables her to communicate.

This…this is incredible. I looked at Pha. Her primate face wore an expression I'd learned to interpret as satisfaction. I had no idea how to make my borrowed face do that.

As I said, this one changes everything.

My thoughts raced. I'd longed to communicate with sentients for so long, and now I couldn't think where to begin. So many questions…

I sat my awkward body on the floor across from her. She met my eyes with a boldness I'd never encountered from her species.

Why did you come here? I asked.

She moved her mouth in the gesture for acceptance or pleasure. *TO STUDY YOU.*

I reeled, both from the force of her transmission and the implications of it.

You *came to study us?*

WHY SHOULD THAT SURPRISE YOU?

I was struck that it didn't. I was amazed, but not surprised.

What do you hope to learn?

EVERYTHING.

Everything…about us?

WHO YOU ARE. WHY YOU ARE HERE. WHY YOU SUBJECT US TO SUCH ABUSE.

Her calm, composed expression filled me with shame. Suddenly I didn't want to be right. This being was sitting before me proving my instincts were correct, and I wished she wasn't. I was newly appalled at everything Doers had inflicted on these bipeds since we arrived. They were complex, intelligent beings, just as I had tried to demonstrate to the Dispenser of Justice. And Nadia was proof.

I didn't want to face her. I exported from the cramped chamber and stood in the corridor, listening to the distant cries of other incarcerated primates. Pha imported beside me and stood silent in her smooth-skinned form.

Aren't you pleased to be vindicated? she finally asked.

I'm ashamed. Ashamed of everything we do to them. Ashamed I didn't try harder to win my case.

I know you Convincers. I find it difficult to believe you could have tried any harder.

What will happen to her? I asked, changing the subject.

It appears she wishes to stay here, so we will keep her, for now at least.

She needs better conditions, a larger chamber, the company of her own kind. Can she be housed with my former clients?

I suppose so. But why don't you ask her what she would like?

I regarded the Studier for a moment and imported myself back into the chamber with a final thought.

I wish to speak with her alone.

Nadia looked at me, her sharp eyes keen and wary. She picked up an inscribing implement and began to scrawl marks on the sheaf of paper before her.

What are you doing? I asked her.

WRITING, she boomed.

Can you explain to me what that is?

THE COMMITMENT OF WORDS TO PAPER. IT ENABLES ME TO RECORD MY THOUGHTS AND OBSERVATIONS AS I INTERACT WITH YOU.

I sagged in amazement. I knew it.

So it isn't just random marks?

WHY WOULD I EXPEND SO MUCH ENERGY ON NONSENSE?

I decided to shift topics. *Nadia, I don't understand. If you know what goes on here, why would you willingly subject yourself to it?*

She stopped writing and met my false gaze. *YOU SOUND AS THOUGH YOU DISAPPROVE OF YOUR OWN EXPERIMENTS.*

They're not my experiments. I have long opposed the way your species is treated.

I sensed surprise from her for the first time. *IS THAT WHY YOU CAME TO SEE ME?*

Yes. I have always believed there was more to your species than mine gave you credit for. You are the living proof of all I have longed to show my fellows.

She turned up her mouth in the approving gesture again. *THEN IT SEEMS YOU ARE MY LIVING PROOF THAT YOUR SPECIES IS NOT BLIND TO OUR SUFFERING.*

You need better living conditions than this. I managed to secure space and plants and simulated daylight for the group of sentients I once represented. Would you like to join them?

She nodded her head. *I WOULD LIKE THAT. VERY MUCH. AND... WE ARE "HUMANS."*

Humans? Their name for themselves?

HUMAN BEINGS.

I will arrange to have you moved.

I exported myself from the room and clamoured my astonishment to Pha. Nadia's revelations were almost too much to take in.

✧

Over the following cycles, I spent almost every moment with Nadia. I held long conversations with her, I observed her interactions with the domestics, I watched her recording her own observations in turn. At no point did she seem distressed, and her calm presence seemed to soothe the others. She told me their language was a less sophisticated version of hers, which was a revelation of its own. These creatures had multiple languages. I still couldn't make out what they said to one another, and despite my requests, Nadia showed no interest in teaching me. I suspected she preferred to keep us ignorant of their communications.

Why you? I asked her one day. *What made you the chosen human for this mutual study?*

I MADE THE DECISION TO COME, THOUGH I WAS ADVISED AGAINST IT. MY LIFE'S WORK HAS BEEN THE STUDY OF YOUR SPECIES, BUT ALWAYS FROM AFAR. I KNEW I WOULD PROGRESS NO FURTHER WITHOUT SPENDING TIME WITH YOU UP CLOSE.

So you are a Studier among humans? You have enclaves, as we do?

OF A SORT. WHAT YOU CALL "STUDIERS," WE CALL "SCIENTISTS."

An interesting concept. Doers of science. And brave ones at that.

You willingly put yourself in danger for your career?

She contemplated this for a moment. *YES. SOMETIMES IT IS THE ONLY WAY TO LEARN.*

These beings were more like Doers than we ever imagined. I was even more determined that their incarceration must end.

✧

You know there is no re-petition once the Dispenser has spoken, Ahn transmitted.

Of course I do. My reply was sharp.

Then what do you propose? another Convincer asked. The Convincers' plane hummed with minds in the darkness. I had sent a wide transmission to my fellows to see what our collective expertise might suggest.

The law is final, came another thought, strongly tinged with disapproval.

I softened my tone. *Has it ever occurred to any of my fellow Convincers that perhaps the law is not always right?*

A slow emanation of shock, outrage, even fear began to fill my mindspace. I had uttered a blasphemy among Convincers.

I have heard enough. This angry transmission was followed by a sudden absence as its emanator exported from the meeting. I immediately sensed several other exports as staunch Convincers departed. I knew some of them personally. Their disapproval stung. I wondered, not for the first time, if this cause was worth the risk to my career and identity. It was too late now. The thought could not be recalled, so I could only plough ahead.

I sensed concern and dismay from those who remained, but mingled with enough curiosity that I believed they'd hear me out. *We do not question the law, and for good reason. It is all we have, all we are as Convincers. But just as new circumstances call for new laws, so new revelations call for re-evaluation of the law. The human Nadia is the proof I lacked during my attempt to convince the Dispensers this species should not be subject to our whims. If she had been here at the time, I believe my convincing would have succeeded.*

But she was not! transmitted Convincer Kav, one of the most experienced among us. I mentally nudged him to carry on.

This human may indeed hold new revelations about their species, but she is not proof they all share her capacity. And even if she were proof now, she was not at the time of your convincing, Vla. Once the Dispenser has spoken, there is no reversing the proclamation. The day a Convincer publicly questions a Dispenser is the day our profession is ruined. And that Convincer would make herself a pariah. An Undoer.

I had suspected the objections would find their way here, but I recoiled at his thought nevertheless. An Undoer was nobody, a being without identity or purpose, caught between two professions or none at all, useless to society. I could yet turn back and steer myself from this path. But the image of Nadia was firm in my mind. Nadia, observing us with the scrutiny we turned on her. Nadia, making her endless, complicated writing marks, recording every observation with exceptional detail. Nadia, meeting my shapeshifted eyes and staring through my disguise in a way the domestics had never done. She was remarkable, shrewd, clever. And whatever Kav had to say, she was proof. Even if only a handful of the humans had her intelligence and capability, we owed rights to them all. A destructive species they may have been, but they were also bright and intuitive and brimming with emotion and creativity. If I turned my back on them now, I would be an Undoer in my own mind. If I risked being so in everyone else's, so be it.

I mustered my thoughts. *Come and visit Nadia. All of you. Come and see her for yourselves. Commune with her. Hear what she has to say. If afterward you still believe the law should remain unquestioned, I will ask no more of you. But if abandoning the humans to our morphological studies and abuses feels unpalatable after meeting her, join me in finding a way to make this right.*

They were silent as they took in my words. Then, one by one, they exported calmly from our plane. I wondered how many would accept my invitation.

What happens when your study is complete? I asked Nadia later that day.

She regarded me with her contemplative expression. *WHAT DO YOU MEAN?*

I mean, what next? You will still be here, imprisoned in this facility. What is next for your science if you have to remain here?

Her mouth twisted upward slightly. *I COULD TURN THAT QUESTION ON YOU AND YOUR KIND. WHAT "NEXT" WHEN YOU ARE THROUGH STUDYING US?*

She had me there. *I suppose we will never be through…discovering new shapes and forms of adaptation is at the core of who we are. There is so much left to learn about your species. So much potential for my fellow Doers to exploit.*

Her eyes bored through my adopted form. *THEN WHAT MAKES YOU THINK MY STUDY OF YOU WILL EVER BE COMPLETE?*

Even so. You cannot intend to remain here forever. What use are your conclusions about us if you cannot share them with others? Is that not the meaning of science?

She lowered her eyes to her writing and refused to engage further on the subject.

Over the ensuing days, I learned that several of my colleagues had been to see Nadia. They had taken my advice on that score, at least…dare I hope they might lend their assistance further?

When I next imported to the Convincers' plane, I found a group mid-discussion. They paused and sent a transmission of invitation my way.

Convincer Vla. Your timing is impeccable, Kav greeted me. *We were just discussing your "human."*

I assume you mean Nadia?

Nadia. Yes. Most intriguing that they name themselves almost as we do.

What are your conclusions? I asked, impatient to hear their impressions.

She is astonishing, Ahn transmitted. *I never imagined these primates had such capacity for thought and reflection.*

Despite all their accomplishments as a species, prior to our arrival? You never once considered there was more at work than the mindless manipulation of their material world? I felt the acid edge to my own transmission and did nothing to soften it. I was so tired of trying to justify the obvious to my own kind.

Their sole dominion of the material world is precisely what makes them so primitive, Vla. Kav's tone was the one he used to make a case in the Dispensing Chambers. *We cannot be derided for overlooking the intelligence of a species so unaware of its own multi-dimensional environment.*

I have never claimed they have the perspective that we do. But our greater awareness does not make us superior.

There was silence for a time. I held my thoughts in suspension, waiting for another to continue.

We have decided. Convincer Kav's transmission was wide, and I realized they had been communing privately. *We will petition the Dispenser of Justice. We cannot ask her to change her ruling, but we can ask that she meet with Nadia herself. Perhaps then she will come to a realization, as we have, that things are not as they seem with this native species. Perhaps she will see fit to make a new ruling without overturning her previous one.*

Yes. Meeting with Nadia could only help. She seemed to inspire awe in all who met her. *It is a start,* I transmitted, muting my hopes.

We launched our petition immediately, gathering our thoughts and citing our sources. Studier Pha and two Handlers agreed to lend their names on the humans' behalf. For the first time, I believed this might work. Nadia was changing minds, one Doer at a time.

Several days later, I was met at the Center by an agitated Studier Pha.

She is here. Her transmission was taut.

Who? I asked.

The Dispenser of Justice. She has come to see Nadia. At your request.

You disapprove of my request?

The Dispenser knows nothing of the humans. She has no understanding of their interactions, no experience in communicating with them, and she refuses to take their form.

What's happening? I forced my limbs into a shambling run. Pha trotted along beside me, her urgency blaring through my senses.

She's frightening them. The domestics are panicking and Nadia refuses to transmit to her.

Anger flared in me. Our request had been that she visit in the company of a Studier and Handler, who could liaise between her and the humans. I had never intended that she come alone and unannounced. What was she thinking?

We reached the chamber and imported ourselves inside. The scene that met me was appalling. Two of the domestic humans huddled in a corner, their faces blanched with fear. A third, the largest male, was grappling with the Dispenser of Justice, who had spread herself to full girth and took up almost a third of the chamber's space. Her blue-gray, putty-like exodermis pulsed with the bioluminescence that marked her status. Her multifaceted light receptors were turned on the male human, whose right fore-limb had merged with the Dispenser's flank as he sought to grasp her or push her away. She radiated strength and terrible beauty, but I could see her display of dominance only terrified the primates. The fourth domestic was shielded by Nadia, who stood firm, attempting defiance despite the fear in her eyes. Two Handlers, in primate form, stood by helplessly, unprepared to challenge the Dispenser's authority despite their superior understanding of the situation.

I had no such qualms.

Dispenser! Please! I transmitted at full force. *They do not understand you!*

Her reply was disparaging. *Your "intelligent" beings. Your marvellous sentients. No, Vla. They do not understand, do they?*

You cannot expect them to make sense of Doers' body language. Why do you think we take their form to interact with them?

You understand theirs, though, correct? As a superior, intelligent being might be expected to make sense of a less intelligent species?

This is unfair. I struggled to keep my bearing civil. *This is not an accurate gauge of their understanding. They have not had the opportunity to study and understand us!*

I had transmitted widely. Nadia, astounding in her bravery, latched onto my thought and transmitted one of her own.

I AM STUDYING YOU NOW. YOUR DISPLAY IS INTRIGUING. GIVEN TIME, I WILL LEARN TO MAKE SENSE OF IT.

The Dispenser of Justice reeled at Nadia's intensity. She let go of the male, whose arm came free of her flesh with a peeling sound. He fell back, clutching his glistening, reddened limb.

Why now? The Dispenser asked, her glittering focus on Nadia. *You would not transmit to me earlier.*

I realized the Dispenser had been attempting to force communication from the reluctant human. Had she been faced with a fellow Doer, her will would have been done immediately.

I DO NOT KNOW YOU. I HAVE NEVER SEEN YOUR KIND IN THIS FORM. YOUR THREAT-ENING BEHAVIOR LED ME TO BELIEVE YOU WERE DANGEROUS AND NOT SOMEONE TO WHOM I WISHED TO TRANSMIT THOUGHT. Nadia's confidence grew as she spoke, and the other humans began to relax at her lead.

The Dispenser contemplated her for a long moment. *I am told you have recorded observations since your arrival. I would like those recordings delivered to me for perusal.*

I CANNOT DO THAT.

We would not be able to make sense of them anyway, Dispenser, Pha interrupted. *We've barely begun to decode the human markings, and Nadia has shown no interest in helping us make sense of them.*

Then she can read and transmit them to us. The Dispenser made it sound final.

I WILL NOT.

This is not a matter for discussion.

Despite her precarious situation, Nadia's posture stiffened and her eyes grew hard. *WHEN HAVE YOU SHARED YOUR STUDIES WITH US? WHY WOULD I SHARE MINE?*

Because you are under our control. Not the other way around. The Dispenser's prejudice was entrenched. My plan was failing in front of me.

Place this one in isolation until she cooperates. The Dispenser's transmission was emphasized toward Studier Pha and the Handlers. She exported before any of us could argue further. I sensed Pha's simmering frustration without her having to transmit a word.

Do you realize what you've done? She sent the thought tightly before turning her back on me to engage with the Handlers.

It took a full day to calm the humans. Pha was furious at the damage to the painstaking trust she had developed with them. She moved Nadia back to her original chamber and entirely refused to communicate with me throughout.

I exported back to the Convincers' plane and closed my mind to my colleagues' questions. I needed time alone.

✿

Vla. Vla...Vla!

The transmission woke me from my semi-transient doze. Convincer Ahn was before me, emitting urgency.

What? My reply was irritable.

Studier Pha requires your presence immediately. She has not been able to contact you.

I was surprised she even wanted to. *What does she want?*

Most likely your human negotiating skills. There is an uprising at the Center.

An uprising?

Wild sentients have descended.

I didn't pause to find out more. I exported to Pha's wing of the Center with Ahn's thoughts echoing in my mind. Pha met me in the receiving area with a decidedly human look of concern on her primate face. I could hear yells, thuds and crashes from outside the building. Pha took my shapeshifted arm in hers and pulled me toward a window overlooking the Center's front square. The outer doors were rarely used; Doers imported in and exported out. The doors were for admitting sentients or other creatures, but now they were besieged by a mass of humans, all of them wild and fabric-draped. There were hundreds, vastly outnumbering the Doers inside.

We cannot keep them at bay, Pha transmitted. *They will be inside before long.*

What about the subduing cannons? I hated to suggest them.

Someone has dismantled the cannons. This is a planned uprising, not a riot. I fear we are betrayed.

"Someone?" One of us?

It's too early to know for certain. The damage was only discovered an hour ago.

Such a level of betrayal would mean full-scale Doer rebellion. Everyone knew Convincers were working hard to amend the law in the humans' favor. I couldn't imagine anybody risking so much without waiting for the machinations of society to run their course. But there was another possibility.

How do you know humans weren't responsible? Perhaps they infiltrated the Center somehow. What if this "uprising" is merely a distraction?

Pha looked at me. I sensed her mind go cold; she hadn't considered this.

Nadia. She exported before my eyes, with a rush of air and a soft "pop." I followed a moment after, but our arrival inside Nadia's chamber was too late.

The door was open, and the human scientist and all her records were gone.

My mind burned at Pha's curse.

Calm down, Pha.

She ignored me and ran into the corridor, hitting an alarm panel on the wall. A siren began to blare. *She may not have gone far. We'll split up—you check this level and I'll head to the lower one.* My orders given, Pha exported from the corridor. No matter; I had a feeling I knew where to find Nadia.

I imported beside the leafy enclosure of my former clients. Nadia and two humans I didn't recognize stood outside, trying unsuccessfully to key the lock.

It's different from the one on your chamber. I startled them all. *This enclosure has restricted access. Only a handful of Doers can open it.*

The other two wild humans, a male and a female, pointed energy-discharging weapons at me. Nadia stepped forward.

ARE YOU ONE OF THOSE WHO CAN OPEN IT?

I hesitated. *Yes.*

THEN DO SO. YOU WANT THEM FREED, DON'T YOU? It was a challenge rather than an appeal to wisdom.

Are you behind all this? I asked her.

DID IT NOT OCCUR TO YOU THAT I WOULD NEVER SUBJECT MYSELF TO THIS PLACE WITHOUT AN ESCAPE PLAN?

It hadn't occurred to me. I felt like a fool.

But…how? How did these two get in? How did they know where to find you?

She exposed her teeth in the gesture of pleasure that I had begun to find endearing. YOU CAN TRANSMIT TO HUMAN MINDS. WHY SHOULDN'T I BE ABLE TO?

I was staggered, not by her admission but by my own stupidity, never mind Pha's or the Handlers'. Nadia had been communicating with her fellow wild humans all along. We had been so fascinated by her that we'd been blind to her cleverness even as we were being charmed by it.

WILL YOU OPEN THIS DOOR?

I looked at her, at her armed conspirators, at the domestics who had crowded around the entrance to their enclosure, anticipating its opening. She was right. I did want them freed. I wanted Nadia out of

here too, before the Dispenser forced her to reveal her observations. Opening that door would leave me teetering on the brink of Undoing.

Leaving it closed would undo me completely.

I keyed the scanner with a clumsy human digit. A beam confirmed my energy signature and the door slid back. The four bare-skinned domestics joined their covered cousins and fled down the corridor, shielded by the weapon-bearers. Only Nadia hesitated.

THANK YOU. IT SEEMS YOU ARE INDEED MY LIVING PROOF. PERHAPS NOW YOU CAN CONVINCE OTHERS AND ELIMINATE OUR SUFFERING.

Your species is remarkable. If I am alienated for assisting you, perhaps I can seek you out.

She inclined her head. YOU ARE ALWAYS WELCOME AMONG US. WE ARE ALLIES. VLA.

A twist of emotion ran over my skin. It was the first time she had addressed me by name.

Nadia.

She turned and ran. I stood listening to her nimble footsteps echo into the distance, knowing, somehow, that I would see her again.

✧

We never discovered how they got in or how they got out. The riotous crowd dispersed soon after Nadia disappeared, proving themselves a smokescreen. Four other sentient chambers had been opened. Two of the occupants fled, presumably with Nadia's group. The other two were found, wandering and jittery, in the hallways. One of them had loose wires trailing from the exploratory implant in his skull, wires I was later told had been keeping him alive. I couldn't decide whether or not he was lucky to survive.

The full extent of the sentients' organized plan forced the Dispenser of Justice to concede their right to their own autonomy.

Despite their limitation to a single dimension, she transmitted across all planes, *these beings have proven their self-awareness and capability. Convincer Vla's earlier case for their intelligence lacked irrefutable evidence until now. I am therefore obliged to amend my previous ruling.*

The domestic breeding plan was halted immediately and all testing began to be phased out.

My part in the escape earned me a severe reprimand and banishment from the Convincers' plane for eight lunar cycles. I returned from my exile to face the Dispenser's final justice, fully expecting to be declared an Undoer. I was prepared for it, having long since made peace with my decision.

Convincer Vla, it seems to me that despite your transgressions, you can be of great use to us. The domestic humans require rehabilitation. Studiers tell me that their best hope is to be united with wild humans. As you have established a relationship with their kind, you would seem to be the one to liaise with them.

But… I was taken aback. With all respect, Dispenser, that does not appear to fall under a Convincer's remit.

No. It does not. As it is, you have brought your role into question through your actions. I consequently strip you of the title of Convincer.

I muted my thoughts.

Subsequently, I hereby establish the new role of Ambassador to Humans, and designate you, Vla, its first Doer.

She emitted her finalizing pulse of light. If I'd been in human form, I would have swayed on my feet. Ambassador Vla.

I was, against all odds, still a Doer.

And the humans were free.

Copyright © 2018 by Eleanor R. Wood

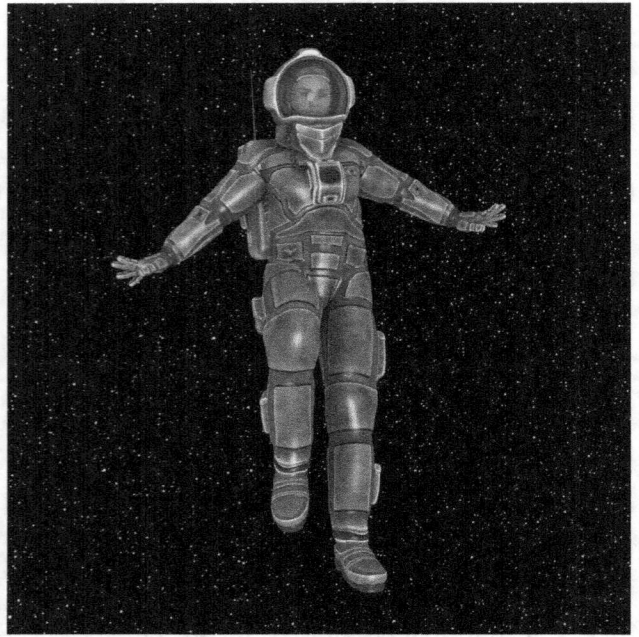

Harry Turtledove is a Hugo winner who seems to live on the bestseller list. The field of alternate history was pretty much overlooked and abandoned until Harry made it his own, and tens of millions of sales later, he still pretty dominates it.

THE MORE IT CHANGES

by Harry Turtledove

Yitzkhak the cobbler loosened the vise and checked to see whether the glue had set between the half-dozen thicknesses of leather. Finding it had, he let out a small grunt of satisfaction. On the topmost layer, he drew an outline of the rears on the pair of boots that needed reheeling. The knife he reached for was sharp but sturdy. Sturdy it had to be, to cut through that much leather.

He bore down with the knife, using all the strength in his right arm. *If I forget thee, O Jerusalem, let my right hand forget her cunning.* The verse from Psalm CXXXVII was seldom far from the Jew's thoughts.

He muttered to himself as he cut. Too many people had forgotten too many things over the course of too many years. To Yitzkhak, it seemed as though more people had forgotten more things lately. That might have been because his rusty beard had more white in it than he cared to remember. Or, on the other hand, it might not. The way things were these days, you never could tell. And no one ever seemed to forget trouble.

After cutting the new boot heels, he used brass nails to fix them in place. Iron nails would have been cheaper, and would have served just as well… till Chaim the butcher walked in mud or splashed through a puddle. After that, they would have started to rust. *Do it right the first time* was one of the rules Yitzkhak's father had beaten into him. The habit was too deeply ingrained now for him to lose it, or even to remember he'd once had to acquire it.

Warm, sweet summer air and light came through the open door and the narrow window of the cobbler's shop. So did the exciting, almost intoxicating gabble of trade. Monday was market day in Kolomija—the town's name could be spelled at least half a dozen different ways in at least three different alphabets. The same was true for Yitzkhak's own name. This was a debatable part of the world in all kinds of ways.

It was summer, yes. Just what the date was was as debatable as the spelling of Kolomija. By the calendar the Catholics used, it was August 24, 1772. To the Orthodox, it was August 13 of the same year. In the Jews' system, which reckoned from the creation of the world, it was the twenty-fifth of Av in the year 5532. The Ottoman Empire lay not far to the south—just on the other side of the Carpathians. To Muslims, it was the twenty-fourth of Jumaada al-awal, 1186. And, by the new reckoning that threatened to swallow all the others, it was the twenty-fifth day of the eleventh month in the year 95.

Even the frontiers in these parts rippled and shifted like a river. Until a few months before, the Jews of Kolomija had paid taxes to a nobleman who mostly didn't send them to the King of Poland. Now, though, Kolomija—and that nobleman—owed allegiance to the Emperor of Austria. If the nobleman held out on Joseph, Yitzkhak suspected he would regret it.

The cobbler looked at the boots he'd just fixed. He looked under the counter. He had to patch a torn upper for Shmuel the rope-maker. That could keep, though. Shmuel was down in Jablonow, fifteen miles to the south, tending his sick mother. Unless the poor woman took a turn for the worse and died (*God forbid*, Yitzkhak thought), he wouldn't come home for a week or two.

Yitzkhak didn't have anything he needed to do right this minute. It was gloomy and stuffy inside the cramped shop. It smelled of leather and sweat and glue. Under that, it smelled musty.

Outside, the sun shone. Outside, the market square would be packed. Kolomija had a fine market day. It wouldn't just be peasants bringing in chickens and white radishes and peas from the countryside. Merchants came call the way from Czernowitz, sometimes all the way from Rowne, to buy and sell and trade. Rowne was on the other side of the border now, but nobody yet had fussed about it.

He closed and latched the shutter, stepped outside, and put a big iron padlock on the front door. The lock was ancient and rusty. A half-witted child could pick it or force it. So far, no burglar had figured that out. With luck, none would till Yitzkhak

got back. *"Alevai omanyn,"* he murmured as he started for the market square.

His own well-made boots kicked up dust at every step. It *was* hot outside. The broad brim of his fox-trimmed black hat kept the sun off his face, but sweat sprang out on his forehead.

He wasn't the only man who might have been working but was heading for the market instead. He called greetings to Jews and to Catholic Poles. Like most people in Kolomija, he could get along in Yiddish or Polish, German or Little Russian, or even Slovak in a pinch. He talked to his God in Hebrew, as the Poles talked to theirs in Latin.

Czeslaw the tavern-keeper had a bottle of plum brandy under each arm. He was on his way back from the square. His red nose and the veins that tracked his cheeks said he drank up some of his profits. He and Yitzkhak nodded to each other. Kolomija wasn't such a big town that everyone didn't know everyone else, at least by sight.

"How's the square?" Yitzkhak asked.

"Busy. Busiest I've seen it for a while. With the roads dry, people from a long way off can get here." Czeslaw frowned. His ice-gray eyes narrowed. "I'm not so sure that's a good thing, not the way it is nowadays. They'll go home and remind their neighbors we're around."

Yitzkhak made an unhappy noise. "I'm not so sure it's good, either. Sometimes—a lot of the time—the most you can hope for is that everybody forgets about you and leaves you alone."

"Too right, it is!" Czeslaw said. "There was talk that *haidamacks* are gathering." He crossed himself to turn aside the evil omen.

"God forbid!" Instead of thinking it, Yitzkhak said it aloud. He wanted to give the Lord a better chance of hearing it. *Haidamacks* meant *rioters*. They were Cossacks and other ne'er-do-wells who swarmed like locusts every so often, killing and looting and burning for the greater glory of their notion of God—and for the fun of it. Yitzkhak went on, "I hope the talk is wrong. The last time they came through was only—what?—four years ago?"

"Yes, that's when it was," the taverner said. "Before that, we didn't see them for fifteen or twenty years, and then another fifteen before that. We were both little boys back then."

"I remember." Yitzkhak touched the brim of his hat once more. "Well, I'd better head on to the square myself and hear it with my own ears. May the Lord bless you and keep you, Czeslaw."

"And you, Jew. And you." Bobbing his head, the Pole headed up the street toward his place of business.

On to the market square trudged Yitzkhak. The joy, the anticipation, were gone from his step. The only thing he had to look forward to now was bad news. The day felt darker, as if clouds covered the sun. They didn't, but the cobbler saw with his heart as much as with his ears.

Wagons and carts filled the square. Women in embroidered head scarves sat on the ground, selling eggs or mushrooms or turnips from baskets they'd made themselves. A donkey brayed. Stray dogs skulked, looking for food they could steal.

Peddlers who'd come to Kolomija from bigger towns shouted their wares: plates; big, clunky clocks with gilded wooden cases; books in German and French and Latin and Hebrew; the brandy Czeslaw had bought; carved meerschaums from Vienna; singing finches in brass cages; and almost anything else someone thought he might be able to sell.

Yitzkhak eyed the meerschaums with longing, especially one in the shape of a bare-breasted mermaid—you smoked through her tail. His current pipe was baked clay. It worked, but it was ugly as the mud it came from. He asked the trader what a meerschaum cost. The answer made him retreat in a hurry. The best haggling in the world wouldn't bring the price down to anything he could afford.

He did buy a bagel for a copper. His jaw worked at the chewy dough as he went through the square, though not before he recited the *brukha* over bread. A sausage-seller held up a link. Yitzkhak politely shook his head. Tadeusz used pork in his sausages; it wasn't forbidden him.

The cobbler wished he had ears like a cat's or a fox's, ears that could swivel and track things he particularly wanted to hear. But he turned out not to need anything like that. People were talking about *haidamacks* in several different languages. They would have talked about a rising storm the same way when clouds were still low on the horizon.

He wasn't the only man from Kolomija whose face got glummer the longer he stayed in the market square. Alter the druggist and Casimir the stonecutter were talking when Yitzkhak came up to them. Alter touched his hatbrim; Casimir bobbed a token bow.

"It doesn't sound good," the stonecutter said.

"They're coming, sure as sure," the druggist agreed sadly. "For our sins, they're coming."

"We must have done something awful, to make God hate us so much," Yitzkhak said. "Another pogrom, so soon after the last one…"

As Czeslaw had before, Casimir made the sign of the cross. "I'm a good Catholic—well, as good a Catholic as an ordinary man can be," he said. "All I want to do is to worship God the way my father and my grandfathers and all my ancestors did before me."

"That's all I want, too." Yitzkhak and Alter said the same thing at the same time. The two Jews looked at each other and laughed. It was that or burst into tears.

Casimir glowered at them from under bushy eyebrows. "That miserable…" The stonecutter growled a Polish obscenity, adding, "He was just a rotten *Zhyd* himself."

"*Nu?*" Yitzkhak shrugged an expressive—and nervous—shrug. He didn't want to tangle with Casimir; the man's trade had given him shoulders broad as a bull's and upper arms bulging with muscle. He tried simple truth instead: "So was the one you go to church for."

"It's not the same," Casimir said, but he stopped glowering.

"Besides," Yitzkhak added, "would it make any difference if he'd been a Turk? He still would have been…what he was. What they say he was, I mean."

"What they say he was, eh?" Casimir seemed to like that. He nodded. "Maybe the God-cursed *haidamacks* will be afraid of the Austrian Emperor. This is his land now. Maybe they won't come. Maybe the town can fight them off if they do." He lumbered away. He'd talked himself into feeling better, anyhow.

Softly, so the stonecutter wouldn't hear, Alter said, "And maybe I'll grown like an onion, with my head in the ground."

"Maybe you will," Yitzkhak said. "You never can tell." They both laughed again. Again, Yitzkhak heard the sorrow under the mirth.

✿

Summer slipped toward fall. The High Holy Days came and went. The Jewish year 5532 gave way to 5533. Yitzkhak fasted and prayed through Yom Kippur, the Day of Atonement. He begged forgiveness of everyone he'd offended the past year, and did his best to forgive everyone who apologized to him. It wasn't always easy, but on that day of days a man had to try.

The fall rains held off long enough to let the peasants bring in a good harvest of barley and wheat. The winter would be hungry—winters usually were. But no one seemed likely to starve.

As soon as the rains came, roads went from dusty tracks to rivers of mud. Travel slowed, or else stopped altogether. The roof in Yitzkhak's shop leaked. He put a chipped bowl under one drip and a dented tin cup that had lost its handle under another. Every so often, he would toss the water into the muddy street.

He didn't mind one bit, not that autumn (during which the new reckoning passed from year 95 to 96). Every time a drop plinked into the tin cup, he would smile. *Forty days and forty nights, Lord*, he thought. The longer it rained, the longer before the *haidamacks* could come, if the *haidamacks* did come. They swept out of the east when they came, and the rains were usually worse in that direction. Everybody said so.

But the rainy season didn't last forever, no matter how much Yitzkhak wished it would. Snow whitened the upper slopes of the Carpathians. Frost traced magic patterns on the glass windowpanes of rich men's houses. Yes, the rich—mostly Poles—in Kolomija had glass windows, as if it were Czernowitz or Kiev or Warsaw.

And the cold weather hardened the ground, as it did toward the end of fall every year. The muddy roads turned to something more like rock. With the crops in, the worst of the year's work was done. Some men out in the countryside lay up through the winter like sleepy bears—though bears didn't have vodka to help make time spin by.

Yitzkhak didn't mind the men who stayed in their houses and drank their way through winter. They were harmless. Oh, they might beat their wives and children, but they might do that sober too. The trouble was, vodka also inflamed other men, the kind who loaded their muskets and pistols, climbed into the saddle, and went riding in the name of the

Messiah—and in the name of kicking up as much trouble as they could.

Haidamacks torched the synagogue in Zastawna. They burned the rabbi in it, and howled with laughter at his screams. Zastawna lay between Czernowitz and Kolomija, west of the one but east of the other. It wasn't nearly far enough away to let anyone in Kolomija feel safe, in other words.

Snyatyn was a smaller town a little southwest of Zastawna—even closer to Kolomija, that is. Two days after people fleeing Zastawna came to Kolomija, people fleeing Snyatyn got there.

"God have mercy on us!" a Catholic woman from Snyatyn screamed in the street as she stumbled past Yitzkhak's house. "Christ have mercy on us! They murdered the priest, the holy father! They cut his throat on the altar in the church, as if he were a hog! Their horses drank from the holy-water fount! Oh, Christ have mercy!"

Yitzkhak's wife was a small, dark woman named Rivka. She was quiet and steady. He could see that those shrieks shook her even so. "They'll be here next, won't they?" she said, her voice not much above a whisper.

"I'm afraid so," he answered.

"They went away the last time," his son Aaron said. "They went away, and we're still here, and we're still Jews." He was fifteen. He thought he was a man. Under religious law, he was. Otherwise…less so. He did have a certain gift for the Talmud, which made Yitzkhak proud. An open volume sat on the table in front of him.

"It's like a bad storm," Yitzkhak said heavily. "It blows for a while. Then it eases back, and you think maybe it's over. But it blows some more, stronger than ever. And before this one is done, if it ever is, it's liable to blow all our houses down."

"What will you do, then, Father?" Aaron asked. "Will you bend to the storm?"

Yitzkhak understood what that meant. He shook his head. "A lot of people have, but I won't. I'll stay a Jew, a proper Jew, as long as I live. *Hear, O Israel, the Lord our God, the Lord is one.* That was the first prayer I learned, and those will be the last words that ever pass my lips."

"Some of the Catholics want to fight the *haidamacks*," Aaron said, his voice cracking with excitement.

Talmud or no Talmud, he added, "I want to fight alongside them."

"What do they say about that?" the cobbler asked. His wife looked horrified. He understood; that was what mothers were for. He knew horror, too, but also a grim determination.

"They say every man with a knife or a hatchet in his hands can help," Aaron answered. "If we don't fight, we'll go under."

No Jew in Kolomija owned anything much more dangerous than a knife or a hatchet. The Catholics had firearms. Some had gone to war; others hunted. That they were willing, even happy, to have Jews stand with them was a telling measure of how desperate they were. Well, by the woman from Snyatyn's cries, they had reason to be desperate. Time was when they'd looked down their noses at Jews. They still did, some; *goyim* were like that. But the passage of Kolomija from Poland to Austria was the least of their worries.

Poland, Austria, Russia, Turkey—even, from what Yitzkhak had heard, Prussia…. The same storm was blowing through all of them, and showed no sign of blowing itself out. If anything, it was spreading. Where it touched, nothing was the same again. Would the proud Catholic Poles of Kolomija want Jews at their side if things were the same as they used to be?

Tell him no. Tell him he's too young—Rivka's eyes begged Yitzkhak. But the cobbler could see that the only way to keep Aaron from doing something like that would be to tie him up and sit on him. Easier to ride a horse in the direction it was already going.

Besides… "Enough is enough. If nobody stands up to the *haidamacks*, they'll ride roughshod over everything," Yitzkhak said. "And if the Catholics will take one Jew who doesn't know much about this fighting business, chances are they'll take two."

"*Vey iz mir!*" Rivka said. Yitzkhak could hardly hear her through his son's war whoop. He didn't feel like a warrior himself. Unlike Aaron, he didn't want to fight. But he didn't think things would turn out any worse for him if he did than if he didn't. There was even some small chance they might turn out better.

He got something better than a hatchet. The Catholics gave him a spear. A spear of sorts, anyhow: an old scythe blade lashed to a staff. He had Rivka's

longest knife on his belt, and a small one from his shop stuck in one boot for a holdout weapon. Aaron hefted a makeshift spear, too.

Casimir carried a stout wooden club with nails driven through it. Yitzkhak wouldn't have wanted to be on the wrong end of a buffet from that, especially not with the stonecutter swinging it. But the *haidamacks* were horsemen. A spear at least gave you extra reach. How much good could a club do?

A couple of Poles had iron helmets. One even wore a back-and-breast that must have come down from his great-grandfather. It might keep out a musket ball. It would surely make the man very slow. Several Catholics shouldered muskets. One was a businesslike modern flintlock. The rest looked at least as old as the corselet: wheel-locks and an ancient matchlock.

Czeslaw had a pistol. A taverner needed something to keep himself safe. He surveyed the ragtag militia. "We're a fine bunch, aren't we?" he said. "Maybe the *haidamacks* will get a good look at us and laugh themselves to death. Christ, it's our best hope!"

"If you feel that way—" Yitzkhak began.

"Why don't I pack it in?" Czeslaw finished for him. "Because I'm a stubborn son of a bitch, that's why. We all are, or we wouldn't fight back. We'd do what the *haidamacks* want, and that would be that. Only then we'd hate our own reflections for the rest of our lives."

Yitzkhak nodded. He felt the same way. He wouldn't have stood there shivering in the cold if he hadn't. So many, though, had gone over to the new reckoning without so much as a backward glance at what they'd once believed.

One of the Poles who'd done some real soldiering before his hair grayed took command of the fighters. He stationed them on the streets just inside the east end of town. "We'll make things crowded for the *haidamacks*, anyway," he said. "We'll run up what barricades we can and hope for the best."

"What if they swing around to the west side?" Aaron asked him.

The veteran scowled. "You're one of those damn smart Jews, are you? If they go over there, they screw us up the ass, that's what. But they won't. They aren't long on tactics, the *haidamacks*. They just charge on in and start smashing things."

Townswomen brought the fighters soup and stew in big, steaming kettles. After a hurried *brukha*, Yitzkhak ate whatever got ladled into his bowl without worrying much about breaking dietary laws. He'd atone for his sins later, if he had a later. When you went to war, you dispensed with a lot of the formalities anyhow.

As night fell, Casimir pointed out into the gathering gloom. "Look! You can see their fires!"

Yitzkhak cocked his head to one side. "Yes, and you can hear them howling, too. If they aren't already plastered, they will be soon."

A drum began to pound out there. The first thud was so deep and sudden, for a panicky moment Yitzkhak took it for a cannon firing. But it thumped again and again and again. The *haidamacks'* drunken shouts coalesced into a chorus that rang out between the drumbeats: "Sabbatai! Sabbatai!"

"God damn Sabbatai," Casimir said in Polish at Yitzkhak's left hand. He spat on the ground.

"God curse Sabbatai," Aaron said in Yiddish at Yitzkhak's right hand. He spat on the ground too.

"God's already done whatever He chose to do with Sabbatai Tzevi," Yitzkhak said, first in the one language and then in the other, though Aaron followed Polish perfectly well. "It's here on earth that we're still sorting things out."

"God damn Sabbatai," Casimir repeated. "God damn him and the Devil broil him black!"

Sabbatai Tzevi had been dead for almost a century; the date of his death marked the first day of the new reckoning his followers used. He'd been born an ordinary Jew in Turkey, but he had messianic ambitions and pretensions. He also had the kind of spellbinding character that made people who heard him take those ambitions and pretensions seriously.

They said he worked miracles. Yitzkhak didn't know the details; he didn't want to know the details. Sabbatai had preached in Asia Minor, and in the Holy Land, and in Egypt. Some from Europe who'd heard him believed his claims as firmly as the folk in the Ottoman Empire.

Finally, in the year the Christians called 1666, Sultan Mehmet IV summoned Sabbatai to Istanbul to hear at first hand what he had to say. The canny Turk listened to the man who called himself the Messiah…and declared that he was changing his name to Sabbatai I.

The new faith exploded through the vast Ottoman domain, and out into Europe as well. Sabbatai Tzevi lived another ten years after converting Mehmet to his cause. Mullahs, cardinals, patriarchs, rabbis—every religious authority called curses down on his head. It did them little good. When people were ready for something, they grabbed at it whether their leaders approved or not. Christianity and Islam had spread the same way.

And when people were ready for something, they were also ready—eager!—to ram it down their neighbors' throats, regardless of whether the neighbors were ready too.

"Sabbatai!" the *haidamacks* roared. "Sabbatai!" They danced around the fires like…like Yitzkhak didn't know what. He vaguely knew there was a New world beyond the ocean far to the west (he only vaguely knew there *was* an ocean far to the west), but tales of its natives had never reached his ears.

He turned to the grizzled veteran who ordered the defenders around. "We ought to go out there while they're drinking and yelling and carrying on—take them by surprise."

"Another Jew who thinks he's a general." The Pole sounded more amused than annoyed. He waved toward the fires. "Go ahead, Jew—be my guest. If you guys were real soldiers, not odds-and-sods, I might try it. But they'd chop you to bits if I did. You don't know how to hold together. No, our best chance is staying where we're at and making them come to us."

"All right." Yitzkhak had no idea whether it was or not. But the gray-haired Pole understood more of war than he did. He pulled his black coat tighter around him, lay down on the ground behind a barrel, and tried to sleep.

He didn't think he would, but he managed a light, on-and-off doze. He was dozing when a *haidamack* rode out of the gray predawn light in the east and shouted, "You misbelievers there! Give your souls to Sabbatai Tzevi, God's great light on earth, and we'll leave you alone! Otherwise, you'll pay for your wickedness in this world and the next!" He sounded like a Little Russian trying to speak Polish, but no one in Kolomija would have trouble following him.

"Go away! Leave us alone! Let us worship the way we want to!" Yitzkhak shouted as he grabbed his spear and scrambled to his feet. Other men yelled variations on the same theme.

"On your heads be it—and it will." The *haidamack* turned his horse and rode back to his encampment. Sabbatai's followers, like those of Muhammad and Jesus before them, were sure they knew the one right answer and had the right, even the duty, to inflict it on everyone else. Jews didn't proselytize—which was, no doubt, why there were so few of them.

The drums began to pound again. When the sun rose, the *haidamacks* came trotting toward the town and its homemade barriers. Some bore lances, some short muskets, some pistols. They wore fur hats; their capes streamed out behind them. As they came, they shouted Sabbatai's name.

One of the defenders steadied his musket on a board and fired. The shot missed anyhow. Yitzkhak was too excited to be afraid—till a pistol ball smashed Casimir's face. The burly stonecutter wailed and gobbled at the same time. Bright blood poured out between his fingers as he clapped his hands to the wound. Then he fell, and it puddled and steamed under him. He never got to use his fearsome club.

A raider's horse went down. The *haidamack* howled—his leg was broken or crushed beneath the thrashing animal. The others kept pushing forward, though. They had more guns and less fear than Kolomija's amateur defenders.

Yitzkhak awkwardly thrust his improvised spear at a horse. The rider didn't get close enough to let the weapon bite. He shot at Yitzkhak, missed, and cursed horribly.

Another *haidamack* skewered a Jew with his lance at the same time as his comrade shot the Catholic next to that Jew. Their horses chested planks aside. Whooping, the *haidamacks* poured through the breach in the miserable barricade and into Kolomija. A couple of them went down, but most rode on.

Some made for the Catholic church, others for the synagogue. That split the defenders: the Poles tried to save the one, the Jews the other. The fire in the synagogue started first.

Aaron lay in the street, bleeding from the head. "No!" Yitzkhak shouted. He tried to skewer one of the raiders. Laughing, the man yanked the spear from his startled hands. "No!" he shouted again. "Your Sabbatai, he was a Jew, the same as we are!"

"He got over it." The *haidamack* aimed a musket at Yitzkhak's belly. "Will you, fool? Admit that Sabbatai was the Lord's chosen, the Messiah, and you can have your worthless life."

Yitzkhak grabbed for the kitchen knife on his belt. "It isn't true," he said. Even as the words came out of his mouth, he wished he had them back. *Why would you condemn yourself like that? Because I am a Jew*, he thought. *Because I can't be anything else.*

Laughing still, the raider pulled the trigger. Maybe the gun would misfire. If it didn't, maybe he would miss. Maybe—

Flame and smoke burst from the muzzle. The bullet caught Yitzkhak square in the chest. It didn't hurt. Then it did, horribly. He crumpled, blood filling his mouth. Through it, he managed to choke out, "Hear, O Israel, the Lord our God, the Lord is one" before darkness swallowed him.

The synagogue burned. A couple of hundred yards away, so did the church. "Sabbatai!" the *haidamacks* cried, over and over again. "Sabbatai!" Like the smoke from the houses of God, the name mounted to the uncaring heavens.

Copyright © 2014 by Harry Turtledove

Larry Hodges has sold more than ninety stories. His third novel, Campaign 2100: Game of Scorpions, *was recently published by World Weaver Press. His* When Parallel Lines Meet, *a Stellar Guild team-up with Mike Resnick and Lezli Robyn, came out in October of 2017.*

THE RAT RACE OF TOMORROW

by Larry Hodges

It really hurts to get thrown out of the only home you've ever known. After four and a half billion Earth years you'd think I'd get some consideration. But I made one mistake—*one!*—and out came the torches and pitchforks. (Why do I feel groggy? My head, or what you'd call a head, feels like a supernova crashing into a black hole of chili pepper.)

Sure, I killed off humanity and most other life on Earth. But it wasn't my fault—just a little careless horseplay in the asteroids, and how was I to know Ceres would go off in *that* exact direction? Just plain bad luck for them. (Wait—the chances of that are next to impossible! I would have had to aim it—did I? *Why can't I remember?*)

But look at all the good I've done. Who do you think planted the seeds of intelligent life on primordial Earth? Who gave nudges here and there—and a big shove during the Cambrian—as they evolved from amoebas to lemurs? Who cultivated and protected human ancestors all these years, from the Stone Age to the Space Age, right up to the rat race of today that you call civilization? That was me.

But of course you invading Crites only recently set up your colony on Ganymede—already a million of you!—so you don't know any of this. To you, I'm just an oozing mass of cold, green plasma that seems to break the laws of physics as I zip around the solar system. But you look like giant, slimy earthworms with two little wiggling worms for eyes, and eight more for arms and legs. *Yuck!* But I won't judge you for your looks, so don't judge mine. I'm really a nice guy. At least I think so, though I'm having trouble remembering much right now.

Sure, I've caused my share of mischief. I kicked Mercury, a former moon of Jupiter, practically into the Sun. Dumped carbon dioxide waste on Venus.

Pretended to be a god on Earth—thought I could teach moral values, silly me. Stole the water from Mars. Punched Jupiter in the solar plexus. Played ring toss with Saturn. Gave Uranus a funny name. Strangled Neptune till it turned blue—who knew it had that much blue-reflecting methane inside! I even tricked those gullible humans into declassifying Pluto as a planet.

But the minute Ceres smashed into Earth—*pow!*—and killed humanity, you Crites hit the galactic roof as if *you* were Earth's protectors—where were you the last 4.5 billion years?—and came after *me.* We had some crazy hide and seek in the asteroids before you got me in a tractor beam and flung me out of the solar system at escape velocity. So began my friendly tour of the Kuiper Belt and the Oort Cloud. Thanks a bunch.

My head is starting to clear. And—I remember! *I REMEMBER!*

The humans, practically my children, they didn't like you Crites any more than I did—they were just scared—but even I don't normally believe in genocide. *My God!* You were the scapegoat for leaders all over Earth to take over. With half the world rallying behind them and against you, they declared war, though you probably never noticed. They created a superweapon to destroy you, a superfusion bomb, and had plans for an even more powerful one.

It was the toughest decision I ever made, but it was either you or them, and they were the aggressors. *That's* why I sent Ceres after them. And *that's* why I blocked their superweapon on its way to Ganymede—it got me smack in the head, *ow!*—to save your silly little tushies. *Boom!*

And my reward for saving you worm-guys was a heave-ho into comet central.

But there's a limit to my goodness, and you've rocketed past it like a crazed Halley's Comet. (Which is right over there.) No more Mr. Nice Oozing Green Plasma Guy. So a little nudge here, a little shove there…well, I'm counting the seconds. It's been a hundred and forty quadrillion seconds since the solar system and I were created together, and I can wait another three billion, about the time it'll take the remnants of Earth to circle the Sun ninety-five times. That's when Halley and about a trillion other comets and asteroids will smack into Ganymede.

And if you Crites show up again, well, last time you caught me a bit groggy, that superweapon-in-the-head thing, but I'll be ready next time. This system's off limits for you.

With you gone, I'll start over on Earth. I learned from the failed human experiment. Some rodentia survived, and I always thought they had promise. This time I'll focus a bit more on moral development. My little rat friends, we're going to have a fun time together as you guys evolve and get smarter. I'm counting the seconds!

Copyright © 2018 by Larry Hodges

Marc A. Criley's work has appeared in Beneath Ceaseless Skies, Syntax & Salt, *and others. This is his first appearance in* Galaxy's Edge.

A MULTITUDE OF SPARKS DESCEND

by Marc A. Criley

Where are you? I trace ringing photons, syncopated cosmic ray beats, attenuated quaverings of taut space-time chords. Entangled atoms vibrating in quantum indecision sustain my faith. I range across light-years, plow gigaparsecs of quantum foam, dark matter tides, neutrino cacophonies. I hear the echo of your joy; your laughter spun into nebula, open cluster, gamma ray jets; imprinted on cosmic dust and intergalactic magnetic fields. An intergalactic palimpsest beneath white noise.

Eons we roamed—I collapsed dust clouds. You kindled stars. We spun whole galaxies into sheets and voids, soared through and sculpted big bang detritus. We twisted gravity, folded space, burned the very atoms of creation.

I kneaded clays, stirred warm brackish waters and thick ice-roofed seas. I shoved tectonic plates, cracked hydrothermal vents. I nudged atoms, finessed self-replicating molecules, wound an amino acid helix; optimized for transcription, mutation, propagation.

You bolted lightning through ultraviolet-ionized gas giants, stirred the coronaspheres of furious suns. You twisted magnetic vortices into helixes! Double helixes! You plummeted into energy-gorged accretion disks, you bent stellar jets. Fractal life amongst the quanta; self-assembling electromagnetic scaffolding draped with plasma sheets. Forged in the magnetic loops of fresh-lit stars!

We primed young worlds; evolve and adapt—or not. Life is hard but life is hardy. Someday a Spark—lit in clay or fire or water or air or plasma—would seek us. *Faith.*

Where are you? I've lost your vector, velocity, position. A few indecisive, entangled atoms my last tether. I am so lonely. Where in all these trillions upon trillions of megaparsecs are you ensnared?

✧

A Spark chances upon me, the first! Seeking its own mystery, its origins. It finds me—but just me, alone. (I had so hoped we'd share this moment.)

They are all that we imagined, moreso! Rooted and forged by the helices of creation. This Spark and I, we devise a *lingua astra*. I share that I am of a pair, entangled. They ask of you. You are lost, I tell them, lost elsewhere.

It—no, *they*, them—they proffer aid. Without hesitation hurling themselves into the void, bestowing an infinitesimal reduction of an infinite search.

Another Spark alights. Then another. Offering aid, spreading the word of an impossible search. Soon more Sparks, calling out, coordinating, vectoring off into the cosmos. Divide and swarm. Oh so many Sparks! By the thousands, millions, the billions they embark; to scour a hundred billion stars in a hundred billion galaxies.

✧

Here! a Spark cyphers in coded space-time, *Here!*

Backtracing the arrow of time to a relativistic super-massive black hole collision. You, so fascinated at the whorls and fractures of space-time infrastructure, was it *your* doing? Spinning quarks top and bottom, charmed and strange? In the quark-gluon plasma and relativistic jets of coalescing singularities did you attempt an interstitial analogue of helices and many-worlds transcriptors?

Seasoned we are, but uncertainty is the universal currency. A picosecond inflation—too fast!—trapped you within the event horizon. Your far-flung field gradients, vortex manipulators, and quantum sheaths came undone, hissed a dissipating echo; reverberating through gravitational lenses and dragged frames.

Entanglement persists, faith persists. An infinite gravity well slows time, I perch on the event horizon, I wait. Are you aware yet of your plight?

Photons flare, signal each miniscule evaporation.

Has even a moment passed for you? I will wait, alone and patient for your release, while the universe darkens and chills.

✧

These others have no patience! A multitude of Sparks descend, the Sparks we kindled, a conflagration infinitely diverse! They seek us! Us! I am alone, I tell each one, for now an entangled uncertainty of faith is the all of you I hold.

Wave upon wave arrives riding blazing blue-shifted quantum twists of matter and energy. Plummeting to the edge of incandescence. They shear away the annihilating event horizon's vacuum energy fringe, intensify the sheeting photon storms of virtual particle evaporation. Soon, my love, soon! All this cosmic vitality joins to disassemble, to disintegrate, to…disentangle.

I will tell you now that the universe is warm and aglow, coruscating with life.

I will tell you we have made many friends…and everyone is here to meet you.

Copyright © 2018 by Marc A. Criley

Nancy Kress is a multiple Hugo winner and a six-time Nebula winner. We're thrilled to have her back in the pages of Galaxy's Edge *again.*

UNTO THE DAUGHTERS

by Nancy Kress

This is not the way you heard the story.

In the beginning, the tree was young. White blossoms scenting the air for a quarter mile. Shiny succulent fruit, bending the same boughs that held blossoms. Leaves of that delicate yellow-green that cannot, will not, last. Yet it did. He always did have gaudy taste. No restraint. Just look at the Himalayas. Or blowfish. I mean, really!

The woman was young too. Pink curling toes, breasts as barely budded as the apple blossoms. And the man! My dear, those long, firm flanks alone could make you ache inside for hours. He could run five miles and not even be winded. He could make love to the woman five times a day. And did.

The flowers were young. The animals, tumbling and cavorting on the grass, were young. The fucking beach sand was young, clean, evenly-shaped grains that only yesterday had been igneous rock. There was virgin rain.

Only I was old.

But it wasn't that. That was the first thing that came to your mind, wasn't it? Jealousy of glorious youth, revenge by the dried-up and jaded. Oh, you don't know, you sitting there so many centuries ahead. It wasn't that at all. I mean, I loved them both.

Looking at them, how could one not?

✿

"Go away," Eve says. "I'm not going to eat one."

She sits cross-legged, braiding flowers into a crown. The flowers are about what you'd expect from Him, garish scarlet petals and a vulva-shaped pistil like a bad joke. Braiding them, her fingers are deft and competent. Some lion cubs tumble tiresomely on the grass.

"I want to give you a reason why you should eat one," I say, not gently.

"I've heard all your reasons."

"Not this one, Eve. This is a *new* reason."

She isn't interested. She knots the crown of flowers, puts it on her head, giggles, tosses it at the lions. It settles lopsided over one cub's left ear. The cub looks up with comic surprise, and Eve explodes into laughter.

Really, sometimes I wonder why I bother. She's so stupid compared to the man.

I bother because she's so stupid compared to the man.

"Listen, Eve. He withholds knowledge from you two because He's selfish. What else would you call it to keep knowledge to yourself when you could just as well share it?"

"I don't need knowledge," Eve says airily. "What do I need knowledge for? And anyway, that's not a new reason. You've said that before."

"A tree, Eve. A fucking tree. To invest knowledge in. Doesn't that strike you as just a teeny bit warped? Mathematics in xylem, morality in fruit pulp? Astronomy rotting on the ground every time an apple falls. Don't you wonder what kind of a mind would do that?"

She only stares at me blankly. Oh, she's dumb. I mean!

I shout, in the temper of perfect despair, "Without knowledge, nothing will change!"

"Are you here again?" Adam says. I hadn't heard him climb over the rock behind us. He has a very quiet footstep for someone whose toenails have never ever been cut. Also a quiet, penetrating voice. Eve jumps up as if she's been shot.

"I thought I told you not to talk to this…thing ever again," Adam says. "Didn't I tell you that?"

Eve hangs her pretty head. "Yes, Adam. You did. I forgot."

He looks at her and his face softens. That blooming skin, those sweet lips. Her hair falls forward, lustrous as night. I don't think my despair can go any deeper, but it does. She is so pretty. He will always forgive her. And she will always forget everything he says two minutes after he says it.

"Be gone! You don't belong here!" Adam shouts, and throws a rock at me. It hits just behind my head. It hurts like hell. One of the lion cubs happily fetches it back, wagging a golden tail. The other one is still wearing the lopsided crown of flowers.

As I slither away, half blind with pain, Eve calls after me. "I don't want anything to change! I really don't!"

The hell with her.

☼

"Just listen," I say. "Just put your entire tiny mind on one thing for once and listen to me."

Eve sits sewing leaves into a blanket. Not cross-legged anymore: She is six months pregnant. The leaves are wide and soft, with a sort of furry nap on their underside. They appeared in the garden right after she got pregnant, along with tough spider webs that make splendid thread. Why not a bush that grows little caps? Or tiny diapers with plastic fastening tabs? Really, He has such a banal imagination.

Eve hums as she sews. Beside her is the cradle Adam made. It's carved with moons and numbers and stars and other cabalistic signs: a lovely piece of work. *Adam* has imagination.

"You have to listen, Eve. Not just hear—listen. Stop that humming. I know the future—how could I know the future unless I am exactly what I say I am? I know everything that's going to happen. I told you when you'd conceive, didn't I? That alone should have convinced you. And now I'm telling you that your baby will be a boy, and you'll call him Cain, and he—"

"No, I'm going to call him Silas," Eve says. She knots the end of her spider-thread and bites it off. "I love the name Silas."

"You're going to call him Cain, and he—"

"Do you think it would be prettier to embroider roses on this blanket, or daisies?"

"Eve, listen, if I can foretell the future then isn't it logical, isn't it reasonable for you to think—"

"I don't have to think," Eve says. "Adam does that for both of us, plus all the forest-dressing and fruit-tending. He works so hard, poor dear."

"Eve—"

"Roses, I think. In blue."

I can't stand it anymore. I go out into the constant, perpetual, monotonous sunshine, which smells like roses, like wisteria, like gardenia, like wood smoke, like new-mown hay. Like heaven.

☼

Eve has the baby at nine months, thirty-two seconds. She laughs as the small head slides out, which takes two painless minutes. The child is perfect.

"We'll call him Cain," Adam says.

"I thought we might call him Silas. I love the na—"

"Cain," Adam says firmly.

"All right, Adam."

He will never know she was disappointed.

☼

"Eve," I say. "Listen."

She is bathing the two boys in the river, in the shallows just before the river splits into four parts and leaves the garden. Cain is diligently scrubbing his small penis, but Abel has caught at some seaweed and is examining how it hangs over his chubby fists. He turns it this way and that, bending his head close. He is much more intelligent than his brother.

"Eve, Adam will be back soon. If you'd just listen…"

"Daddy," Abel says, raising his head. He has a level gaze, friendly but evaluative, even at his age. He spends a lot of time with his father. "Daddy gone."

"Oh, yes, Daddy's gone to pick breadfruit in the west!" Eve cries, in a perfect ecstasy of maternal pride. "He'll be back tonight, my little poppets. He'll be home with his precious little boys!"

Cain looks up. He has succeeded in giving his penis the most innocent of erections. He smiles beatifically at Abel, at his mother, who does not see him because she is scrubbing Abel's back, careful not to drip soapstone onto his seaweed.

"Daddy pick breadfruit," Abel repeats. "Mommy not."

"Mommy doesn't want to go pick breadfruit," Eve says. "Mommy is happy right here with her little poppets."

"Mommy not," Abel repeats, thoughtfully.

"Eve," I say, "only with knowledge can you make choices. Only with truth can you be free. Four thousand years from now—"

"I am free," Eve says, momentarily startled. She looks at me. Her eyes are as fresh, as innocent, as when she was created. They open very wide. "How could anyone not think I'm perfectly free?"

"If you'd just listen—"

"Daddy gone," Abel says a third time. "Mommy not."

"Even thirty seconds of careful listening—"

"Mommy never gone."

"Tell that brat to shut up while I'm trying to talk to you!"

Wrong, wrong. Fury leaps into Eve's eyes. She scoops up both children as if I were trying to stone them, the silly bitch. She hugs them tight to her chest, breathing something from those perfect lips that might have been "Well!" or "Ugly!" or even "Help!" Then she staggers off with both boys in her arms, dripping water, Abel dripping seaweed.

"Put Abel down," Abel says dramatically. "Abel walk."

She does. The child looks at her. "Mommy, do what Abel say!"

I go eat worms.

✧

The third child is a girl, whom they name Sheitha.

Cain and Abel are almost grown. They help Adam with the garden dressing, the animal naming, whatever comes up. I don't know. I'm getting pretty sick of the whole lot of them. The tree still has both blossoms and fruit on the same branch. The river still flows into four exactly equal branches just beyond the garden: Pison, Gihon, Hiddekel, Euphrates. Exactly the same number of water molecules in each. I stop thinking He's theatrical and decide instead that He's compulsive. I mean—really. Fish lay the exact same number of eggs in each river.

Eve hasn't seen Him in decades. Adam, of course, walks with Him in the cool of every evening. Now the two boys go too. Heaven knows what they talk about; I stay away. Often it's my one chance at Eve, who spends every day sewing and changing diapers and sweeping bowers and slicing breadfruit. Her toes are still pink curling delicacies.

"Eve, listen—"

Sheitha giggles at a bluebird perched on her dimpled knee.

"Adam makes all the decisions, decides all the rules, thinks up all the names, does all the thinking—"

"So?" Eve says. "Sheitha—you precious little angel!" She catches the baby in her arms and covers her with kisses. Sheitha crows in delight.

"Eve, listen—" Miraculously, she does. She sets the baby on the grass and says seriously, "Adam says you aren't capable of telling the truth."

"Not *his* truth," I say. "Or His." But, of course, this subtlety of pronoun goes right over her head.

"Look, snake, I don't want to be rude. You've been very kind to me, keeping me company while I do my housework, and I appreciate—"

"I'm not being kind," I say desperately. Kind! Oh, my Eve… "I'm too old and tired for kindness. I'm just trying to show you, to get you to listen—"

"Adam's back," Eve says quickly. I hear him then, with the two boys. There is just time enough to slither under a bush. I lie there very still. Lately Adam has turned murderous toward me; I think he must have a special dispensation for it. *He* must have told Adam violence toward me doesn't count, because I have stepped out of my place. Which, of course, I have.

But this time Adam doesn't see me. The boys fall into some game with thread and polished stones. Sheitha toddles toward her daddy, grinning.

"We're just here to get something to eat," Adam says. "Ten minutes, is all—what, Eve, isn't there anything ready? What have you been doing all morning?"

Eve's face doesn't fall. But her eyes deepen in color a little, like skin that has been momentarily bruised. Of course, skin doesn't stay bruised here. Not here.

"I'm sorry, dear! I'll get something ready right away!"

"Please," Adam says. "Some of us have to work for a living."

She bustles quickly around. The slim pretty fingers are deft as ever. Adam throws himself prone into a bower. Sheitha climbs into his lap. She is as precocious as the boys were.

"Daddy go back?"

"Yes, my little sweetie. Daddy has to go cut more sugar cane. And name some new animals."

"Animals," Sheitha says happily. She loves animals. "Sheitha go."

Adam smiles. "No, precious, Sheitha can't go. Little girls can't go."

"Sheitha go!"

"No," Adam says. He is still smiling, but he stands up and she tumbles off his lap. The food is ready. Eve turns with a coconut shell of salad just as Sheitha is picking herself up. The baby stands looking up at her father. Her small face is crumpled in disappointment, in disbelief, in anguish. Eve stops her turning motion and looks, her full attention on Sheitha's face.

I draw a deep breath.

The moment spins itself out, tough as spider-thread. Eve breaks it. "Adam—can't you take her?"

He doesn't answer. Actually, he hasn't even heard her. He can't, in exactly the same way Eve cannot hear Him in the cool of the evening.

You could argue that this exempts him from fault. Eve picks up the baby and stands beside the bower. Fragrance rises from the newly crushed flower petals where Adam was lying. When he and the boys have left again, I slither forward. Eve, the baby in her arms, has still not moved. Her head is bent. Sheitha is weeping, soft tears of vexation that will not, of course last very long. Not here. I don't have much time.

"Eve," I say. "Listen—"

I tell her how it will be for Sheitha after she marries Cain, who is not as sweet-tempered as his father. I tell her how it will be for Sheitha's daughter's daughter. I spare her nothing: not the expansion of the garden until the home bowers are insignificant. Not the debate over whether women have souls. Not foot-binding nor clitorectomy nor suttee nor the word "chattel." Sheitha, I say. Sheitha and Sheitha's daughter and Sheitha's daughter's daughter... I am hoarse before I'm done talking. Finally, I finish, saying for perhaps the fortieth or fiftieth time, "Knowledge is the only way to change it. Knowledge, and truth. Eve, listen—"

She goes with me to the tree. Her baby daughter in her arms, she goes with me. She chooses a bright red apple, and she chews her mouthful so completely that when she transfers it to Sheitha's lips there is no chance the baby could choke on it. Together, they eat the whole thing.

I am tired. I don't wait around for the rest: Adam's return, and his outrage that she has acted without him, his fear that now she knows things he does not. His arrival. I don't wait. I am too tired, and my gut twists as if I had swallowed something foul, or bitter. That happens sometimes, without my intending it. Sometimes I eat something with a vitamin I know I need, and it lies hard in my belly like pain.

☼

This is not the way you heard the story.

But consider who eventually wrote that story down. Consider, too, who wiped up the ink or scrubbed the chisel or cleaned the printing office after the writing down was done. For centuries and centuries.

But not forever.

So this may not be the way you heard the story, but you, centuries about Eve's screams on her childbed, and Sheitha's murder at the hands of her husband, and Sheitha's daughter's cursing of her rebellious mother as the girl climbed willingly onto her husband's funeral pyre, and her daughter's harlotry, and her daughter's forced marriage at age nine to a man who gained control of all her camels and oases. You know all that, all the things I didn't tell poor Eve would happen anyway. But you know too—as Eve would not have, had it not been for me—that knowledge can bring change. You sit cross-legged at your holodecks or in your pilot chairs or on your councils, humming, and you finally know. Finally— it took you so fucking long to digest the fruit of knowledge and shit it out where it could fertilize anything. But you did. You are not stupid. More— you know that stupidity is only the soul asleep. The awakened sleeper may stumble a long time in the dark, but eventually the light comes. Even here.

I woke Eve up.

I, the mother.

So that may not be the way you heard the story, but it is the way it happened. And now—finally, finally—you know.

And can forgive me.

Copyright © 1995 by Nancy Kress

Dantzel Cherry has recently sold stories to Cast of Wonders *and* Timeless Tales. *We're happy to welcome her back for her fifth appearance in* Galaxy's Edge.

LIVECASTING MY DESCENT INTO THE MARTIAN UNDERWORLD

by Dantzel Cherry

I maneuver around an outcropping of rocks in my trusty Rover, kicking up red dust into the pristine Martian canyon, and find the permafrost waiting for me in all its unexplored glory. On either side the cameras swivel, livecasting my every movement to the viewers back on Earth.

"This is a great shot," I say into my comm, bringing Rover to a stop and manually focusing Camera A on my establishing shot. I give a thumbs-up and wide-mouthed grin at the camera. "This will look awesome back home."

"Perfect, Sandeep," our producer Sally says in my left earpiece. "Do you have any lines prepared? Because I can—"

"Not this again," Commander Dosela says in my right earpiece. "Drive to the collection point on the map, get the soil sample, and get out. We aren't ready to explore this riverbed in depth yet."

"Who said 'explore?'" I say. "I'm boosting our ratings. It'll only take another minute."

I roll forward a couple of inches.

Sally, of course, backs me up. "The HAB isn't cutting it for the viewers."

Commander Dosela ignores Sally's reminder about our funding. "Adjust course, Sandeep. Move that giant space heater the hell off the permafrost."

"I only need ten seconds!" Sally says. "Pan Camera A left for ten seconds, then zoom in and tighten your focus on the peaks."

"*No.* We'll schedule a drone next week and capture all the footage your little hearts desire," Dosela says in my right.

But Sally's right. We need the human element. Man versus nature and all that. Exciting shots make for increased funding, whether Dosela admits it or not. I'm doing this for her own good.

I pause and twist my shoulders slightly—a better angle for the camera—and Rover's boom zooms closer.

The ground under Rover groans.

"Are you sinking?" Dosela says. "Get—"

Another groan. Rover trembles.

I pull Rover into gear, but it's too late. Mars has taken the wheel now.

"Sandeep? Repor—" Dosela cuts out on my right.

"The boom is out! Sandeep, tell us how you feel!" And then Sally's voice shorts out.

My suit protects me from the initial blows, but it can't protect my neck when Rover slams into a rock. I fly backward, cracking the windows. Metal screeches and crunches.

Another hard bounce.

A sharp pain lances my thigh.

The lights in Rover flicker through the dust.

I've stopped moving. I think.

My vision reels, my ears ring, and I'm distracted by the warm blood pooling in my suit from whatever is spiking my thigh.

I rip it out. Scream. Feel sick.

With clumsy gloved hands I pull supplies from the med kit and staunch the flow, but I probably sealed the suit leak wrong. Guess I'll find out soon enough.

"Dosela? Sally?" I first whisper, then shout into my comm. "I'm ready to turn around now, Commander!"

Radio silence.

At the very least the receiver's crushed. I'm alone down here.

Well, maybe. Most of the lights in Rover are working—most of the important ones anyway. And if the cam in my helmet is still working and being underground isn't running interference with my video, then I might have a captive audience of one billion watch me bleed out in the remains of an underwater river on the Red Planet.

That's enough motivation to spur me forward.

The dust has nearly settled. I grunt as I push Rover's door open and hobble out, feeling weak.

"Dosela? Sally?"

Above me glows a dull red haze. Up the walls I climb, but the rocks crumble and down I slide. Up. And down again. I circle the hole, hoping for just one viable escape route. I take another run at a likely-looking spot and slip a few steps in.

I stand up, ready to admit defeat, but a lump catches my eye. I pull it closer.

Limestone? Really?

Fully awake from the adrenaline rush, I lug the precious rubble over to Rover for testing. I rest and inspect it while the test is running. The skeletal fragments twist and wrinkle in a way that the coral, foram, and molluscs back on Earth do not, but my trained eye understands what they are.

The test comes back positive for calcite and aragonite: unquestionable proof of life on Mars, and Rover and I are sitting in the middle of it.

"Dosela! Sally? Is anyone seeing this?"

I bask in my own glory for a moment. If my transmitter's still running, everyone back home sees this and Sally's weeping with joy over the ratings. Florence is plunked down at the terminal next to Dosela, capturing screen shot after screen shot of the hollow spaces where water once carved a path through the sediment with insistent vigor, and someone is running a side-by-side comparison of Martian limestone and Earth limestone for the viewers back home. If the transmitter's still running, someone is shrieking "Life on Mars! Life on Mars!" at their TV screen, and everyone at NASA is gnashing their teeth that they didn't get to this first.

But—oh hell, if the cameras *are* out? Then Sally's prepping the rescue team's on-screen eulogies for me even as they come searching for my body.

I'm cold. And tired. My foot is sticky with the pooling blood. I'm not sure which will kill me first: lack of blood or lack of oxygen.

"Dosela? Sally?"

I could probably attempt a couple more climbs before passing out, but I'm not going to fool myself, and anyway, I'm not leaving my limestone behind.

I make myself comfortable in Rover, and use the rest of the medical wrap to tie my limestone to my waist. If someone gets here in time, I can explain my discovery. If they don't—well, they can't miss this.

My vision's too fuzzy to see properly now, but I'm not worried.

This is a great shot.

This will look awesome back home.

Copyright © 2018 by Dantzel Cherry

This is Canadian lawyer David L. Hebert's second published story, and we're pleased to be the ones to present it to you, as we did with his initial effort. Clearly he's honed his art by spinning fantasies to Canadian judges.

THE RESURRECTION OF ABIGAIL

by David L. Hebert

The last thing Abigail Florence Wright could remember was dying.

Dying had carried with it an indescribable feeling of peace and relaxation. Once the cancer had become more aggressive, the chemo couldn't keep up. Death was to be a welcome respite after eighty-six years of slogging through words to build stories and novels to pay her bills. Those last few months really wore her down. When death finally came it was a beautiful, reassuring silence.

But that was then, and this was now.

A man stared down at her. He had dark hair and appeared to be in his mid-forties. "Hello, Abi."

"Only my friends call me Abi," she croaked. She tried to sit up, but restraints held her snugly in place.

The man gingerly pressed his hand on her shoulder, encouraging her to lie back flat on the bed. "You can't get up yet. There are more tests and more scans to complete."

Abigail stopped struggling, cleared her throat, and asked, "Can you tell me where I am, and what I'm doing here?"

The man smiled. "You've been revived. Your body has been genetically replaced."

Abigail almost started to object and insist that she had never asked to be revived, but she noticed that the man was turning a knob on one of the many tubes that seemed to be connected to her. Within seconds she was asleep.

✧

There were no restraints on her when she awoke. She felt rested. She could feel silk against her skin and warmth from the covers of the bed. She was alone in the room.

Revived, he had said. *How?* And better still, *why?* She wasn't wealthy. There was no way her estate could afford this. True, she'd won several awards as a mildly-renowned science-fiction writer, but accolades didn't necessarily translate into money. She'd had a couple of category bestsellers, and the sales of her other books had been respectable, but nothing to cause George R. R. Martin or Stephen King to lose any sleep over. She had never been wealthy.

She was surprised to find that she could sit up easily on the edge of the bed. She gingerly placed her feet on the floor, standing with ease, perfectly upright, which she hadn't been able to do in years. She took a tentative step, then another. The bed was at the center of a large room. The tubes and wires were gone, as was the equipment that had surrounded her. There was a door, but there was no handle. The only other decoration in the room was a mirror. She walked over and looked into it.

The octogenarian with the sagging skin and the myriad wrinkles was nowhere in evidence. Her body felt different, and it *looked* different. She had grown accustomed to the combined effects of gravity and aging, but from the image before her, she appeared to be in her late twenties or early thirties. Instead of her hard-fought reality, her reflection was an idealized image, and more like a teenage fantasy than any realistic expectation of what a real woman actually looked like. She noticed something hanging on a hook on the wall beside the curtain. It was a white dress. She slipped it on over her naked form. It hugged her curves and was cut too low and too short for her taste, but it was all there was to wear.

She went back to the bed and sat. After a few moments, the door slid open and the man stepped into the room.

"Abi! You have awakened!"

Abigail smiled back at him. "Please call me Abigail. And I'm glad you're back. Now you can tell me what all this is about."

"You are my favorite author," he said, smiling. He moved to the edge of the bed and sat.

She'd heard that one before, ages ago, usually from guys who were hoping to talk or flatter her into bed. He explained that he was a scientist, and he had combined his life's work with his fascination with her work. He told her about his experiments and his scientific achievements, his history as a geneticist

and neurobiologist, and his attempts to reconstruct her, using her DNA.

"And I was successful!" he concluded. "I was actually able to reconstruct your neurology from a series of scans of your remains."

"My remains?"

"I had them exhumed. I am not without resources." There was that damned smile again. "The dry heat of the Arizona mausoleum preserved the brain tissue well enough that the scans allowed me to reproduce your consciousness, with most of your memories intact."

"Why would you want to do that?" she asked him.

Something in his eyes changed. There was an almost wistful look to them. "There's never been another writer like you! I want to see you create still more masterpieces!"

She had no idea how to respond to that.

"Your stories are magical," he enthused, "and contain insight that still rings true today, nearly twenty years after your passing. The world has been deprived of your exquisite voice for far too long. You will be able to sing again!"

Isn't he poetic? she thought dryly. "What makes you think I want to continue writing?" Obviously this guy hadn't lived through it, spending hours on the phone per month with customer service reps from the utilities, trying to stall for weeks while waiting for publishers' increasingly late checks to arrive.

"Your words make the world a better place." He seemed so very passionate about this, though he was clearly a crackpot, scientific achievements be damned.

"So you are suggesting that I write?" she asked carefully.

He nodded enthusiastically. "The scans I've done of your reconstructed neuro-cortex show complete congruity. I was working from twenty-year-old desiccated tissue, so there's bound to be some slight memory issues with regards to specific incidents, but I believe that they'll all come back with use. Your creativity should be a part of that, combined with your extensive knowledge and talent."

Suddenly he stood up. "Come with me," he said, moving to the doorway. He waved his finger over a small metal plate near the jamb, and the door slid open. She followed him out into the hall. They walked a few steps to another doorway, he waved his finger again, and that door also slid open.

The room was huge, but it felt almost cramped by the aisles of shelving filled with neatly-organized boxes. A large table near the entrance was strewn with papers. Abigail glanced at it. She didn't have to look too closely to recognize her unique scrawl.

Plot notes. Character descriptions. Snippets of dialogue. Handwritten stream-of-consciousness conversations with herself about how situations would develop. Collectively, it was the behind-the-scenes work of everything she'd ever written.

She gave him a sideways glance. "I donated these to the University of Florida in 2012."

He flashed that knowing grin again. "They had digitized the whole collection by 2022. After that, the papers themselves were just taking up space. They agreed to let me have them for the cost of removing them." He looked almost smug as he picked up a box stuffed with used envelopes from a shelf. "I also managed to collect a number of your letters to publishers and fans. In fact, they helped me to reconstruct your genetic profile using the DNA I obtained from them." He returned the box to the shelf. "Come now, and I'll show you where you will write."

He led her out the door and down the hall to another room. Inside were four desks. On one sat an IBM Selectric typewriter, on another a generic PC, on the third a futuristic contraption that Abigail didn't recognize, and the surface of the fourth desk was clear, save for some pens in a holder and a stack of blank paper. There was a chair at each desk. Nothing adorned the walls.

"I read in one of your interviews that you prefer your writing quarters to be rather bland."

He explained that she had admitted to having preferences, over time, for various machines on which to write—hence the Selectric and the computer, which was loaded with various versions of different software programs she had preferred over the decades. "You can use whichever you happen to prefer." He took her to the third desk. The futuristic-to-her machine was simply a computer with a holographic display. He turned it on, and the screen floated into view. Using gestures and voice commands, he explained, she could have access to the Omninet to research whatever she chose.

"The Omninet?"

"The Omninet is a subscription past all paywalls. You can research anything, including medical journals and newspaper archives, without a password." He gave her a brief introduction to its use as they sat together at the terminal. She picked up the basic commands quickly.

"I have an additional room to show you," he said, standing and walking toward the hallway. Directly across from the writing room was another door, which he activated. "This," he said as the door slid open, "is the library."

The library was larger than the writing room, and each wall was lined with shelves that were crammed with books. A mixture of hardcovers, trade paperbacks, and normal paperbacks covered all the available shelf space. There was a set of couches in the center of the room with tables between them. Abigail stepped closer to a shelf to examine the titles. She was only mildly surprised to find the nearest set of shelves covered with her own books, all of which looked to be in excellent shape. On the lower shelves sat collections of magazines and anthologies that contained stories she had written. Looking at her collected writings all together like this, Abigail concluded that there was no wonder it had felt like a hell of a lot of work.

"I've read a great many of the books in this library. This collection contains most of the important science fiction works of the twentieth and early twenty-first centuries. And, naturally, your section is complete."

He led her to a couch, and they sat.

"I hope you will find the library satisfactory. You mentioned in one of your interviews that you love to read old classics from the field."

Jesus Christ. What *hadn't* she said in these interviews? "Yes, it's a source of inspiration for me, at times."

"Well, you'll find the complete works of C.L. Moore, Henry Kuttner, and Robert Heinlein, including the pseudonyms they also published under, to name but a tiny handful. And in the balance of the books here, you'll find quite a few of your own contemporaries, and most of the greatest works in the field up until the time of your death in 2015."

"So you expect me to write and find inspiration from re-reading books I've read before. What else is there to this life you've built for me?"

"All in good time," he said. "Your physiology, neurology, and biology all appear to be working harmoniously, but we need to keep monitoring you to make sure that remains the case. As I gain more confidence in your physical abilities, we will establish a routine that suits you." He stood and held out a hand to her. "We will be more comfortable in the lounge. Come." He helped her to her feet and led her to the door.

He led her down the hallway to another nondescript door, which he opened by waving his hand over the panel mounted beside it. They then entered a small lounge with comfortable upholstered chairs placed around an expensive wooden table. He beckoned her to sit and, after she was seated, took the chair beside her.

"I am a neurobiologist by training," he began. "My parents were both scientists. I am an only child, and my parents were opposed to the mindless entertainment of television and movies. They encouraged me to embrace reading as a hobby, and filled the house with books. My father was a science fiction fanatic."

He was lost in his memories as he recounted his story. "My mother was also a voracious reader, although her tastes were more devoted to titles from the nonfiction field, and so I was surrounded by an incredible selection of both science fiction and educational books about science and technology. I must have been eleven or twelve when I stumbled across one of your books, and, frankly, I was hooked. I worked my way through the titles of yours that we had in the family library, and when I exhausted those, I begged my father for more. He was happy to encourage my reading habit, and he ordered the books I requested. By the time I was sixteen I had read all of your works. I had also read the works of many other authors of the various periods over the years that marked the rising popularity of the genre, but none contained the unique qualities that yours possessed."

Abigail supposed that she should take his interest as a compliment, but she sensed some inconsistencies in his thinking. "What are these unique qualities you've mentioned?"

She was trying to be cordial to stay on his good side, but she was genuinely curious. Had he seen something the rest of the world hadn't? Any success

Abigail had created was generated by hard work, but it seemed that he was placing some form of reverence in the words of the stories themselves. For Abigail, the hard work had been cranking out the words, one by one, that would ultimately tell the story. The story, not the turn of phrase, was what paid the bills, and each month there would be more bills to pay, so new words went into new stories, and the process continued. But the words were just the necessary first step.

"I don't know that I can explain it any better than I already have," he said. "Your words speak truth, and life, and vitality. All of your characters, even the ill-intentioned ones, have an inner decency that runs through everything you write. Your characters always do the right thing."

"I would tend to agree," she said in measured tones, "that my characters do what's right at the first available opportunity."

He continued. "Your novels truly spoke to me during my formative years. I honestly believe your books helped define my sense of self, my morality, and my role as a human being. I am the person I am because of you."

"But you already have shelves of my books. Why is it so important to you that I continue to write?"

He became animated and expressive. "I want to read more of your work! I created the resurrected you! Who knows what your work will inspire me to do next? You can devote all your time now to writing," he concluded, placing his hand on her knee and gripping it with a firmness that sent a shiver of alarm through her body.

She gently removed it. "All in due time," she said. After a brief pause, she turned to face him. "If you expect me to spend my time writing, I'm going to need my uniform."

He looked at her quizzically. "Uniform?"

She nodded. "Wasn't it in the interviews you read? Did none of them ever ask what I wore when I wrote? I need flannel nightgowns. Roomy ones. And silk or satin robes to wear over them. And I'll need comfy underwear, and a couple of bras."

She watched his expression begin to blanch as she stated her litany of demands. "That, of course," she continued, "is for when I'm writing. But I'll also need some casual clothes to wear during downtime and for supper. And perhaps clothes for any other functions that I'm not aware of as yet." She tugged at the snug skimpy white dress that hugged her figure. "*This* is definitely not going to cut it."

He was quiet for a moment, then assured her that her needs would be met. Suddenly he stood up. "I almost forgot! I'll be right back!" He rushed out the door, returning in a few moments with a crystal vase filled with a dozen fresh-cut white roses. He'd obviously stumbled upon some interview where she admitted to admiring them.

She stood and thanked him, taking them from him and placing them on the table. "They're absolutely beautiful!" They were, but she still felt the chill from earlier. She spent a moment fussing over them, moving a few around in the arrangement, and then turned to thank him again. He excused himself, and told her to get ready for supper.

☼

He led her into the dining room. Their place settings were at alternate ends of a long table. It was only after she was seated that she noticed that her silverware included no knife. The haute cuisine was served by robots; if there was any live staff in the kitchen, they were ghostly silent.

"Do you realize," she began, and paused to take a sip of her wine, "that you haven't even told me your name?"

"I am Dr. Josef Frankl—but I would appreciate it if you would call me Joe, Abi."

"I would appreciate it if you called me Abigail."

He set down his glass and arched an eyebrow. "It was my understanding from the writings about you that you preferred to be called Abi."

Abigail shook her head. "Do you believe everything you read?"

"By you? Yes."

"People called me that. I may not have corrected them, but I never said I preferred it, *Joe*." She smiled wryly as she stretched out his name.

"So be it, *Abigail*." His broad smile looked almost lewd.

She could feel the skin crawling on the back of her neck. She was not enjoying this charade of flirting with him, but it was necessary. While she was secretly harboring fantasies of stabbing him in the eye with a fork, such an action would not get her out

of this place. Her objective was to escape, not kill him and be trapped down here. What she needed was a plan—but while she'd be polite and pleasant, she wouldn't fawn over him. She had never been a fawner, and she wasn't about to start now.

"When can I leave this wing?" she asked.

"It is best," he answered, "to keep your existence under wraps for the time being. You are one of the biggest scientific breakthroughs of the century. Perhaps *the* biggest."

"So why keep me a secret?"

"The world is not ready to know you yet."

She shot him a glance that told him to cut the bullshit.

"You successfully recreated me twenty years after my death. Nothing you have said gives me any indication that you were involved in the creation of the technology. So why is it such a secret?"

"Oh, I have every intention of unveiling you to the public, Abigail," he said reassuringly. "As I've told you, we still have testing to complete before I can be certain that we won't face any medical complications. As of this moment, I'd say you are perfect, but I want to satisfy myself beyond doubt. It would be imprudent to announce your presence before I have reached that level of certainty. Until then, you will remain here in the citadel."

Citadel. Interesting name for it, she thought. "I have one more question, Joe."

He smiled at her. "And that is?"

"What you did—resurrecting me. Is it legal?"

He did not answer.

☼

When Abigail awoke the next morning, a white chest of drawers and a white wardrobe had been moved into the room. Inside was an assortment of the types of clothes she'd requested the day before. She was mildly impressed that he had acquiesced to her demands so quickly, and she was relieved that she was going to have something comfortable to wear while she figured out how to get out of this place.

The interior doors now opened for her as she approached. She wandered from her sleeping chambers out into the hall.

She turned left and began walking down a corridor she hadn't yet explored. A small alcove held a single painting on its wall. It caught her attention, but only because she didn't recognize it at first. Then recognition came flooding back: It was the cover art for what was quite possibly the worst book she had ever written. Oh, hell, who was she kidding? It may well have been the worst book *anybody* had ever written. The only reason it sold the few copies it had was because her name was on the cover.

The Goddess of Tartarus. Who the hell had she been trying to kid?

She had churned that one out in the middle of her divorce, when she was more often drunk than not, and the book was filled with inconsistencies and contradictions and what might have even been entire passages lifted word-for-word from her prior works, as various bloggers had suggested. She'd have made out better writing a cookbook—but then maybe the market wasn't quite ready for a cookbook where every recipe called for three fingers of scotch per serving.

There was some bitter irony that one of the central issues of the divorce revolved around her name and her ex-husband's persistent attempt to make her give it up. It was marital property, he said. She should have to pay him half of all future earnings, including anything she subsequently wrote, since it was his name to begin with. She'd lose ninety percent of her following if she had to switch names mid-course. It would be like starting her career over, and she wanted to avoid that at all costs.

The worst part was that it looked like the court was going to agree, and maybe *Goddess was* actually a subconscious attempt to trash any value the name had left in it. Maybe it was even the reason he asked for a temporary injunction to keep her from using the name until the case was decided, or unless she agreed to his exorbitant settlement proposal. Maybe it was just the booze. No wonder she didn't recognize the cover at first—she had only ever let herself look at it once, and in the haze, her memory of it had been successfully repressed.

At some point in the middle of those dark days she found the spark of inspiration to move past the alcohol, but more importantly, she moved past the self-pity that was making her turn to the booze in the first place. She signed off on her ex-husband's settlement proposal, abandoning most of her fortune

but hanging onto her rights. With those rights, foreign and reprint sales could hold her creditors at bay long enough for her to start writing saleable books again.

So she started once more, living in a basement apartment and subsisting on noodles and eggs. She paid her dues all over again, and within a few years she had regained her former prominence.

She studied the painting. It was actually a gorgeous piece of cover art, she decided. Her shame arose from the contents, not from the painting. After all, she decided, you can't judge a cover by its book.

The dress that she had found hanging on the hook in the bedroom was the same as the dress worn by the woman on the cover. The cover's white hallways of the glistening palace were reminiscent of the long white corridors she had wandered down to get here. For the first time in years she wished she could remember that damned book.

The complete collection of her works was just down the hall in the library. The novel had been written over a half a century ago, and she had very little memory of what had gone into the damned thing in the first place.

Well, she was about to find out. She made her way to the library and found the paperback copy, which was its only form of release. She sat down on one of the couches, put her feet up on the table, and began to read.

She had often said that she could write a novel in her sleep, and here was proof that she had pretty much done just that. None of it seemed familiar. There was a citadel of some sort where Abigail had placed her heroine, trapped, unable to escape from the clutches of her tormentor. The evil and grotesque figure was obviously her ex-husband, and she herself was the virtuous and troubled heroine. It was a sad novel, dystopian in tone, and different from the titles she had been previously known for.

Yet somehow she had pulled this one off. The book had enough of the elements to satisfy, and something quirky in the telling had resonated with enough readers that the book became its own petite classic in her collection. The story elements were all there. The things that would draw the reader in, those little hidden unanswered questions that unfold as the story progresses, the little pieces that come alive in the imagination. Yes, the novel was minimally passable, and in more than a couple of places she actually found herself feeling mildly impressed. In retrospect, if this book hadn't had so much negative attachment to it, she might have revisited it and turned it into something worthwhile.

And Frankl was one of the ones who had become a devotee. Abigail suddenly understood. She had written the script, and he planned to produce it. But not for film or television—no, he was producing a real-life performance for an audience of one. Himself.

Suddenly Abigail rushed to the writing room.

✧

The computer ran smoothly enough, and she was simply typing up the story that had come to her. She proofread it once and made some minor corrections, but she was satisfied with the overall structure of the short piece.

In the first-person story, she cast herself as the heroine, captive in the dreaded prison on Silonurus III. She wrote in a romantic interest, a genius geneticist who worked for the prison but whose loyalties lay with her. She didn't escape, but with the help of the geneticist her life became tolerable. But the key to the story was that the protagonist's romantic interest was richly and continuously rewarded when he gave in to her various demands. Abi hoped it would be enough to set her plan in motion.

Just before she sent it to the printer, she changed the title to all caps as the finishing touch: YOU MAY CALL ME ABI.

✧

That evening, at supper, she made small talk. After dessert, she reached into the pocket of her pantsuit and pulled out the few pages she had printed and folded in half. She smoothed them out on the table.

"I've written a new story," she told Frankl. "I'd like your opinion."

The expression on his face was unlike anything she had seen before—a little bit shocked, a tad stunned, and accompanied by a touch of awe. She carried it over to him. "Maybe you can read it tonight before bed, or in the morning after you wake up."

She wanted to encourage him to read it immediately, but it was very important that she did not come across as eager. She hadn't written the romantic interest as anyone in particular. In fact, she'd left out as much detail as possible about the character. With Frankl's apparent penchant for projecting his own wants and desires onto a situation, she hoped that he'd identify with the male character simply because that character appeared to be on the receiving end of what Abigail suspected Frankl truly wanted. With luck, he would embrace the written word in the same way he had with *Tartarus*, and Abigail could use it to escape from this prison that he had built around her.

He gathered up the pages. "I will go and read it now."

She finished her wine and set down the glass. "I'll be in the library."

✧

As the door slid open, the mix of emotions on Frankl's face was hard for Abigail to read. He stepped slowly and quietly into the library.

"I have read your story," he said slowly, as he came to a stop in the center of the room. He smiled broadly and met her gaze directly. "It is quite possibly the best story you have ever written." He became more animated as he spoke. "The character development is incredible! The slight tension giving way to the growing love between the two characters in the face of punishment for their illicit affair, and the risks they take to share that love—it's such a beautiful story!"

"I am so glad you enjoyed it. It was fun to write." She smiled at him. "As you see, I borrowed your occupation."

"I noticed."

"I'm a few years out of date as far as current events go, and I have no idea what kind of jobs people have nowadays, or even what they wear. I needed something, so I used it. I hope you don't mind," she said apologetically. She had to play this coyly; she hoped that she was convincing.

"How could I mind? It's a fabulous story!" he exclaimed, and the excitement in his voice seemed genuine. Abigail was relieved. It wasn't even a story at all. It was just a couple of scenes stuck together with a lot of dialogue about forbidden love and undying loyalty. But she had hoped that it would resonate with him and his fantasies, and it looked like she'd hit the mark.

Now it was time for the next phase of her plan.

☼

"Have you been working on new stories?" asked Frankl as he stepped into the library the next day.

She looked up from her seat on the couch. "I've tried," she said, feigning weariness. "The ideas haven't been coming very easily. Every time I think I've got one, it fizzles. There's nothing that holds my attention. If I'm going to be able to write, I need to get out into the world and experience it again. I need to see some shows, go to the theater, and the opera, and the ballet. It's getting out there and living that gives a writer the ability to construct scenes and build characters. You can't create in a vacuum—and this place is a creative vacuum."

"What do you need to do?"

"Isn't there an opera we can go to? A ballet? Some live theater—Shakespeare, Albee, even Neil Simon? Anything that shows real human beings doing something creative." She smiled at him. "Don't you think it would be a wonderful evening—going out on the town to enjoy some high arts, and especially to engage in the art of people-watching, to see what they're wearing, what they're saying, how they're reacting, wondering what kind of lives they live?"

He stared at her rather blankly.

She shook her head sadly. "You still don't quite get it. This is how a writer creates. Ideas don't just pop into her head with no input from the outside world. Asimov never met a robot, and Clarke never met an alien. Story ideas come from clashes of observed real events colliding with ideas of 'What if *this* happened to cause it?' or 'What if *that* happens as a result?' This writer's block I'm experiencing is because I've got no outside stimulation to trigger the creative reaction."

He acquiesced. "If you think it will help alleviate the writer's block, I'm happy to do it. And nobody knows who you are. We should be able to attend in near anonymity." He brushed a lock of hair from her forehead to the side, tucking it behind her ear. "Aside from whatever attention your beauty may bring."

She forced a big smile. "I'll need a dress."

☼

Abigail was taken aback with the beauty of the Opera House's lobby. The gilt decorations and the lush red draperies created a truly elegant atmosphere, blending with the walls and their coverings of red and gold textured wallpaper. They were early enough that there were not yet a great many people.

She truly felt stunning in the dress Frankl had chosen. It was sleek and black with a rolled collar that showed off her figure but left more to the imagination than his typical selection might have. She was relieved to have most of her skin covered for once.

She glanced around the room at the exit signs, noting their locations. One was close to the front entrance, beside the coat check area and the door to the manager's office. The others were next to stairwells on the sides of the lobby. She looked at the gold-and-red walls beside the exits, straining to see details but having a difficult time. Finally, gazing in the direction of wall by the manager's office, she could see what she had been striving to see. She turned back to Frankl.

"Let's stay in the lobby for as long as we can," she said. "I haven't been in a crowd for so long, I forget what it feels like. Five minutes before show time should give us plenty of time to get to our seats."

Frankl was looking around the room. "Have you found anything interesting to watch?"

She smiled at him. "You never know what's going to interest you. An idea can be sparked by anything. An earring, perhaps. Or the decorative handle on a cane. Or a drunk uttering unpopular truths. There's no telling what might spark that creative imagination. You just have to be ready when it finally happens." She took his hand and pulled. "Come. Let's circle the room."

They made their way around the large lobby, casually observing the people around them. Abigail took note of their mode of dress, their accessories, and the styles of their hair, but also their countenances, and the worries and emotions that showed through. She was actively masking her own, but she was taking total stock of those around her.

"Now why don't you grab us some drinks before show time?"

"Gin and tonic," he said knowingly.

"I knew that had to have been in an interview somewhere," she said dryly as he ambled off toward the bar. She waited a moment, and as he settled in line she moved toward the wall beside the manager's office. She looked around the now-crowded lobby as Frankl slowly made his way up to the bar. He was third in line when she reached up and pulled the fire alarm.

✧

Abigail had arrived at the restaurant for a late dinner with her recently-acquired attorney. She shook hands with him as she sat down next to him.

"Frankl is still in custody," the attorney told her. "He's been denied bail. If he pleads not guilty, you may have to testify."

"Better than introducing me as an exhibit. Have they pressed charges?"

The attorney shrugged. "Cloning is still highly illegal, but I'm not certain they've settled upon a charge. Would you like me to check?"

Abigail shook her head. "Don't bother. Any luck on the stuff I hired you for?"

He nodded. "I've done the research. This is unprecedented, but the rights to your prior works should be yours."

"It's that simple?"

He nodded an affirmative. "We have the DNA results to prove who you are."

"And the memoirs? Have you heard anything yet?" she asked.

"I was waiting to surprise you. The auction for your memoirs was held this afternoon. The successful publisher has pledged a half-million-dollar advance."

She smiled and held up her champagne glass. "Thank you, Mr. D'Amico."

He clinked glasses with her. "Please call me Matt, Ms. Wright."

She took a sip in celebration. "Please call me Abi."

Copyright © 2018 by David L. Hebert

Mercedes Lackey is the author of more than a hundred novels, creator of the Valdemar universe, occasional collaborator with Anne McCaffrey, Eric Flint, and Andre Norton, and frequent bestseller. We're happy to welcome her back to the pages of Galaxy's Edge.

A BETTER MOUSETRAP

by Mercedes Lackey

If there was one thing that Dick White had learned in all his time as SuperCargo of the CatsEye Company Free Trader *Brightwing*, it was that having a cat purring in your ear practically forced you to relax. The extremely comfortable form-molding chair he sat in made it impossible to feel anything but comfortable, and warm black fur muffled both of Dick White's ears, a steady vibration massaging his neck. "Build a better mousetrap, and the world will beat a path to your door," Dick said idly, as SCat poured himself like a second fluid, black rug over the blue-gray of his lap. It was SKitty who was curled up around his shoulders, vibrating contentedly in what Dick called her "subsonic purr-mode," while her mate took it as his responsibility to make sure there was plenty of shed hair on the legs of his gray shipsuit uniform.

"What?" asked Terran Ambassador Vena Ferducci, looking up from the list of Lacu'un nobles petitioning for one of SKitty's latest litter. The petite, dark-haired woman sat in a less comfortable, metal chair behind a stone desk, which stood next to a metal rack stuffed with archaic rolled paper documents. The Lacu'un had not yet devised the science of filing paperwork in multiples yet, which made them ultra-civilized in Vena's opinion. This, her office in the Palace of the Lacu'ara and Lacu'teveras, was not often used for that very reason. When she dealt with *Terran* bureaucracy, she needed every electronic helper she could get.

The list she perused was very long and made rather cumbersome due to the Lacu'un custom of presenting all official court-documents in the form of a massively ornamented yellow-parchment scroll, with case and end caps of engraved bronze and illuminated capital-initials. Dick had a notion that somewhere in the universe there probably was a collector of handwritten documents who would pay a small fortune for it, but when every petitioner on the list had been satisfied, it would probably be sent to the under-clerks, scraped clean, and reused.

"It's an old Terran folk-saying," Dick elaborated, and gestured to the list by way of explanation. "One which certainly seems to be borne out by our present situation."

"Yes, well, given the length of this list we're doubly fortunate that SKitty and SCat are so—ah—*fertile*, and that BioTech is willing to send us their shipscat wash-outs." Vena stretched out her hand towards SCat's head, and the huge black tom cooperated by craning his neck toward her. Even before her fingers contacted his fur, SCat was purring loudly, giving Dick an uncannily similar sensation to being strapped in while the ship he served was under full power.

Dick White could well be one of the wealthiest supercargoes in the history of space-trade—his share of the profits from CatsEye Company's lucrative trade with the Lacu'un amounted to quite a tidy sum. It wasn't enough to buy and outfit his own ship—yet—but if trade progressed as it had begun, there was the promise that one day it would be.

Not that I want my own ship yet! he told himself. *Not until I know as much as Captain Singh. There are easier ways to commit suicide than pretending I know enough to command a starship when all I really know is how to run the cargo hold!*

Not that Captain Singh would *let* him take his profit-share and do something so stupid. Dick grinned to himself, imagining the captain's face if he showed up in the office with *that* kind of hare-brained proposal. Captain Singh's expression would be one to behold—following which, Dick would probably find himself stunned unconscious and wake under the solicitous attentions of a concerned head-shrinker!

The Captain *had* been willing, even more than willing, to let Dick stay on-planet for a few Terran-months though, after SKitty and SCat announced the advent of a litter-to-be. One of her last litter was co-opted to serve as shipscat pro tem, while Dick and his two charges waited out the delivery, matura-

tion, and weaning of eight little black furballs who were, if that was possible, even cuter than the last batch. It was a good thing that they all *were* on-planet too, because the Octet managed to get themselves into a hundred times more mischief than the previous lot.

The trouble is, they have a lot of energy, absolutely no sense, and no fear at all at this age. Brainless kitten antics rapidly begin to pall when you've fished a wailing fuzz-mote out of the comconsole for the fifteenth time in a single shift.

But every Lacu'un in the palace, from the Lacu'teveras down to the lowliest scullery-lad, was thrilled to the toes—or rather, claws—to play with, rescue, and cuddle the Bratlings. If SKitty and SCat had not taken their duties as parents, palace-guardians, and role models so seriously, they wouldn't have had to do anything but lie about and wait for the kittens to be carried in to them for feeding.

Fortunately for all concerned, their parents had powerful senses of responsibility toward their offspring. Both cats were born and bred—literally—for duty. Yes, they were cats, with a cat's sense of independence and contrariness, but they took duty very, very seriously. And their duty was Vermin Control.

This was a duty that went back centuries to the very beginnings of the association of man and cat, but until BioTech developed shipscats, never had a feline been better suited to or more cooperative in the execution of that duty. Furthermore, Dick now knew what few others did—that the shipscats so necessary to the safety of traders and their ships were actually a highly profitable byproduct of other research, secret research, designed to give the men and women of the Patrol uniquely clever comrades-in-arms.

These genetically altered cats were not just clever, it was not just that they had forepaws modeled after the forepaws of raccoons—oh no. That was not enough. Patrol cats were telepaths.

SCat had been a patrol cat—but although he could understand the thoughts of humans, he couldn't speak to them. This was a flaw, so far as the Patrol was concerned, though not an insurmountable flaw. However, when criminals took over the ship he served on and killed all of those aboard, SCat was the only survivor and the only witness—unable to call for help or relate what he had witnessed, he had sought for help from his own kind and found it in SKitty. When the same criminals learned SCat was still alive and tried to eliminate him and the crew of the Free Trader ship *Brightwing*, for good measure, it had been Dick's research and deductive reasoning that had learned the truth in time, and with SCat's and SKitty's help he had foiled the plot.

As for SKitty, she was something of an aberration herself—ordinary shipscats were not supposed to be telepathic *or* fertile; she was both.

As far as Dick could tell, she was telepathic only with him—though, given that she was all cat, with a cat's puckish sense of humor, she might well choose not to let him know she could "speak" to others. Everyone on the ship knew she was fertile, though—when they had first come to the world of the Lacu'un, she'd already had one litter and was pregnant with another. That first litter—born and raised in the ship—had shown just what kind of a nightmare two loose kittens could be within the close confines of a spaceship. Dick had not been looking forward to telling Captain Singh of the second litter when SKitty had solved the problem for them.

The Lacu'un, a race of golden-skinned, vaguely reptilian anthropoids, suffered from the depredations of a particularly voracious, fast, and apparently indestructible pest called *kreshta*. The only way to keep them from taking over completely was to lock anything edible (and the creature could eat practically anything) in airtight containers of metal, glass, ceramic, or stone, and build only in materials the pest couldn't eat. The pests did keep the streets so clean that they sparkled and there was no such thing as a trash problem, but those were the only benefits to the plague.

The Lacu'un had just opened their planet to trade from outside, and the *Brightwing* was one of several ships that had arrived to represent either themselves or one of the large Companies. Only Captain Singh had the foresight to include SKitty in their delegation, however, for only he had bothered to research the Lacu'un thoroughly enough to learn that they placed great value on totemic animals and had virtually *nothing* in the way of domesticated predators themselves. He reckoned that a tame predator would be very impressive to them, and he was right.

SKitty had been on her best behavior, charming them all, and taking to this alien race immediately. The Lacu'teveras, the female co-ruler, had been particularly charmed, so much so that she had missed the presence of one of the little pests, which had bitten her. Enraged at this attack on someone she favored, SKitty had killed the creature.

For the Lacu'un, this was nothing short of a miracle, the end of a scourge that had been with them since the beginning of their civilization. After that moment, there was no question of anyone else getting most-favored trading status with the Lacu'un, ever.

CatsEye got the plum contract, SKitty's kittens-to-be got immediate homes, and Dick White's life became incredibly complicated.

Since then, he was no longer just an apprentice supercargo and Designated Shipscat Handler on a small Free Trader ship. He'd been imprisoned by Company goons, stalked and beaten within an inch of his life by cold-blooded murderous hijackers, and had to face the Patrol itself to bargain for SCat's freedom. He'd had enough adventure in two short Standard-years to last most people for the rest of their lives.

But all that was in the past. Or so he hoped.

For a while, anyway, it would be nice if the most difficult decision I had to make would be which of the Lacu'un nobles get SKitty-babies and which have to make do with shipscat washouts.

Those "washouts" were mature cats that for one reason or another couldn't adapt to ship life. Gengineering wasn't perfect, even now; there were cats that couldn't handle freefall, cats that were claustrophobes, cats that were shy or anti-social. Those had the opportunity to come here, to join the vermin-hunting crew. Thus far, thirty had made the trip, some to become mates for the first litter, others to take up solitary residence with a noble family. There were other washouts who didn't pass the intelligence tests, but those were never offered to the Lacu'un—they already filled a steady need for companions in children's hospitals and retirement homes, where the high shipscat intelligence wasn't needed, just a loving friend smart enough to understand what not to do around someone sick or in pain.

There were still far more Lacu'un who urgently craved the boon of a cat than there were cats to fill the need. Thus far, none of SKitty's female offspring had carried that rare gene for fertility—when one did, that one would go back to BioTech to be treated like the precious object she was, pampered and amused, asked to breed only so often as *she* chose. There was always a trade-off in any gengineering effort; lack of fertility was a small price to pay in a species as notoriously prolific as cats.

Meanwhile, the proud parents were in the last stages of educating their current offspring. There was a pile of the dead vermin just in front of Vena's desk; every so often, one of the half-grown kittens would bring another to add to the pile, then sit politely and wait for his parents to approve. Sometimes, when the pest was particularly large, SCat would descend from Dick's lap with immense dignity, inspect the kill, and bestow a rough lick by way of special reward.

Dick couldn't keep track of how many pests each of the kittens had destroyed, but from the size of the pile so far, the parents had reason to be proud of their offspring.

The kittens certainly inherited their parents' telepathic skills as well as their hunting skills, for just as it occurred to Dick that it was about time for them to be fed, they scampered in from all available doorways. In a moment, they were neatly lined up, eight identical pairs of yellow eyes staring avidly from eight little black faces beneath sixteen enormous ears. At this age, they seemed to consist mainly of eyes, ears, paws and tails.

The Lacu'un servant whose proud duty it was to feed the weanlings arrived with a bowl heaping with their imported food. She was clothed in the simple, silky draped tunic in the deep gold of the royal household. The frilled crest running from the back of her neck to just above her eye-ridge stood totally erect and was flushed to a deep salmon-color with pleasure and pride. She started to put the bowl on the floor, and the kittens leapt to their feet and ran for the food—

But suddenly SCat sprang from Dick's lap, every hair on end, spitting and yowling. He landed at the startled servant's feet and did a complete flip over, so that he faced his kittens. As they skidded on the slick stone, he growled and batted at them, sending them flying.

"*SCat!*" Vena shouted, as she jumped to her feet, horrified and angry. "What are you doing? Bad cat!"

"No he's not!" Dick replied, making a leap of his own for the food bowl and jerking it from the frightened servant's hands. He had already heard SKitty's frantic mental screech of :*Bad food!*: as she followed her mate off Dick's shoulders to keep the kittens from the deadly bowl.

"The food's poisoned," Dick added, sniffing the puffy brown nodules suspiciously, as the servant backed away, the slits in her golden-brown eyes so wide he could scarcely see the iris. "SCat must have scented it—that's probably one of the things Patrol cats are trained in. *I* can't tell the difference, but—" As SKitty held the kittens at bay, he held the bowl down to SCat, who took a delicate sniff and backed away, growling. "See?"

Vena's expression darkened, and she turned to the servant. "The food has been poisoned," she said flatly. "Who had access to it?" They both knew that Shivari, the servant, was trustworthy; she would sooner have thrown herself between the kittens and a ravening monster than see any hurt come to them. She proved that now by her behavior; her crest-frill flattened, she turned bright yellow—the Lacu'un equivalent of turning pale—and replied instantly.

"I do not know—I got the bowl from the kitchen—"

She grabbed Vena's hand and the two of them ran off, with Dick closely behind, still carrying the bowl. When they arrived at the kitchen, Vena and Shivari cornered all the staff while Dick blocked the exit. He had a fair grasp of Lacu'un by now, but Vena and Shivari were talking much too fast for him to get more than two words in four.

Soon enough, though, Vena turned away with anger and dissatisfaction on her face, while Shivari began a blistering harangue worthy of Captain Singh. "There was a new servant that no one recognized on staff this morning," Vena said in disgust. "Obviously they were smart enough to keep him away from the food meant for people, but no one thought anything of letting him open up the cat food into a bowl."

"Well, they know better now," Dick replied grimly.

"I'll put the Embassy on alert—and give me that—" Vena took the bowl from him. "I'll have the Marines run it through an analyzer."

Embassy guards by long tradition were called "Marines," although they were merely another branch of the Patrol. Dick readily surrendered the poisoned food to Vena, knowing that if SCat could smell a poison, the forensic analyzer every Embassy possessed—just in case—would easily be able to find it. Relations with the Lacu'un were important enough that Vena had gone from being merely a trade advisor and titular Consul to a full-scale Ambassador, with the attendant staff and amenities. It was that promotion that had persuaded her to remain here instead of returning to her former position in the Scouts.

Dick himself went to the storage vault that held the imported cat food, got a highly-compressed cube out, and opened it over a freshly washed bowl. The stuff puffed up to ten times its compressed size once it came into contact with air and humidity; it would be impossible to tamper with the packages without a resulting "explosion" of food. The entire feline family flowed into the kitchen as soon as his fingers touched the package; the kittens swarmed around his legs, mewling piteously, but he offered the bowl for SCat's inspection before allowing them to engulf it.

His mind buzzed with questions, but two were uppermost—who would have tried to poison the kittens, and why?

✩

SCat and SKitty herded their kittens along like a pair of attentive sheepdogs when they'd finished eating, following behind Dick as he left the palace, heading for the Embassy. The Marine at the entrance gave him a brisk nod of recognition, saving her grin for the moving black-furred flock behind him.

A second Marine at a desk just inside, skilled in the Lacu'un tongue, served double-duty as a receptionist. "The Ambassador is expecting you, sir," he said. "She left orders for you to go straight in."

Dick led his parade past the desk—a desk of cast marble reinforced with plastile, which would serve very nicely as a blast-and-projectile—proof bunker at need. The door to Vena's office (a cleverly concealed blast-door) was slightly ajar; it sensed his approach and opened fully for him after a retinal scan.

"Have you ever wondered why our peaceful hosts happen to field a battle-ready army?" Vena asked him, without even a preliminary greeting.

"Ah, no, I hadn't—but now that you mention it, it does seem odd." Dick took a seat, cats pooling around his ankles, as Vena tossed her compuslate aside.

"Our hosts aren't the sole representatives of their race on this dirtball," Vena replied, with no expression that Dick could see. "And *now* they finally get around to telling me this. It seems that there is another nation entirely on this continent—we thought that it was just another fief of the Lacu'ara, and they never disabused us of that impression."

"Let me guess—the other side doesn't like Terrans?" Dick hazarded.

"I wish it was that simple. Unfortunately, the other side worships the *kreshta* as children of their prime deity." Vena couldn't quite repress a snarl. "Kill one, and you've got a holy war on your hands—we've been slaughtering hundreds for better than two years. The attempt on the Octet was just the opening salvo for us heretics. The Chief Minister has been here, telling me all about it and falling all over himself in apology. Here—" She pulled a micro reader out of a drawer in her desk and tossed it to him. "My head of security advises that you commit this to memory."

"What is it?" Dick asked, thumbing it on, and seeing (with some puzzlement) the line drawing of a nude Lacu'un appear on the plate.

"How to kill or disable a Lacu'un in five easy lessons, as written by the Patrol Marines." Her face had gone back to that deadpan expression again. "Lieutenant Reynard thinks you might need it."

The prickling of claws set carefully into his clothing alerted him that one of the cats was swarming up to drape itself over his shoulders, but somewhat to his surprise, it wasn't SKitty, it was SCat. The tom peered at the screen in his hand with every evidence of fascinated concentration too.

He was Patrol, after all… was his second thought, after the initial surprise. And on the heels of that thought, he decided to hold the reader up so that SCat could use the touch screen too.

It was easier to disable a Lacu'un than to kill one, at least in hand-to-hand combat. Their throats were armored with bone plates, their heads with amazingly thick skulls. But there were vulnerable major nerve-points at all joints; concentrated pinpoint pressure would paralyze everything from the joint down when applied there. When Dick figured he had the scanty contents by heart, he tossed the reader back to Vena, though what he was supposed to do with the information was beyond him at the moment. He wasn't exactly trained in anything but the most basic of self-defense—that was more in Erica Makumba's line, and she was several light-years away at the moment.

"The Lacu'un Army has been alerted, the Palace has been put under tight security, and the caretakers of the other cats have been warned about the poisoning attempt. However, the mysterious kitchen-helper got clean away, so we can assume he'll make another attempt. My advisors and I would like to take him alive if we can—we've got some plans that may abort this mess before it gets worse than it already is."

SCat's deep-voiced growl showed what he thought of that idea, and Vena lowered her smoldering, dark eyes from Dick's to the tom's, and smiled grimly.

"I'd like to put a Marine guard on the cats—but I know that's hardly possible," Vena continued, as SCat and SKitty voiced identical snorts of disdain. "But let's walk back over to the Palace and talk about what we *can* do on the way."

SCat looked up at him and made an odd noise, easy enough to interpret. "SCat thinks he and SKitty can guard the kittens well enough," Dick replied, as Vena waved him through the door, a torrent of cats washing around his ankles.

"I'm sure he does," Vena retorted. "But let's remember that he's only a cat, however much his genes have been tweaked. I hardly think he's capable of understanding the danger of the current situation."

"He isn't just a cat, he was a *Patrol* cat," Dick pointed out, but Vena just shook her head at that.

"Dick, we don't even know exactly what we're into—all we know is that there was an attempt to poison the cats by an assassin that got away. We don't know if it was a lone fanatic, someone sent by our hosts' enemies, if there's only one or more than one—" She sighed as they reached the street. "We're doing all the intelligence gathering we can, but it's difficult to manage when you don't look anything like the dominant species on the planet."

The street was empty, which was fairly normal at this time of day when most Lacu'un were inside at their evening meal. The sky of this world seemed a bit greenish to him, but he'd gotten used to it—today, there were some clouds that might mean rain. Or might not, he didn't know very much about planet-side weather.

SCat's squall was all the warning Dick got to throw himself out of the way as something dark and fast whizzed through the place where he'd been standing. SKitty and the kittens fairly flew back to the safety of the Embassy, SCat whisked out of sight altogether; a larger, cloaked shape sprang from the shadows of a doorway, and before Dick managed to get halfway to his feet, the gray-cloaked, pale-skinned Lacu'un seized Vena and enveloped her, holding a knife to her throat.

"Be still, blasphemous she-demon!" it grated, holding both Vena's arms pinned behind her back in a way that had to be excruciatingly painful. She grimaced but said nothing. "And you, father of demons, be still also!" it snapped at Dick. "I am the righteous hand of Kresh'kali, the all-devouring, the purifier! I am the bringer of cleansing, the anointed of God! In His name, and by His mercy, I give you this choice—remove yourselves from our soil, take yourselves back into the sky forever, or you will die, first you and your she-demon and your god-killing pests, then all of those who brought you." Its voice rose, taking on the tones of a hellfire-and-brimstone preacher. "Kresh'kali is the One, the true God, whose word is the only law, and whose minions cleanse the world in His image; His will shall not be flouted, and His servants not be denied—"

It sounded like a well-rehearsed speech, and probably would have gone on for some time had it not been interrupted by the speaker's own scream of agony.

And small wonder, for SCat had crept up unseen even by Dick, until the instant he leapt for the assassin's knife-wielding wrist and fastened his teeth unerringly into those sensitive nerves at the joining of hand and wrist.

The knife clattered to the street, Vena twisted away, and Dick charged, all at the same moment; his shoulder hit the assassin and they both went down on the hard stone paving. But not in a disorderly heap, no; by the time the Marines came piling out of the Embassy, alerted by the frantic herd of cats, Dick had the miscreant face-down on the ground with both arms paralyzed from the shoulders down. And, miracle of miracles, this time *he* wasn't the one battered and bruised—in fact, he was intact beyond a few scrapes!

He wasn't taking any chances though; he waited until the Marines had all four limbs of the assassin in stasis-cuffs before he got off his captive and surrendered him.

"Do we turn him over to the locals?" one of the Marines asked Vena diffidently.

"Not a chance," she growled. "Hustle him into the Embassy before anyone asks any questions."

"What are you going to do?" Dick asked *sotto voce*, following the Marines and their cursing burden.

"I told you, we've got some ideas—and a couple of experiments I'd rather try on this dirt-bag rather than any Lacu'un volunteers," was all she said, leaving him singularly unsatisfied. All he could be certain of was that she didn't plan to execute the assassin out-of-hand. "*We* caught him, and we've got a chance to try those ideas out."

He continued to follow, and was not prevented, as Vena led the way up the stairs to the Embassy med-lab. The entire entourage of cats followed, and Vena not only *let* them, she waved them all inside before shutting and locking the door. The prisoner was strapped into a dental chair and gagged, which at least put an end to the curses, though not to the glares he cast at them.

But Vena dropped down onto one knee and looked into SKitty's eyes. "I know you're a telepath, SKitty," she said, in Terran. "Can you project to anyone but Dick? Could you project into our prisoner's mind? Put your voice in his head?"

SKitty turned her head to look up at Dick. :*Walls*,: she complained. :*Dick has no walls for SKitty*.:

"She says he's got barriers," Dick interpreted. "I understand that most nontelepathic people have and it's just an accident that the two of us are compatible."

"I may be able to change that," Vena replied, with a tight smile, as she got to her feet. "SKitty, I'm going to do some things to this prisoner, and I want you to tell me when the barriers are gone." She turned to a

cabinet and unlocked it; inside were hypospray vials, and she selected one. "We've been cooperating with the Lacu'un Healers; putting together drugs we've been developing for the Lacu'un," she continued. "There are hypnotics that are proven to lower telepathic barriers in humans, and I have a few that may do the same for the Lacu'un. If they don't kill him, that is." She raised an eyebrow at Dick. "You can see why we didn't want to test them even on volunteers."

"But if the drugs kill him—" Dick gulped.

"Then we save the Lacu'ara the cost of an execution, and we apologize that the prisoner expired from fear," she replied smoothly. Dick gulped again; this was a ruthless side of Vena he'd had no notion existed!

She placed the first hypo against the side of the prisoner's neck; the device hissed as it discharged its contents, and the prisoner's eyes widened with fear.

An hour later, there were only two vials left in the cabinet; Vena had administered all the rest, and their antidotes, with sublime disregard for the strain this was probably putting on the prisoner's body. The effects of each had been duly noted, but none of them produced the desired effect of lowering the barriers nontelepaths had against telepathic intrusion.

Vena picked up the first of the last two, and sighed. "If one of these doesn't work, I'll have to make a decision about giving him to the locals," she said with what sounded like disappointment. "I'd really rather not do that."

Dick didn't ask why, but one of the two Marines in the room with them must have seen the question in his eyes. "If the Ambassador turns this fellow over to them, they'll execute him, and that might be enough to send cold war hostilities into a real blaze," the young lieutenant muttered as Vena administered the hypo. "And the word from the Palace is that the other side is as advanced in atomic physics as our lot is. In other words, these are religious fanatics with a nuclear arsenal."

Dick winced; the Terrans would be safe enough in a nuclear exchange, and so would the bulk of city-dwellers, for the Lacu'un had mastered force-shield technology. But in a nuclear exchange there were always accidents and as yet it wasn't possible to encase anything bigger than a city in a shield; he'd seen enough blasted lands never to wish a nuc-war on anyone, and *certainly* not on the decent folk here.

SKitty watched the prisoner as she would a mouse; his eyes unfocused when the drug took hold, and *this* time, she meowed with pleasure. It didn't take Dick's translation for Vena to know that the prisoner's telepathic barriers to SKitty's probing thoughts were gone.

"Excellent!" she exclaimed with relief. "All right, little one—we're going to leave the room until you send one of the kittens to come get us. Let him think we've lost interest in him for the moment, *then* get into his head and convince him that *he* is a very, very bad kitten and *you* are his mother and you're going to punish him unless he says he's sorry and he won't do it again. Make him think that you are so angry that you might kill him if he can't understand how bad he's been. In fact, any of you cats that can get into his head should do that. Then make him promise that he'll always obey everything you tell him to, and don't let up the pressure until he does."

SKitty looked at Vena as if she thought the human had gone crazy, then sighed. *:Stupid,:* she told Dick privately. *:But okay. I do.:*

Dick was as baffled as SKitty was, as he followed Vena out into the hall, leaving the cats with the prisoner. "Just what is that going to accomplish?" he demanded.

She chuckled. "I rather doubt he's ever heard anyone speak in his mind before," she pointed out. "Not even his god."

Now Dick saw exactly what she'd had in mind—and stifled his bark of laughter. "He's going to be certain SKitty's more powerful than *his* god if she can do that—and if she treats him like a naughty child rather than an enemy to be destroyed—"

"Exactly," Vena said with satisfaction. "This is what Lieutenant Reynard wanted me to try, though we thought we'd have to add hallucinogens and a VR headset rather than getting right directly into his head. My problem was finding a way to tell her to act like an all-powerful, rebuking god in a way she'd understand. In the drugged state he's in now, he'll accept whatever happens as the truth."

"So *he* won't threaten the cats anymore—but then what?" Dick asked.

"According to Reynard, the worst that will happen is that he'll be convinced that this new god of his

enemies is a lot more powerful and real than his own, and that's the story he'll take back home."

"And the best?" Dick inquired.

She shrugged. "He converts."

"Just what will that accomplish?"

She paused, and licked her lips unconsciously. "We ran some simulations, based on what we've learned about Lacu'un psychology and projecting the rest from history. Historically, the most fanatic followers of a new religion are the converts who were just as fanatical in their former religion. In either case, imagine the reaction when he returns home, which he will, and miraculously, because we'll take a stealthed flitter and drop him over the border while he's drugged and unconscious. He'll probably figure out that we brought him, but there won't be any sign of how. Imagine what his superiors will think?"

The Marine lieutenant standing diffidently at her elbow cleared his throat. "Actually, you don't have to guess," he said respectfully. "As the Ambassador mentioned, we've been running a psych-profiles for possible contingencies, and they agree with her educated assessment. No matter what, the fanatics will be too frightened of the power of this new 'god' to hazard either a war or another assassination attempt. And if we send back a convert—there's a seventy-four-point-three percent chance he'll end up starting his own crusade, or even a holy war *within* their culture. No matter what, they cease to be a problem."

"Now *that*," Dick replied with feeling, "is really a better mousetrap!"

Copyright © 1989 by Mercedes Lackey

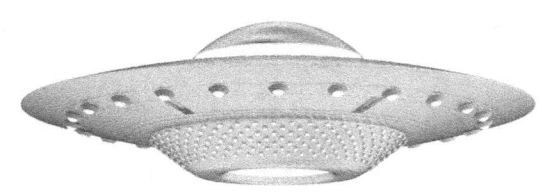

"Cat Lady" marks Susan Taitel's first professional sale. We expect to see more of her work in the months to come.

CAT LADY

by Susan Taitel

Another missing cat. Sixth one this week. A handsome seal point gazes disdainfully from the flyer. I tear the page from the tree, return to my Toyota, and take my collection of flyers from the glovebox. Fanning them out on the dash, I search for a pattern. All of the cats went missing from Uptown or Loring Park. All appear healthy and attentively groomed in the pictures. All of the owners have offered a reward between two hundred and one thousand dollars. One or two lost cats doesn't signify much, but six? My hackles are raised…pardon the pun.

After a brief rehearsal, I dial the number on the most recent flyer.

"Oh my god, you found him?" an anxious female voice asks.

"I'm sorry, no, but I was hoping I could speak to you in person."

"Why, exactly?" The cat's owner is justifiably suspicious"I believe I can find your cat, but I need to have a look at his environment."

"And you are?"

"My name is Vivian Kotek. I'm a detective." Kinda sorta.

"I'm not looking to hire a detective."

"All I want is the reward if I find him."

The owner identifies herself as Brenda and gives me an address near the Greenway. The concierge eyes me warily before buzzing me in. Maybe I should've changed out of my work clothes before coming over.

"This is his nest." Brenda gestures to a cardboard box lined with a threadbare towel. Next to it stands a virtually pristine, ultra-plush carpeted cat tree. "Those are his toys." She points out a feathered wand and several hand-felted mice. "He loves bottle caps too, but I worry about BPAs, you know?"

"Of course." I nod. "Did you get him from a breeder?"

"No, Gene was a shelter rescue. Louise too." She inclines her head toward a bookshelf, where a gray tabby peers down with feigned disinterest. "Poor thing is sick with worry."

At these words, Louise drops from her perch and casually leaves the room.

"Any idea how he got out?"

"I don't know! I don't let either of them near the door when it's open. The balcony is always locked. He's not an adventurous cat."

"Uh-hm," I agree, biting my tongue. Trying to pin down a cat's personality is like tying a ribbon on a wave.

I ask Brenda a few questions about Gene's eating and sleeping habits, his relationship with Louise, if he'd been acting strangely, etc. Then I have a look around the small but upscale one bedroom. There are no obvious escape points. I note the accumulation of bottle caps and hair ties behind the combination washer-dryer. Gene had secrets. Well done, Gene.

All appears normal. Which unsettles me. It's possible Gene is a feline Houdini, but my instincts say otherwise.

All appears normal at the next three houses as well. None of the owners know how their cat got out. They all woke up to find an absence of cat. With no signs of how it escaped. No doors left open and not a cat-flap in sight. They've put up flyers, posted on message boards, and offered rewards. To no avail. All are concerned and anxious. All simply want their cats home safe. I want the same. And if I collect a few rewards along the way? I can pay my bills, fill my gas tank to the top for once, and prove to my mother that I don't need to move back to Brainerd.

A ripped window screen in the basement at the fourth house hints at a conventional disappearance. As does the mangled robin corpse left near a gap in the backyard fence. I take kitty number four off my roster.

At the fifth house, I'm shown a photo of a bundle of white fur named Ophelia. The owner is beside himself.

"A Persian?" I ask, examining the photo.

"Yes." It's a pricy breed. That could be a factor, but none of the others were purebred.

"How old is she?"

"Nine weeks." He sniffles into a hankie. "She must be so scared."

"I'm sure she's fine." She's definitely not fine.

"But she's an indoor kitty. I don't know how this happened."

I pat his arm, making nebulous comforting sounds. I still haven't found a pattern. What am I missing?

His other cat, a hairless sphinx, jumps into his lap with a concerned "mrr." The owner absentmindedly strokes Horatio's wrinkled pink skin.

"Are you allergic to cat hair?" I ask.

"My ex was. But I wanted a cat so much we compromised and got a hairless breed. I got Ophelia as soon as we broke up. She sheds like crazy, but she's just so cute." His voice catches.

The pieces drop into place. The thief took Ophelia but ignored her more valuable, but bald, housemate. Louise, a garden-variety American Shorthair, was also left behind. The one thing all the missing cats have in common is their full, luxurious coats. The catnapper likes them fluffy!

I call in a favor with an ex who lives dead center of the disappearing-cat-zone. Okay, I don't call in a favor so much as break into his condo. But he owes me one, and he's always at a conference this time of year.

I spend most of the day planting evidence of cat residency all over Chris's condo. A litter box here, a well-dented, cat hair coated pillow there. Toys and paper bags strewn over the rug. Claw marks on the door frame and couch. Chris won't be happy about that, but what the hell…Chris is a weasel. I should eat all of his fancy cheese.

At sundown, I bait my trap. I remove my clothes and let my body shrink and contort. Four legs, a tail, downy ears, the works. I take a strut in front of Chris's mirrored closet, admiring the long tortoiseshell coat I've willed up. Normally I go ginger shorthair, for ease of care, but I'll be damned if this isn't working for me. I give it several go-overs with tongue and paws to maximize the floof.

My mom would be so happy to know I was putting a little effort into my appearance. Of course, that would mean calling her. Which would mean listening to a gently-worded lecture on the dangers facing a young shapeshifter in the big city. Dangers she can't possibly know about since she's never lived more than one house away from her parents. My dad's parents are in the house between. All four of her siblings live across the street and the next few blocks are mostly first and second cousins. She doesn't understand why I want to live somewhere I have a chance of socializing outside my gene pool. I do miss her pierogi though. I've yet to find any in the Cities as good as hers.

Nothing to do now but wait and see if the cat thief appears. To keep myself occupied I run a few laps across the condo; under the bed, over the dresser, and through the vertical blinds. Then take some pleasure in unraveling the toilet paper roll. I've always been a method actor.

I give up the watch at dawn. No point, all the cats went missing at night. I get a few hours of sleep before my shift at the groomers. It's a slow day. I get a decent tip for shearing a badly matted Pomeranian but the rest of the day is just shampoo, rinse, repeat. If I don't find one or two of the missing cats I'll be able to pay my rent, but groceries are off the table.

During my break, my best work-friend, Candace, shows me a compilation video of cats being startled by cucumbers. They leap and flail and trip over themselves while running away. It's got over ninety million views. Between customers, we go on a cat-video binge. Cats knocking things off ledges. Cats falling off tables. Cats attacking walls for no reason. Even celebrity cats who do tricks. Candace laments that her cat's only trick is somehow managing to pee on the floor from inside his litter box.

When I get back to Chris's street, I find a new flyer on a signpost. A cat went missing last night from a house one block over. Judging by the thick ruff, it's part Siberian or Main Coon. It fits the profile. I call the owner and ask a few questions. No history of running away, no obvious escape point. It happened again, right under my nose.

I change into cat form and curl up in Chris's front window. The one with a perfect view of the street. I groom myself in the late afternoon sun. I stay in the window as long as possible, preening.

Once the sun has completely sunk below the horizon, I get to patrolling. I trot the perimeter of the condo for hours, searching for anything out of the ordinary.

A little past three a.m., I hear something. A faint scraping coming from an air vent near the ceiling. I inch under the log stand in the fireplace Chris never uses. A little man, around four inches tall, wriggles through the vent, ass first. He skitters down the wall like a gecko, a limp sack slung over his shoulder. His head is too big for his spindly body and covered in sea urchin-like spikes. My ears twitch in anticipation. He hasn't spotted me yet. Keeping one hand on the wall, he makes his way to my last napping spot. He scoops up a handful of fur from the rug and sniffs it. He runs it along his cheek. He nods, takes a look around, and spies me in the fireplace.

The creature moves toward me and my back fur bristles. I swat at him, he dodges. I don't want him near me, his scent is acrid and rude. He smells like danger. Forgetting my mission, I display my claws and hiss. Instead of fleeing, as a wise creature of his size should, the little man reaches into his sack. Smiling a too-wide smile, he holds up a tiny silver hammer and disk. He beats the hammer against the disk, producing a tinkling beat. Slow then fast, slow then fast. Tink, tink, tink. Tink-tink, Tink-tink. The man dances in circles to his own tattoo.

Unwilling, I creep out from the logs. The tink, tink, tink of the hammer draws me forth. It's undeniable, inevitable. I must go to the little man.

Tink-tink, tink-tink.

A snare closes around me.

Tink, tink, tink.

✿

This is humiliating.

By the time the compulsion wore off, I was already in a cage. A cage in a kitchen. A cage in a kitchen in a restaurant run by trolls.

Utterly humiliating.

Humility is not a concept often associated with cats, but I'm not a true cat, just a shapeshifter with an affinity for felines. Naturally, I can't return to human in such a confined space.

The little spiky guy sold me to a troll chef for a bottle of ten-year-old port. Honestly, I'm worth at least a twenty year.

It's bad enough we're going to be eaten, Fred the Ragdoll in the next cage sniffs. *Must you subject us to your self-pity?*

He's right, wallowing isn't going to fix my troll problem. Trolls in the Twin Cities, pretty sure that's new. There were trolls in the Old Country, according

to Granny Kotek. It was one of the reasons our ancestors emigrated. That and the pogroms.

On the upside, I've found the lost cats. All except Ophelia the Persian kitten.

On the downside, we're to be the filling to the enormous piecrust the troll chef is assembling.

On the so-far-down-it-may-as-well-be-underground-side, we're also providing the sauce. Why is that worse than being minced and baked in a crust? It's a hairball sauce.

Every few minutes, one of my fuzzy companion's back will ripple, their shoulders roll, a noise resembling a misfiring lawnmower signals the intent, and SPLAT.

The chef then retrieves the deposit with a pair of tongs and adds it to the simmering pot of stomach acid and fur.

Before one gets too judgmental about the epicurean tastes of trolls, consider haggis.

I'm not seeing a way out of this. The cage openings are too small to smoosh through, even for such a smooshable creature as a cat. The inevitable question is why don't I shift into a mouse or a fly? I only do cats. It's a mental block. I've tried other animals, but the closest I've gotten is a furry, four-legged catfish. My brother Elliot calls it shapeshifter dyslexia. I look at it as an asset, not a liability. I'm a specialist.

And look at the heights to which it's taken me.

The chef adds a troll-sized handful of smoked herring to the sauce pot. A few chunks fall to the floor. A tiny white paw shoots from under the oven and snatches them. I almost chuckle but it would sound like I'm contributing to the sauce.

I have to wait twenty minutes, but the chef finally trudges out of the kitchen on some errand.

Ophelia. Opheeeeeelia, I coo.

A dusty fluff-ball emerges.

✿

How did you get out of the cage, Ophelia? I swish my tail. Even with as high a fur-to-flesh ratio as hers, she couldn't have fit more than a paw through the bars.

What cage? I'm not in a cage. Are you in a cage? She blinks adorably.

Who me? Maybe. Probably by choice. If I were to choose not to be in a cage, how might I do that?

Ophelia flops onto her side and stares blankly.

I'm sure it was a very clever escape. I wish I had seen it.

It was. She flicks her tail on the linoleum.

If I currently had fingers and could reach her, I'd wring her precious neck.

Little one, we don't have time for games. The troll could return at any minute. How did you get out?

She curls inward and begins grooming her stomach.

Ophelia! Desperation is such an ugly look on a cat.

Leave it, Miss Elinor Scratchwood, a calico, interjects. *The infant probably forgot how she did it in the first place.*

Did not! Ophelia glares at her. *I got the door thingy open with my paw.*

She undid the latch with her paw? I already tried that. I could reach the latch through the bars, but I couldn't turn the knob and push the rod at the same time. Cat paws don't work like that.

Impossible, Miss Elinor taunts.

Not for me. Ophelia stretches, splaying her front paws. Each bears an extra toe. The fuzzy little freak has opposable thumbs!

I flex my own paws, willing myself to grow an additional toe. That does the trick. I drop to the floor, stretch my cramped but blessedly human again legs, and release the rest of the captives.

Unfortunately trying to get nine cats to follow a simple instruction is like…well exactly like trying to get nine cats to follow a simple instruction.

Imagine a cat who's just been rescued from impending doom, what does that cat do? Quietly follow the nice naked lady to safety? Or knock over a giant piecrust and cause a ruckus to satisfy your need for furry vengeance? I think the answer is obvious.

The troll bursts back into the room. Roaring over the loss of his entree, he grabs a butcher's knife. The cats scatter. The troll flashes me a murderous look and lunges. My bones expand, tendon and tissue mushrooming under my skin. Fur prickles into place. The troll hesitates.

One Bengal tiger vs. troll fight later, I'm walking up Hennepin Avenue, naked but for a very large chef's coat, and trailed by eight bedraggled felines. Ophelia is hitching a ride in a pocket.

I lead them back to Chris's, get dressed, and one by one return the cats. All but four. Gene has decided to stay with me. Brenda, he says is trainable,

but Louise has made it clear she prefers to be a one cat household. There's another three I don't have flyers for. I asked them where home was, but the answers were less than illuminating. Unless someone can tell me where *back of the closet, behind the tall shoes* is. I collect nearly $2,000 in reward money. But after this month's bills, food and supplies for my new—hopefully temporary—roommates, and the $300 I owe Chris for a new couch, I'm nearly broke again.

There's always YouTube.

Copyright © 2018 by Susan Taitel

Gregory Benford is a Nebula winner and a former Worldcon Guest of Honor. He is the author of more than thirty novels, six books of non-fiction, and has edited ten anthologies. He has been our regular science columnist from the get-go, but opted this month to deliver a brand-new story instead. His column will return next month.

A WALTZ IN ETERNITY

by Gregory Benford

When on some gilded cloud or flow'r
My gazing soul would dwell an houre,
And in those weaker glories spy
Some shadows of eternity.

Henry Vaughan, *The Retreate*, 1690

Falling in. She can *feel* somehow the gossamer sailcraft's long nose-dive into the red star's grav potential, as if her own body were there, plunging arrow-quick, dozens of light-years away.

Her pod hummed, using her entire body to convey connections through its induced neural web. Sheets of sensation washed over her skin, bathed in a shower of penetrating responses, all coming from intricate flurries of her nervous system—the burr and tang of temperature, particle plasma flux, spectral flickers, kinesthetic glides and swivels, sharp images in the unending dark, lit by a smoldering dot of a sun.

These merged with her own in-board subsystems, coupled with high-bit-rate feeds the Artilects had already processed and smoothed from the sailcraft's decades of laser-beamed signals back to Earthside.

She went to fast-forward and the sailcraft plunged, its magnetic brakes on full. Down the potential well it flew in star-sprinkled dark. It heard no electro-magnetics bearing patterns, from radio through to optical. Yet Earthside knew from a few pixels that one world here held an atmosphere out of equilibrium, clean signs of life that used oxygen and methane. So: life, perhaps minds, but no technology that spoke in waves.

This L-dwarf star was of the commonplace majority, perhaps seventy-five percent or more of those stars in the disk, fully half of the total stellar mass in the Galaxy. Small but many, ruddy crucibles for life.

The craft chose its own path, looping intricately through repeated grav-wraps around three gas giants in the outer system, losing delta-Vs all the while. Now it had lost enough of its interstellar velocity to rummage among the inner worlds—one cold and gaunt, then the prize, long known from Earthside 'scopes: a superEarth.

The sailcraft folded in its mag-web brake and deployed 'scopes as it swanned into a high orbit around the cloudy world, 1.63 Earth masses. Its burgundy star glowered down on cloud decks thick as pancakes in the morning.

Rachel licked her lips. Here was the tasty truth, a world for the unwrapping. Smart and sure, the white metal bird blew itself into full plumage. Its inflatable beryllium sails shone in ruddy daylight, hollow-body banners just tens of nanometers thick, the body swelled by low-pressure hydrogen. These it used to steer into lower orbit, scanning the orbit space for satellites—and finding none.

The overseer Artilect inserted == correlates with the spectral strength of water, with strong water absorption lines as seen in clear-atmosphere planets, with the weakest features suggesting clouds and hazes—and she cut it off.

Now the main show: a self-guided human artifact plunging into a fresh solar system, embodying her; a hairless biped, so noble in reason, so infinite in faculties, heir to all creation; and an animal trapped in a box, really, just lying in a pod and sensing inputs that had flown on wings of electromagnetic song across the light years.

This world she dubbed, to herself, *Windworn*. For such it was. A thick atmosphere ripe with oxygen, smothered in good ol' nitrogen, yet beset with methane too—clearly a world-air out of chemical balance. Good!—life.

Pearly cloud decks prevented much down-seeing. The Artilect aboard the craft had elected to deploy its one great immersion resource: the balloon.

The smart aero package fell away on its own braking wings and soon enough, slammed through the cottony clouds, its brake shell burning away—and into a realm of thick, filmy air. Blithe spirit, bird thou never wert—blazing through alien skies as a buzzing firework.

The balloon popped into a white teardrop, lighter than this sluggish air and with its heater able to stay buoyant. Ten kilometers below the land opened, solemn dark green and cloud-shrouded.

The first clear glimpse below was of big smooth whitecap ocean waves that crashed like armies against the rearing snow-white mountains guarding the continents. *I should have called it Rawworld*, she thought.

Below the balloon she watched alien vistas unfurl—big broad brown rivers, lakes, crags. The vegetation was gray and black, not green. Just as the astrobio people had said: around small red stars, plants needed to harvest all the ruddy glow. So they evolved to take in all the spectrum, with little to fear from the small slice of ultraviolet, since it was weak.

She watched the land and air carefully as the balloon skated tens of kilometers above, its cameras panning to take it all in. She did a close-up of the data feed, saw small birds flapping below—and roads.

She froze the image. Small dots that might be vehicles. *Yes*—she watched them crawl along. They went to—caves. Entrances to large hills that had slits of windows in their slopes, rank upon rank of them, orderly, horizontal…all the way to the summit.

Hills upon hills, marching to the distant horizon. Hills of grassland, hills of rumpled brown rectangular stone, hills with great clefts sharpening their edges. Artificial hills.

Hailstones rattled on the balloon. Microphones recorded long shrills, the trembling of tin in sheets, snapping steel strands. Harsh, brittle rings. Distant bellows, perhaps from the barrel-chested six-footed ambulating creatures far below in their herds of many. Once the hail cleared, the balloon could see things the size of houses burrowing into moist soil, after something. Yawning herbivore throngs looked up at the balloon, showing great rows of rounded molars. Forests, animals, birds—all moved before the surging winds.

The balloon acoustic microphones caught a huge manta ray-like thing conning *fwap fwap fwap fwap* across the roiling sky, somehow navigating through. She thought, Crazy *thing, looks like it escaped from a cartoon on video*, with its long lazy strokes and manic grin that she saw was a scissor smile sporting long teeth…on a bird.

Then—black.

End of craft report #3069

a flat statement told her.

An interstellar spacecraft moving at a hundred kilometers per second does not have accidents; accidents have it. The craft turns into a blur of tumbling fragments inside a second.

She let herself drift up from the immersed state—slowly, letting the alien landscapes seep from her mind. It was over. She knew going in that the mission had snapped off, never heard from again. The balloon, its gossamer thin carbon nanotube and graphene covered in conductive metal skin, the super-lightweight rectenna—all gone. Something had blocked their transmissions—accident, intervention? No one knew. The mission report ended in a blank wall.

But she had needed to *feel* it. She knew full well this encounter lived only in thick bricks of data, info-dense and rigid. The lived experience was real, just turned into 0s and 1s, bringing across light-years their stuttering enlightenments to the SETI Library. Still, it mattered as an abrupt lesson in how hard interstellar exploration through sailcraft was, and how sudden the deaths of such adventurers.

When she climbed from the pod she ached all over, stretched, wheezed. Yet she had done no true exercise, except in her mind.

She was late for her appointment, but she paused to look up through the crystal dome at good ol' Earth, a multicolored crescent marble in the Lunar sky.

All but the last few centuries of human history had played out there. Throughout that history men and women had filled in the dark unknowns with imagination. So expeditions crossed oceans and high vacuum until new lands came into view—in just a few thousand years. Go back that far and you would see Sumerian ziggurats whose star maps cartooned the sky with imagined constellations and traced destinies through star-based prognostications.

Someday a robotic follow-up probe might fall again toward the red star she had just seen to become the Schliemann of this alien Troy.

That might happen; there were so many stars to reach out and see, and more candidates by the day. Now she could swim by other strange distant worlds and feel them, fed by slabs of data—and still sense the great dark unknowns. Which was her job.

✡

The Prefect raised an eyebrow, pursed his leathery lips. "I gather you are behind in your summations."

A flat fact. "I am, yes. I have been taking a careful review of some expedition records."

"You are a Trainee, not a Librarian. Nor, if you continue this way, much hope of becoming one. Best to shape your skills to the essentials."

"I think I can better fathom records if I see the planetary explorations in direct sensing."

His face soured more, lips turned down, his frown a ladder of creases. Legendarily, he favored the scowl over the smile. She had to change the dynamic here.

She stood. "My, you have a window." She had never seen one in a Lunar office.

"I like to have some perspective."

Outside was the sweep of the plaza, pearly in the Earthshine. "A view, yes, I can see—"

"I like some separation from the rest of all this. Also the glass is a constant temptation."

"To…what?"

"Throw something through it. Usually a student. Sometimes a Trainee, such as you."

"Ah, I—"

"Fly-in recordings will not reward mere poking around. They have been studied in great detail and can yield nothing more. Especially this red dwarf you just sensed."

"I am not just reviewing—"

"No, you are taking up pod time with full-sense flyby data.

"It was odd, how it suddenly cut off—"

"Many expeditions simply died, yes—accident, equipment failure. Those were the early days, full of verve, over a century ago. Ignore them. I want to see more of your time spent in the *hard* work. Take up third level Messages and work with the Artilects

to advance our understanding. Remember, these are not linear languages at Level Three."

"I, I will try."

"And do not use the pods to simply joyride on old explorations." He turned toward the view and she realized her appointment was over. At least she didn't have to exit through the window.

✡

Quick!—a world in a few passing hours. Then to sum it up in the brittle frame of linear sentences, the frail girders of mere flat words:

A ruddy world with lesser grav. One huge sprawl of a continent, plus lesser land mass in the other hemisphere, of humped and dirty rock-rimmed mountains. Skies the color of crisp sand. Spiky mountains cut into curiously precise pie slices by iodine rivers that flowed to the continental center, making a vast somber bay of jade waters.

Go closer, lower: Giant caterpillars stretched in trees as tall as mountains. The low grav here made for monsters.

Forested slopes in close-up were mushroom trees of violent orange. Huge blue birds with wings like parachutes, bills shaped like Death's sickle, feathers like flapping palm fronds. A plain of plants evoking erect oak leaves. Smaller growths resembling inside-out umbrellas.

Rain turning to snowflakes at high noon on the equator. Rain like drops of blood in the rocky high-lands. Mists glowing like white fire in the valleys. Chasms radiating in mountain ranges like fractures in frosted windowpanes. Winding rivers in the fevered tropics, shapely as women's torsos or slim violins. Icecaps featuring swollen growths like blue berets. Storms that solidified like hurled hammerheads across tropical isles. Clouds drifting like pregnant purple cows. Wind-blasted rockwork in curious curved forms, like frozen music. Lurching beasts all angles and ribs, grazing across mustard grasslands.

The sailcraft played out its fat helium balloons, which went roving roving roving until they ran out of lift. These captured close-up the many odd beasts, eyed landscapes for buildings, assayed the sweep of land for betraying rectangles—signs of intelligence, or else of obsessive animals who knew Euclid in their souls.

Grazers aplenty swept by under the balloon's down-looking eyes, plus carnivores, big and furred and fanged. The craft saw big floater insects too, with steering wings and armor plates and strange inexplicable leggy bits like antennae. These creatures eyed the balloon uneasily, braying roars into the acoustic balloon ears. Some angular beasts gazed upward warily, as if the balloon were a new foe in their air. They bristled, blared and thrust up narrow snouts that ended in the blunt truth of mouths like a pair of pliers. Some, in a narrow canyon lined with goat-like shambling monoliths, shot lances at the balloon eye, which fell far short. Still, perhaps a compliment of sorts.

And again: roads. Towns tucked under ample tree canopies. No electromagnetic emissions beyond the faint and local. Cities under regular humps of hills. Ships dotted the inland sea, white and slender. Yet this advanced society had only a weak signature in the radio, microwaves, and in the other bands, no signals at all.

Then the pod went silent, done. Another failed expedition.

She lingered a while in the quiet. Biting her lip, she wondered if silence was not the true state of the universe, now that the ancestral acoustics of the big bang had faded into scratch-marks in the microwave sky. Silence: far more noble than humanity's squeaks.

This world had been a treat, really. She took planetary records at random, not really knowing what she was seeking. Most worlds in the habitable zone were of a sameness. Solemn planets sleeping in the silence of ice and stone. Seaworlds awash in dark purple waters betraying no life, only its eventual prospect. Baked plains of ancient lava, unblessed by seas or even ponds, a likely match for a collision with a wandering waterworld, should orbital dynamics ever bring one from farther out: a Newtonian miracle awaiting. Black volcanic corkscrews spiraling up to the atmospheric roof of planets still in process, getting baked to oblivion. Vast planets of crawling slime. Oceans lapping against barren shores. Plankton mats the size of continents.

To find a mature, thriving biosphere was a blessing. She savored them in the sensory auditorium of her snug pod.

She began to favor the dwarf suns and their narrow habitable zones. Such stars lived long, as old as the galaxy's ten billion years, yet scarcely a fraction along their stable lifespans. So too, their worlds had millions of millennia to work their slow, gravid marvels. She studied them whenever she could manage the time, outside her own work and research at the Interstellar Library. These labors, she felt, were perhaps foolish but also a proud thing to do, as a fleck of dust condemned to know it is a fleck of dust.

☼

Rachel said to her friend Catkejen, "I'm going crazy. Or maybe I've already arrived."

"Brain-fried with work, maybe," Catkejen said with a sardonic eye-roll, sipping a barely acceptable red wine—but also the only available, fresh from the fragrant farm domes deep underground.

Rachel still wore the single white patch on her collar—"the mark of the least" as they were known. One-patchers were greener than summer grass. Catkejen had two, so was one leg up in the ladder from Trainee to Librarian. Amid the hub and bub of techtalk of the other Trainees, she was sporting a fine plum-colored coat with a laced waistcoat in a deftly contrasting shade, crossed diagonally with a red ribbon. With leggings and heater shoes, current Lunar fashion stressed subtle resistance against the creeping cold of their world, despite the ferocious warmth shed by their reactors. Rachel just wore heavy pseud-wool dresses in severe gray, plus close weave black tights—all free downloads and printouts, but yes, dull. Thrifty was not nifty here, but she didn't care. She wanted to escape notice, to tend her own internal gardens.

"I've added to my historical studies of the dwarf stars," Rachel made herself say amid the babble of the open-air restaurant, gazing down on the gray work expanses of the Lunar plain below. "Something odd going on there."

"Great era, that was," Catkejen said, distracted by the stellar displays that coursed across their social area ceilings. Rachel thought the images odd, skies of galaxies and erupting stars. The psychers said such spectacles fended off the boxed-in phobias that plagued many Loonies. "Centuries ago, right? First closeups of the neighbors, the 550 'scopes just getting started."

"I'm looking at the old missions, the microwave-beamed sail ships that scoped out the nearbys."

Catkejen eyed a passing guy, maybe looking for an evening elsewhere; some of the higher-ups had their own singleton rooms—great for parties, and of course a romantic perk. Catkejen yawned, a clear come-on signal, but the guy just kept moving. "Yeah, long before we knew what a web of interstellar messaging there was."

Rachel leaned forward to keep Catkejen from diversions. "I'm looking at the 550 lens data too. Plenty of life-bearing planets around the galaxy's dwarfs, that says. Some with signs of a civilization too. But most dwarf-star globes are shrouded in clouds, hard to see."

Indeed, Rachel loved roving through the images gathered from coasting telescopes at the great theater in the sky, the worlds of the galaxy itself on display. The sun's focus spot was 550 A.U. out, where gravity gathered starlight into an intense pencil. The many sailship telescopes there fed back distorted images of faraway solar systems, as if seen through a funhouse mirror.

Rachel had learned much by scanning those images. The talent for not dying was distributed undemocratically. Few worlds could dance blithely through a gigayear, or far from their parent star. So many planets—crisp and dry, cloudy and cool, cratered yet with shimmering blue atmospheres—and stars, sometimes in crowded clusters, at times seen close-up and going nova in bright, virulent streamers, or in tight orbits around unseen companions that might be neutron stars or black holes. After a while even exotic alien landscapes became repetitious for her: blue-green mountain ranges scoured by deep gray rivers, placid oceans brimming with green scum, arid tan desert worlds ground down under heavy brooding brown atmospheres. Many ways for life to blossom, or die: ice worlds aplenty beneath starry skies, grasslands with four-footed herds roaming as volcanoes belched red streamers in the distance, oceans with huge beasts wallowing in enormous crashing waves, places hard to identify in the swirling pink mists. *Life adapts, indeed.*

Catkejen rolled her eyes. "Um. That improves your stats?"

"In time, sure. Mostly I just…follow my nose."

Catkejen leaned forward too, her ironic wry grin mocking. "Look, your nose should lead you to use the Seekers of Script more. You're behind in code-processing—*way* behind, gal!"

Meaning, of course, *Look, I have two patches already.* The Seekers of Script were supposedly below Trainees, but more experienced in deciphering SETI messages, using brute force methods from cryptology. They assisted Trainees and reported to Librarians. Rachel reported to a Prefect and Catkejen, at a higher level, now answered to the enigmatic Noughts. All this staff layering the SETI Library had amassed through two centuries of calcification.

Rachel dodged the advice. "How's your Nought?"

"Let's say he—uh, it—relishes the cadences of the language."

"Ah! You mean it's an incorrigible windbag." Apparently having no actual sexual organs lead to verbal ejaculations instead. Just another gender choice, it seemed.

"Right, downright gushy." Catkejen had changed her hair to tarnished silver but her voice was still of scrap brass. Rachel envied her ability to conform to Library's Byzantine styles. Clothes and skin enhancers were the classic methods of competition and display. Men wore Rapunzel hair down to the shoulder blades at the moment. Women had great tangled thickets of hair in the armpits, often displayed in string-shirts. All this, despite the strange blend of decadent excess and harsh asceticism that prevailed in elite Library culture. To Rachel this was a special puzzle comparable to a labyrinthine SETI message.

"I heard they thinned some Trainees last week," Catkejen whispered, glancing around. "No announcement, just—*poof!*—you notice some are missing."

"Part of the method," Rachel said. They had seen this before. Those Trainees of both sexes, or even none, who had gotten by Earthside by being pert, pretty, perky were soon memories.

The Library had begun as a minor academic offshoot, back when there were few SETI messages and none had been well deciphered. Under rigorous mathematical methods, Artilects, and objective though human minds like the Noughts, it had grown in prestige and influence, into a citadel where there was a five-year wait for a windowless office.

Rachel said, "I hear some Trainees are planning a demonstration against these abrupt firings."

Another of Catkejen's patented eye-rolls. "I mentioned that rumor to my own Prefect. I got one of her rare laughs. She said, 'Demonstrations never achieve anything—if they did, we wouldn't allow them.'"

"Ah. A word to the wise?"

"Look, my nun-like friend—you've got to get *style* here. Dig into the ramified SETI messages—thousands of 'em, thick as bees—lurking back there in the vaults." Catkejen let her exasperation out in darting phrases. "Learn the pleasure in dispute, in dialectic, in dazzle. Get some freelance dash, peacock strut, daring hypotheses, knockabout synthesis—and get laid."

Rachel felt her face tighten, struggled to manage a smile. "I'm, you know, wrong time of the—"

"Month? Come on, gal!" Eyes flaring, grin spreading, hands shooting out. "When I'm on my period, I just stand in the shower and watch blood run down my legs into the drain and imagine I am a warrior princess who is standing in the aftermath of a battle where I murdered all my enemies."

At the moment Rachel was mostly about cramp diarrhea. Which meant maybe stay away from the claustrophobic pod and the dwarf stars?

"You don't want to be in the next culling, my friend."

Rachel allowed herself a thin, uncertain smile. "Maybe they keep me on simply to serve as a warning to others."

☼

The Library reception was on the rampart walk above the main plaza. The setting implied antiquity: vaulted and corbelled ceilings, columns sporting reverse flutings and crowned with Corinthian elegance. In a community that spent most of its time in small rooms with faintly oily air, taking advantage of views was essential for social functions. Crescent Earth was just a sliver, a comma, a single eyelash in the star-rich sky.

She looked for the Prefect but he was not in the murmuring crowd. *Probably feasting inside on Muscovy duck with pears and greens balsamico*, she thought,

succumbing to the Lunar cliché of fixating on food. The Library hierarchy emerged most visibly in what luxuries one could afford. Rumors proposed fragrant, exotic dishes none had ever seen, but thought they scented in the closed air of the Library. To the nose, there were seemingly few secrets. Whatever a Muscovy duck might be, keeping one a secret seemed impossible. Still, there were ever more rumors about the sealed and secured portions of the Library, where only Prefects or better could venture.

A mecha band played its typical klunketta-klunketta rhythm and she found herself among some other Trainees, buzzing with talk about Earthside matters. She joined the line for the stand-up banquet—in 0.18 g, not a problem. Above, moon birds looking like paint-splattered sparrows banked and swirled. These had plenty of parrot genes, and others swooped in flocks of sharply elongated eagles, and even a huge impossibility she called Moby Hawk.

There was sweet-smelling bread made from an unpronounceable root vegetable, molasses, something called hoppin' john and tart collard greens, plus rich butter from goat's milk. She favored the usual pickup food of crickets, bugs and odd crispy-fried creatures with Byzantine names, and the obligatory pork and chicken. Considering, she pitied the vegetarians; most went back Earthside soon enough.

She wandered, not spotting any friends, and into a circle discussing the deaths in the latest human cold-sleep method.

"…and they *all* died, within a two-year span," a slim woman said mournfully. "I wish they would stop inflicting such torture on us."

Torture? Scan the news at your own risk, she thought.

She was a bit tired of the Lunar sophisticates' habit, their narcissism of borrowed tragedy. It came from viewing from afar—or at least far enough—the perpetual disasters on overcrowded Earth. It struck her as inverted empathy—relate some tragedy from the news and express your sad-eyed care, and soon enough, other people's suffering becomes about you. You convey with raised eyebrow or warped lips that you're owed some measure of the deference and compassion that the victims are.

"They knew the risks going in."

The thin woman frowned. "Well, I'm sure, but—"

"And chose to take them. Too bad it failed, but honestly—how likely is it that we mammals, whose sole hibernators are bears and the like, could take decades of cold sleep?"

"Well, they've been working on this for—what, a century?—and I think the scientists know what they're doing." The woman gave Rachel a sharp look that should have stuck several centimeters out of her back.

"Seems not. They *all* died?"

"Uh, yes. Twenty-five. Some made it for the six years mark, but none past eight."

"How'd they die?"

"The connectomics scientists say their slowed metabolism just stopped. Wouldn't restart."

A light-haired brown man added with a smack of lips, "The report said when they opened the life chests, there was a distinct smell of porcini risotto. Armpits filled with fungus."

A big laugh. This was enough to disband the group before Rachel got in too deep. But something in the issue tickled her mind. Did a century of trying cold-sleep mean it just wasn't possible for complex animals, including aliens?

If so, no visitors, no crewed starships. Even if civilizations arose and persisted, they could only visit other stars robotically. Then all interstellar contacts were the province of artificial intelligences... A glimmering of an idea.

Maybe—

"I have noted that you are disobeying," the Prefect said at her elbow.

"Oh! You startled me." Somehow the Prefect's bald head loomed large out here in the open. *Or maybe it just reminds me of how many dead worlds I've seen.*

"You are spending pod time on old reconnaissance. I will have to write a report." Not a flicker of emotion. *Write a report* meant blocking her from becoming a Librarian, maybe forever.

"I have an idea I'm pursuing." Not quite a lie.

A long, slow blink, as if thinking. "I give you three days to stop."

The Prefect turned and walked away with the long lope those born on the moon made in a graceful sway.

✿

At every stage of her life she'd been reasonable, dutiful. But now a vague intuition made her bat away the advice of her friends, and the everyday world of what people said, of tips and tales, theories and tidbits that might add to the Library's already vast stores of alien messages.

The Library had evolved into a factory, producing minds distended out of all proportion—force-fed facts, as unlucky geese are force-fed corn. The succulent foie gras of such mind was then to be dined on by the Library, digesting alien 0s and 1s into a digital aesthete's wisdom. A Librarian's life, like the goose's comfort, was certainly secondary.

Even the Prefect, and that Librarian constriction, she shrugged off; her ascetic trainers Earthside had been Dionysic compared him. But she was mature now, nearing fifty and the end of her obedient-student mode.

Instead of worrying, she worked through the latest stellar evolution theories, well buttressed by myriad data links and erudite commentaries. Astronomers loved their data-mountains, indeed.

A star lived very long if it had a tenth of a solar mass and so a tenth of its radius—a pigmy, glowering at its close-clustered children in sullen reds. So a planet in the thin habitable zone of a typical dwarf M star remained in that zone for a hundred billion years. In essence, such stars lasted so long the length of habitability becomes more of a planetary than a stellar issue. If an intelligent species properly managed its environment, it could persist far longer than any around a Sol-like star, which would grow unstable after about ten billion years and swell to fill a world's sky, baking it. Any dwarf-star civilization might have begun billions of years before fish crawled up a beach on Earth and learned to breathe the rising oxygen in the air. Such societies had to manage their worlds or die out.

Pondering this, she booked pod time again.

✿

She knew from her Artilect that the Prefect's boss, the Nought Siloh, was checking on her work, so while her period lasted she actually spent time on the message inventory. She made little progress, even with the ever-helpful Seekers of Script. Picking tiny feelers of meaning from myriad messages—some seemingly simple, many blizzards of digital chaos—was like trying to hear a moth in a hurricane.

To the deep translation problem came also that many Messages were ancient, coding bronzed into memories of dead alien cultures, their beamed hails simple funeral pyres. Many could be solved by a lost wax method of digital abstraction, but that often yielded cries of despair in alien tongues.

After a week of work she got a call to report for review.

✿

The Nought named Siloh frowned, apparently its only expression. "Your performance lags. I suppose insights gathered from your inspection of planetary observations could augment your Message work, yes. But." It stopped, eyeing her.

Noughts had intricate adjustments to offset their lack of sexual appetites and apparatus, both physical and mental. They had been developed in the 2330s to give them a rigorous objectivity in translating the Messages. Somehow this evolved into the 2400s to mean management of the Library itself.

"I assume your but implies that you hold doubts?" She managed a smile with this but the Nought's frown did not budge.

"I solely wish to remind you that such interests are a diversion," Siloh said, drawing out vowels, eyes lidded.

"Perhaps not. I have found some…curiosities."

"You will find in working with your Artilect—the Transap one, I see, excellent choice—saying no more than you mean is essential."

"I looked back at a classic case of direct exploration today, Luhman 16. An old flyby, 6.5 light-years out, the nearest L-type dwarf. For a while the third-closest known star to Sol, after the Centauris and poor lonely Barnard's star. Point is, it's a binary and both stars had planets—a bonanza, but both held remnants of shattered cities, billions of years old."

The Nought sniffed. "Of course."

The obvious rebuff made her bear down. It was easier to act herself into a new way of thinking than to think her way into a new way of acting.

"There's a pattern here. Dead civilizations around dwarf stars."

"The universe is cruel to the unwise. You are ignoring your essential tasks. Does that seem wise?"

✿

She made herself be systematic.

The dwarf stars were marvels, in their way. She had always been impressed by their efficiency at packing hydrogen, the stuff of flammable zeppelins, into such a small space; some were more than twice as dense as lead. The density of Sol was bubblegum by comparison.

Many were tide-locked, or nearly so. Some had a spin/orbit resonance like Mercury, which rotates three times every two orbits around Sol. Others were split worlds, with a twilight border rich in black and gray forests, with mostly minimal animal life. The best were those who spun lazily in the ruby furnace of their skies.

There were systems whose sun was but a tarnished penny above a world where three moons played at their races. Winds were whips, polishing continents to smooth mausoleums. Such hells of sand gave her itchy flashes as the centuries-old probe explored. She rejected these, and many stony rocks and super-Jovians who circled burning circles in the sky.

There were even worse. Some circles lose enough to their star that atmospheric temperatures exceed the boiling point of water. Clouds of unlikely mixtures of potassium chloride or zinc sulfide, lifted high into the atmosphere, yielding a flat, dull spectrum.

Yet even here brightly glowing plumes reminded her of an underwater scene with turquoise-tinted currents. Strange nebulous strands reached out, echoing starfish, giant beings aloft in an atmosphere that would have crushed a dinosaur. If anything lived there, she did not wish to know of it.

✿

She had two more days to comply with the Prefect's orders. But she couldn't. She kept on mining the recon files, experiencing them whole-body.

In her mind swarmed filmy ideas. She slept restlessly, tossing in sweaty sheets—and alone; no social life seemed worth the lost moments. She skipped meals and snacked on garlic-flavored fried beetles.

Then back in the pod. The Prefect could have cut off her privileges, but no such order came.

Among the dwarf stars Earth had explored, or had seen through the lenses coasting out beyond 550 Astronomical Units, there were some worlds on which fancy sorts of watery membrane learned to think—and made great wet beasts from green crusts and reddish films and fizzing electricity. These were often on warmer, cloudy L-class dwarfs and cooler T-dwarfs, whose atmospheres were clear and sharp. In the solar corona something like manta rays coasted—life on a star. But their client planets were even stranger.

A dawn like a gray colloid. The dwarf's ruddy glow stirred the air like a thick fluid, sending blue streamers through the clotted air, bringing soon enough sharp shafts to bear on black forests below. They already knew, from SETI messages and innumerable probes, both human and alien, some sad truths. A million worlds had brimmed with life but like a puzzle with a sole dreary solution, the show ended soon. Ice or fire snuffed out life's promise.

But on living worlds, there was a plentitude of wonders. There was even oxygen—the slow fuse to the explosion of animal life. On Earth around 635 megayears ago, enough oxygen supported tiny sponges. After 580 million years more, strange creatures as thin as blue crêpes lived on a lightly oxygenated seafloor. Fifty million years later, vertebrate ancestors glided through warm, oxygen-rich seawater much as she had done as a girl.

So dwarf stars with oxygen-rich children had billions of years of advantage over latecomer Earth.

They used their eons, she saw. Probes dropped into the atmospheres of these planets heard distant calls like screechy toots on a rusty trombone, gut-bucket growls, sighing cries—from creatures that looked as dull and gray as sluggish rutabagas. Then—goodness gracious, great balls of fire! Odd beings who burst into flame at mating season, apparently after passing on their genes—and leaving the stage in hasty crimson blisters.

Her heart jumped like a mullet, quick and hard, just as she recalled seeing them in the salty warm Gulf bay air where she grew up. *Angels we have heard on high; Sweetly singing o'er the plain*, she thought, as she played back the sounds of distant animals she would never see, beyond mere pixels.

Then the entire vibrant world was gone in a sharp instant.

☼

She staggered a bit, going away from the yawning mouth of the pod. Looking back, it seemed indeed like a giant grin that had swallowed her, and now spat her out, altered. The experience had turned her inside-out, like a pocket no good for holding much anymore.

Somehow the sensorium had been fuller, more invasive this time. Smell carried memory, carried history. She bore now an after-memory of the shimmering redlands she had seen, somehow transmorphed into smells, sounds, and textures in her recollected sum of all she had experienced. The pod made that transition across senses, embedding the past into the sensual present. The pod was an Artilect and so learned her too, and each new world had held greater impact, from that.

She had seen shattered worlds, those at one with the dull, the indiscriminate dust. Those who could pour no more into the golden vessel of great song, sent across the eons and light-years. Their Messages might once have sung of alien Euclids who had looked on beauty bare, and so stitched it into Messages of filmy photons, sent oblivious into the great galaxy's night…

Such fools we mortals be…

She stopped for a glass of wine and some snack centipedes, delaying the inevitable. A passing friend gazed into her eyes and asked, "Hey, what's biting your bum today?"

Rachel opened her mouth, closed it, and the whole idea she had been seeking came together in that second.

"Shut up," she explained. And went to see the Prefect.

☼

"I'm aware that I'm not the fastest fox in the forest here," she began, after seating. "But I have an idea."

The Prefect brightened. "Ah. Fastest fox—I do appreciate bio analogies, since we live on a dead world." He steepled his hands on the desk and took up an expectant face, eyebrows arched.

She took a deep breath, nostrils flared at the antiseptic air of the Nought's shadowy preserve. "The older dwarf stars with rich biospheres—they're lying low."

"From our probes?"

"Yes—that's why they shot down our observing craft."

"Aha." A salamander stare.

So he wants me to spell it out. "I estimate the rejecting biospheres are several billion years old. They let us approach, even drop balloons, then—wham."

"Indeed. You have done the required statistics?"

"Yes." She let her inboard systems coalesce a shimmering curtain in the air, using the Prefect's office system. The correlation functions appeared in 3-D. The Prefect flicked a finger and the minamax hummocks rotated, showing the parameter space—a landscape covering billions of years, thousands of stars.

"Perhaps significant." A frown formed above his one cocked eyebrow. She recalled that the Prefect was the sort who would look out a window at a cloudburst and say, *It seems to be raining*, on the off-chance that somebody was pouring water off the roof.

"They're probably the longest-lived societies in the galaxy, since they're around red stars that hold stable. If they can't do cold-sleep, either—and so can't go interstellar voyaging, like us—they're stuck in their systems. And they're still *afraid*."

The Prefect nodded. "Correct, yes—the cause of the dwarf-star worlds' insularity lies in the far past. An antiquity beyond our knowing, from eras before fish crawled from our seas."

"Whatever could have made them fear *for so long*?"

"We do not know. It is a history…" Mixed emotions flitted across his face, as if memory was dancing within view. "…for which adjectives are temporarily unavailable."

"We have to be alert!" She got up and paced the office. "These aliens hunkering down around their red and brown stars, they have lasted by being cautious."

A shrug. "That seems obvious."

She had hoped for help, not a blasé, blunt assessment. "So we need to find out more," she said, realizing it was lame.

He leveled a stare. "Intelligence is defined by sufficient detachment from one's own case, to consider it as one of many. A child becomes humanly intelligent the moment it realizes that there are other minds just like its own, working in the same way on the same world available to them. It seems to be the same with societies across the galaxy."

She nodded. "Other worlds, other minds, strange—but they have suffered the same past."

"True. This is not a matter of dry certainties. It is a quest for archeological wisdom."

She whirled, her mouth a grimace, eyes wild. "Whatever they're afraid it could be, be—*comin' right atchya!*"

He was calm, further confusing her. He gave her a cautious, precise, throat clearing. "I have an allergy to dogma, including my own."

"What's your dogma?"

"Placing the Library on Luna, safely away from the torrents of Earth, was a primary motive. Best to contemplate the stars where one can see them anytime. In other words, take the long view."

She was getting more frustrated by his blithe manner but resisted raising her voice. "Look, you wanted me to go back to studying decrypting SETI messages, but this, this—I just couldn't give it up."

"Research is not devised, it is distilled."

She let out a loud, barking laugh. "Building logic towers from premises wrung out of thin air, more like it."

"You have got it nearly right."

"Nearly?"

He eyed her narrowly. "We think of the Elizabethan world as one we perceive through our own reductive devising. We think of it as populated by the Queen and Ben Jonson and the Dark Lady and the Bard and a raucous theater full of groundlings. That's what *we* know, from some texts. But the real Elizabethan world had a lot more people in it than that, and countless more possibilities. Here at the Library, we deal with not a mere handful of centuries. We have received messages sent across thousands of light-years, from beacons erected by societies long dead."

"Well, yes—"

"So we need to know more, before deciding anything."

She finally let her anger out. "Nonsense! This is a threat! People need to know." She spread her hands, beseeching him.

"Go and think some more. You are following the right path."

With a wave he dismissed her.

✿

Catkejen came in from a date, all fancied out in a maroon bioweb Norfolk jacket with fluorescent yellow spirals down the arms, and found Rachel calculating some ideas. "Actual penciling out! Pushing graphite! You should get outside sometime, y'know."

Feeling every inch a pedant, Rachel rose, stretched. "I was backtracking those red stars that had hunkered down."

"You mean the ones that prob'ly knocked out our probes?"

"Yes, plus ones we've seen from the 550 AU telescopes that had ruins on them."

"So you're running backward their orbits around the galaxy?" A disbelieving frown.

"Yes, it's a tough, many-body problem—"

"Hey, another example of cross-field confusion. We already have that!"

This was how Rachel learned that astronomers had developed a reverse-history code of extraordinary ability. They had first evolved it to study galactic stellar evolution of spiral arms. Which led to her next audience with the Prefect.

✿

She walked—no, she decided, she *skipped* with schoolgirl joy in the low grav—out of the advanced computational dome, feeling as if she had returned from a great distance.

She blew past the Prefect's office staff and marched straight in on the great man, who was staring at a screen. He looked up, not showing any surprise. "You have more." Not a question.

She flipped on her personal Artilect interface so it projected an image on the office 3-D display. "This shows the dwarf stars our probes and the 550 AU 'scopes found to be defensive or destroyed. No particular correlation between their locations, notice."

He merely nodded. She had tagged the forty-three cases in bright green. They were scattered through a volume more than a thousand light-years on a side—still a mere bubble in the colossal galactic disk. "Now let's run the galaxy backward."

The green dots arced through their long ellipses. The slow spin of the galaxy itself emerged as the bee swarms of stars glided in stately measure. The Sun took a quarter of a billion years to cycle in its slow orbit at about two hundred kilometers a second, taking more than a thousand years to move a light-year. Humanity's duration was less than a thousandth of one galactic cycle. From SETI messages marking funeral pyre societies, the Librarians knew that humans were mayflies among sentient cultures, the newest kids on the block.

The Prefect watched the backward-running swarm and raised his eyebrows as the green dots slowly drew nearer each other. "They follow somewhat different orbits, bobbing up and down in the galactic plane, brushing by nearby stars, suffering small tilts in their courses," she said, as though this wasn't obvious. *Was she making too much of this?* She told herself a sharp no and went on.

"I can see some, well, clumps of several green specks forming," the Prefect said. "They seem to be..." —surprise pitched his voice into a tenor note— "...occasionally passing within a few light-years of each other. There! And now..." —a pause as four dots swooped together— "...another cluster."

Rachel made herself use her flat, factual voice. "Stats show these were nonrandom, four sigmas out from any bell curve odds."

"They...group...at different times. How far into the past are we now?"

"Six million years."

He frowned, pursed his lips. "I have never seen this before."

"Astronomers study star dynamics. This is about the hunkered-down planets, or the ones destroyed, orbiting those stars."

The Prefect gave her a sour smile. "So this is another example of the perils of specialization."

"Um, yes, sir." Let the idea percolate...

The Prefect bit. "Which means?"

"The endangered worlds were near each other, millions of years ago. Whatever attacked them—killing some societies entirely, scaring others so much they still remember it, guard against it—came at them when they were close to each other."

She paused. *Let him figure it out...*

"Whatever menace does this..." The Prefect let his puzzled sentence trail off.

"Wormholes lie somewhere in those intersecting orbits."

The Prefect stiffened. "We know of no wormholes!"

"Right. Absence of evidence is not evidence of absence, as some philosopher said."

A furious head-shake. "But—where could wormholes *come from*? We know they're impossible to build—"

"The big bang? We know it was chaotic. Maybe some survived that era. Got trapped into the galaxy when it formed up later. Goes coasting around, just as the stars do."

He blinked, always a good sign. "So when a wormhole mouth gets near a group of stars…"

"Something comes through it. Someone—some *thing*—that found a wormhole mouth. Y'know, theory says wormholes aren't simple one-way pipes They can branch, like subways in space-time. So something comes through, attacks inhabited planets."

The Prefect looked puzzled. Maybe this was coming too fast? Explain, girl. Go technical.

"We—well, I—saw it in the planets around dwarfs, because there are more of them. Better statistics, the pattern shows up."

She let that sink in while the Prefect watched the galaxy grind into its past. More green dots swooped along their blithe paths, nearing each other, coasting on, apart…the waltz of eternity, Newton meets Mozart, on and on through thousands of millennia, down through the echoing halls of vast, lost time.

The Prefect was a quick study. His sharp, piercing eyes darted among the bee swarm stars, mouth now compressed, lips white with pressure. "What are the odds that there's one near us?"

This she had not thought about. "Given the number of dwarfs nearby… Um. Pretty good."

He smiled, an unusual event. "This is utterly new. When you found the ancient tragedies, I was impressed. If you were wondering, only one in several thousand Trainees catch on to that fact—that secret, I should say."

"Really? And this—the clustering—how often has any Trainee turned that up?"

A quick shake of head. "Never. This is a new discovery."

"Really?" She had thought she would surprise him, get some reward, but…*new?*

"No one knows this. Wormholes! Maybe nearby? So—if there's one nearby—where is it?"

This was going too fast for her. "I sure as hell don't know. I'm not an astronomer! I want to be a Librarian."

The Prefect nodded. "So you shall be, in time." He paused, gazing at the slow, sure grind of the galaxy. "We have a saying, we Prefects. 'Creativity may be hard to nurture, but it's easy to thwart.' You have proven that we do occasionally let talent get through."

She sat silent, not knowing where this was going.

"Also… Congratulations."

"What?"

"You have found the unsaid. The essence of research."

"What…?"

"The Library is not a mere decoding society. We must use the full range of exploration, not just the messages. You saw that. You first ferreted out a truth we Prefects do not wish to make known—the deaths of whole worlds, the closing in of others. Your discovery now, the proximity of the stricken worlds—is a gift."

"Gift?"

"Yes. Much we discover needs time to…digest. But we become calcified, mere decoders. To become a true Librarian, one must show innate curiosity, persistence, drive."

"I, I just got interested. You leaned on me hard to keep up my studies, not fall behind the others—"

"It is *they* who have fallen behind. We cannot drill creativity into our Trainees. They must display it without being asked."

She gaped at him, not following. "So…"

"You are now promoted. You shall not tell your fellow Trainees why. Let them bathe in mystery. Do not say a word of what you have learned."

"But, but—"

For the first time ever, she saw the Prefect smile. "Welcome. I will see to getting you a private office now, as well."

Outside, the night Earth seen through the vast dome was a glowing halo, sunlight forming a thin rainbow circle. She saw his point. Earth was always there, and so were the waiting stars.

And something dark hid in the yawning dark beyond, something even a Nought or a Prefect did not know. Something shadowy in the offing out there in the galaxy, waiting, patient and eternal.

Wormholes? Through which something horrible came? They were out there, hanging like dark doorways between the stars.

It came in a flash she would recall all her life.

Now she knew what she wanted to solve, an arrow to pierce the night beyond and find the doorways. To see across eternity and into the consuming dark above that awaited all humanity.

Copyright © 2018 by Gregory Benford

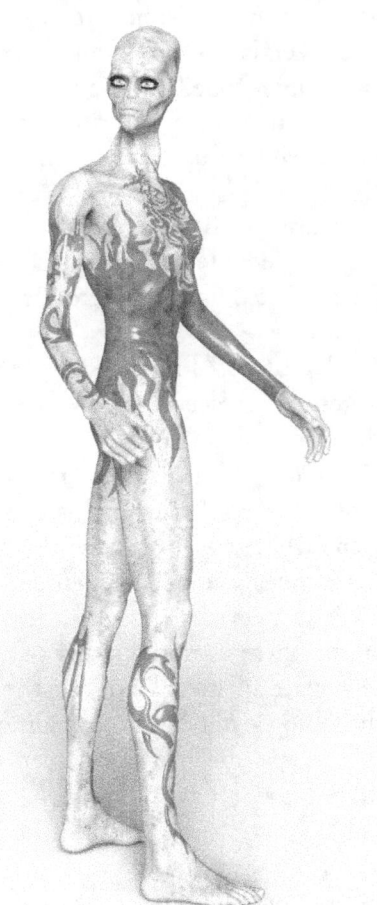

Robert Silverberg is one of the true giants of science fiction. He is a multiple Hugo winner, a multiple Nebula winner, has been a Worldcon Guest of Honor, and is a Nebula Grand Master and the author of numerous acknowledged classics in the field.

JENNIFER'S LOVER

by Robert Silverberg

Finch had married very young—he had been only twenty-three, and Jennifer even younger—and even so he hoped they would live happily ever after. Marriage had been back in fashion for a few years then, but all the same it was unusual to do it so early, and friends and relatives warned them of the risks. Get out and live in the adult world for a while, they said. There's plenty of time later for settling down.

But marrying was more than a matter of fashion for Finch. He had, since adolescence, felt himself to be a basically married person. Like one of the primordial creatures of Plato's *Symposium* is how he saw himself—a twofold being that somehow had been divided and could not be happy until it had been reunited with its missing half. He searched diligently until he found Jennifer, who seemed to be that separated segment of himself; and then he quickly took care to join her securely to him once again. They settled in a sleek and snug Connecticut suburb. He sold portable computer terminals for a dynamic little hi-tech outfit in Bridgeport, and she worked for a publishing company in Greenwich, and before long they had a daughter named Samantha and a son named Jason, after which Jennifer quit her job and began doing some volunteer work at the local museum. Their parents, who had been pretty wild items in their own day, doing dope and marching for peace and trashing campuses, were amazed at the way everything had come around full circle in just one generation.

Finch was on the road a lot, making sales calls in a territory that stretched from Rhode Island to Delaware, and occasionally he wondered if Jennifer might someday amuse herself with a lover. But the idea was really too alien to make sense to him.

Even when he was away from home three or four nights in a row, sleeping in drab motels in New Jersey or Pennsylvania, he saw no need to go outside his warm and secure marriage, and he imagined Jennifer felt the same way. He wondered if that was naive and decided it wasn't. As a couple they were complete, a single entity, a unity. Naturally the early raptures were only warm memories now, but the expectable cooling of passion had been followed by deep friendship. They were together even when they were apart; a lover would be a superfluity; Finch told himself that if he learned Jennifer had been unfaithful to him, he would not so much be jealous as merely mystified.

And of course there were the children to bind them always: Samantha was already beautiful at seven, a slim golden creature who was as apt to speak French as English. She awed them both, and they were immensely proud of her precocious elegance. Jason, not quite six, was of a different substance, a stolid and literal person whose toys were made of microprocessors and LEDs. He had his father's love of technology, and Finch saw in him a chance to create what he himself had not managed to be—a genuinely original scientific intellect rather than a peddler of other people's inventions. Whenever he returned from a long trip he brought gifts for everyone, a book or a record for Jennifer, something pretty for Samantha, and invariably a computer game or mechanical puzzle for Jason. They were splendid children, and he and Jennifer often congratulated one another on having produced them.

At a computer showroom in Philadelphia one rainy autumn afternoon, Finch bought a wonderful toy for Jason, a little synthesizer that played lively tunes when you tapped out signals in a binary code. Not only would it develop Jason's musical skills—and that side of the brain needed to be trained too, Finch thought—but it would sharpen his ability to count in binary. It was so expensive that he felt guilty and eased his conscience by getting the new supercassette of *Die Meistersinger* for Jennifer and a sweater of some glittering furry fabric for Samantha; but on the long drive home he thought only of Jason creating buoyant melodies out of skeins of binary digits.

Jason accepted it politely but seemed not very interested. He watched as Finch demonstrated it, and

when it was his turn he generated a few fragmentary atonal squawks. Then a call from Jennifer's parents interrupted things, and afterward, Finch noticed, the child wandered off to his room without taking the synthesizer with him. That was disappointing, but Finch reminded himself that six year olds had a way of being preoccupied with one thing at a time, and possibly Jason's preoccupation of the moment was so compelling that even a wondrous new device could not gain much of a grip on his attention.

After dinner, feeling a little miffed, Finch took the synthesizer to Jason's room and found him hunched over an odd glowing thing the size of a large marble. When he saw Finch enter, the boy disingenuously pushed it into the clutter on his tabletop and pretended to be busy with his holographic viewer. "You left this in the living room," Finch said, giving him the synthesizer. Jason took it and obligingly hit the keys in his mild, obedient way, but he looked uncomfortable and impatient. Finch said, pointing at the little glowing thing, "What's that?"

"Nothing much."

"It's very pretty. Mind if I see it?"

Jason shrugged. He generated a jagged screeching tune. Finch picked up the sphere. Jason looked even more restless.

"What does it do?" Finch asked.

"You press it in places. It turns colors. You have to get it the same color all over."

"Rubik's Cube," Finch said. "An old idea brought up to date, I guess." He put his fingertips to the sphere and watched in surprise as colors of eerie indefinable hues came and went, blending, shifting. Touch it a certain way and there were stripes; another and there were triangular patterns; another and the surface of the sphere burst into thick, brilliant, throbbing patches of color, almost like a Van Gogh landscape. He had never seen anything like it. "Where'd you get it?" he asked. "Jennifer buy it for you?"

"No."

"Grandpa Finch send it?"

"No."

Finch felt himself growing annoyed. "Then who gave it to you?"

The child looked momentarily troubled, tugging at his lower lip, twisting his head at a peculiar angle.

Then he began to contemplate the synthesizer, and the old serene Jason, imperturbable, studious, returned.

"Nort gave it to me," he said.

"Nort?"

"*You* know."

"I don't. Who's Nort?"

Jason was manipulating the synthesizer, quickly getting the hang of it, making something close to a tune emerge. He had dismissed Finch from his awareness as thoroughly as though Finch had been transported to Pluto. Gently Finch said, "You aren't answering me. Who's Nort?"

"He plays with me sometimes."

Finch decided to drop it. Jason would tell him about Nort in his own good time, he supposed. Meanwhile the boy was mastering the synthesizer with gratifying swiftness; no point distracting him from that. Finch picked up the sphere again, stroked it so that it went through a whole new series of color changes, and brought it almost to the single hue that apparently one was meant to achieve. But he did something wrong and kicked it into a geometrical pseudo-Mondrian pattern instead. A clever gadget, he thought, and went off to find Jennifer and to catch up on local gossip. The mysterious Nort quickly slipped from his mind, and he might never have thought of him again at all if Samantha had not remarked, when he was in her room to say good night to her, "I'm glad you're back. I don't like Nort, really. I hope he doesn't come here any more."

Very calmly Finch said, "Oh, he was here again?"

"Two days, this time. Tell him not to come, will you?"

"I don't know if I can do that. You know who Nort is, after all, don't you?"

"Sure. *Maman's* nephew. A nephew is something like a brother, *n'est ce pas?*"

"A little bit," said Finch. He kissed her lightly. "I'll see what I can do about Nort, all right? And if he comes back when I'm gone, you tell me about it, sweet. I don't think I like him either. But let's not say anything about this to *maman*, okay? She's very fond of her nephew, you know, and it would upset her if she knew that you and I didn't like him."

He paused a moment in the hallway, pressing his forehead against the wall, catching his breath. *Maman's nephew.* Jennifer had no nephews. Finch was trembling. Visiting lovers usually claimed to be uncles, he thought. A nephew? *Jennifer's lover?* It was craziness, a phantasm, a melodrama of a tired mind. Jennifer had no lovers. Finch could visualize their marriage, that abstraction, as a solid concrete thing, a gleaming polished marble sphere rather like Jason's glowing toy, and in the perfection of that sphere there was neither need nor room for lovers. In his own way he would find out who Nort was, he resolved, but above all else he would stay calm. He poured himself a drink and rejoined Jennifer, studying her covertly as if looking for signs of adultery on her forehead, in her cheeks. She was playing *Meistersinger*, humming along with the jollier choruses. When they went to bed, he turned to her as he always did when he came home from a long trip, but he imagined that something strange had descended between them like a curtain of metal links, and he was unable to embrace her. The unknown Nort lay as a barrier in their bed. Finch ran his hands halfheartedly over her breasts and flanks but did nothing else. "You must be very tired," Jennifer whispered.

"I am. All that rain—the traffic skidding around—"

She kissed the tip of his nose. "Get a good night's rest," she said.

He had trouble sleeping. He felt her presence inches away as a pulsating vibration that made his fingers and toes tingle disagreeably. That she might have a lover frightened him, for it meant he held faulty assumptions about their relationship, that his evaluation of reality was defective. And he had to admit that he was upset on a much simpler level: a stranger was creeping into his bed, and he hated that as a violation of his rights. He found his reaction embarrassing. Mere jealousy, he thought, is ugly and stupid and very much beneath me. Nonetheless, beneath him or not, he felt what he felt, and it hurt him keenly.

Eventually he fell asleep, and when he woke to brilliant October sunlight streaming through the blazing leaves of the red maple outside their bedroom everything seemed normal again. Jason was using the synthesizer, getting it to play something that almost might have been *Three Blind Mice*. Finch was intensely pleased by that. At work that day he thought sometimes about Nort, but not in any very painful way—some neighborhood person, he supposed, an artist Jennifer had met at the museum, maybe, who drops around for a drink and some artistic chitchat, most likely gay, gentle, fond of children, harmless. He was much more interested in that peculiar glowing sphere. That night he went into Jason's room to examine it again. Ingenious, the play of colors, the tantalizing way it *almost* went one-toned as you handled it and then slipped away into patterns. He had no idea how it worked. Sensitive to skin-temperature fluctuations, perhaps, or possibly even pressure-sensitive, though it was solid as a marble. And what generated the changing colors and projected them to the surface? He was tempted to ask Jason to get a second sphere from Nort that he could try to take apart.

The week after next he was up in Boston for three days on his regular monthly trip. The first two went well; but on the evening of the third, as he returned to his motel after an overly winy dinner with a buyer from a Cambridge data-shop chain, the incandescent image of Jennifer getting into bed with Nort suddenly blazed in his soul. The Nort that Finch invented was older than he, perhaps thirty-seven, dark and muscular, with a dancer's supple body and an easy, self-assured manner. Finch bit his lip and tried to force the unwanted vision away, but it grew ever more vivid and ever more graphic, and the pain of it was astonishing. He thought seriously of driving home in the middle of the night. But that would be insane, he realized.

He came home on schedule with the usual gifts, and when he gave Jason his—a little screen on which he could draw with a light-pen—he feared the boy, still enthralled by some phenomenal incomprehensible thing that Nort had just brought him, might snub it. But Jason said nothing about Nort and was instantly fascinated by the screen. Finch felt a surge of relief until Samantha drew him aside, an hour later, to tell him, "He was here again."

"Nort?"

"Oui. Mardi et marcredi."

"Mercredi," he corrected automatically. Her French still had some flaws; but she was only seven. He turned away to hide his look of torment. Two nights, again. Tuesday, Wednesday. He had no idea what he was supposed to do. Confront her with his suspicions and demand an explanation? They had never even had a real quarrel. Swallow his agony and

count himself grateful that there was someone here protecting his home and family while he was away? Sure. Sure. In a dull voice he said, "What do Nort and *maman* do when he's visiting her?"

"They have dinner after we go to sleep. Then they stay up late and talk. In the morning he asks us questions about school and things and tries to be nice to us."

In the morning. Finch winced.

He forced himself to make love with Jennifer that evening so she would not suspect that he suspected, but he was without desire and barely managed to enter her, which made it all even worse. Guilty herself, she would want to assume the worst in him, and this uncharacteristic failure of virility after three nights away from her probably would lead her to think he had been with women in Boston, which would encourage her to give herself even more flagrantly to her own lover, which—

In the two weeks before his next road trip he thought constantly of what would take place between Jennifer and Nort while he was away. He was jittery, remote, short-tempered, and morose; Jennifer seemed to be trying to please him, but whatever she did was counterproductive, and he was reduced to pleading business worries and headaches to keep from having to blurt out what was really on his mind. He wanted no confrontations with her. The love he bore her should be great enough to allow scope for a little discreet adultery, and if it did not, well, he would try to work on his attitudes.

But as he drove off toward Hartford under gray November skies, he imagined Nort's car gliding into the garage, Nort entering the house, Nort with his hands on her breasts, Nort leading her toward the bedroom. The absurd intensity of his obsession alarmed and dismayed him. But he could not control his feelings. In Hartford he checked into his motel and drifted like a man in a daze through his first three calls; he must have seemed in terrible shape, because everyone commented on the way he looked; he had two drinks before making his fourth call, which he never did, and then he canceled the call and returned to the motel. There he had another drink, ate a hamburger in the coffee-shop, and stared unseeingly at the television set until midnight, when he abruptly rose, dressed, stumbled outside, and grimly began to drive homeward. He knew that this was absolute madness. He would let himself into the house and catch them in bed together, and then the three of them would sit down and discuss things. And he had no idea what would happen after that.

Just before two in the morning he parked in front of his house and saw, with perverse satisfaction, that a lamp was lit in the bedroom. Strangely calm, Finch peered through the garage window, but saw only Jennifer's station wagon inside. So Nort was a neighborhood person, Finch thought. She phones him and he walks over here and she lets him in.

Noiselessly Finch unlocked the door, punched in his identity code on the burglar-alarm keyboard, slipped off his shoes, and tiptoed upstairs. His heart pounded with such startling force that he began to fear real damage to it. At the top of the stairs he paused, paralyzed with shame and misgivings. Leave them alone, he told himself. This is unquestionably the most stupid and reckless and self-defeating thing you've done in your life. He was quivering. He did not dare go forward.

"Dale?" Jennifer called from the bedroom. "Dale, is that you? It *better* be you!"

"Me," he croaked, and lurched into the room.

She was alone, sitting up in bed, looking frightened and surprised. Finch, ashen and shaking, still had the presence of mind to scan the room for spoor of Nort, an overlooked wristwatch, a stray sock. Nothing. Jennifer was naked. She slept that way with him, but she had once told him that she always wore pajamas when he was away, for warmth. Certainly Nort was still here. Nobody jumps out a second-floor window to escape an angry husband. In the closet? In the bathroom? Under the bed? Finch knew he had created a preposterous farce.

"I felt ill," he mumbled. "Dizzy—hot flashes—I couldn't be alone. I just climbed into the car and headed for home—to be with you—the kids—"

"Dale, what's the matter? What hurts you?" She was as tense and anguished as he was, but she seemed to be recovering her poise. She got out of bed—were those the red imprints of Nort's fingers on her breasts and thighs?—and pulled on her robe and came to him. "If you were so sick, you shouldn't have tried to drive all the way from Hartford. Why didn't you call first? Why didn't you try to have the

motel get you a doctor?" He swayed. His legs felt like concrete. He leaned against her, sniffing for the other man's cologne or even the smell of his sweat, and let Jennifer ease him down to the bed. He wanted to ask her where she had hidden Nort. But the words would not come. She helped him undress and brought him aspirins, and turned the thermostat up because he was shivering so violently, and clasped him in her arms. Her body was so warm and yielding and tender against him that he nearly began to cry. He let himself relax in her embrace, and to his amazement his desires rose and he reached for her. She tried to quiet him, telling him she was too exhausted for any such thing, but there was no halting him and he took her quickly and with uncharacteristic force. Jennifer met his thrusts with a vigor he had not encountered in months. It must be because Nort's done all the foreplay for me, he thought bitterly, and came at once, with a sob, and collapsed against her breast. At once he was asleep, and in the morning it all seemed like a dreadful dream, nothing more. Finch insisted on going back to Hartford and making his rounds, and would hear no objection from Jennifer. But first he went into Samantha's room and, cutting short her expression of surprise at seeing her father return from his trip so soon, asked her bluntly whether Nort had come for dinner the night before.

"Yes," she said. "He was here when I got home from school. Is he still upstairs with *maman*?"

Finch asked himself, as he drove shakily back to Hartford, whether to seek the advice of friends, his parents, the local minister, a therapist. He had never done any of that. His life had always been an amiable progression toward deeper happiness. By the time he reached the motel, he knew he would consult no one, would take no action at all, would simply wait and see. He would let Jennifer make the next move.

But she said nothing and he said nothing and after his next trip, a brief one, he found Jason with another strange new toy, an arrangement of gleaming wires that crossed and recrossed and seemed to disappear at one juncture into a baffling uncharted dimension, visible only as a dazzling flicker of green light. Yes, the boy said, Nort had given it to him. Finch felt a surge of frantic anger. He was almost desperate now to bring this thing to some sort of resolution, for it was devouring him. Jennifer remained tender and loving and outwardly unchanged. Finch suffered. He could not push his fears and confusions below the threshold of awareness for more than an hour or two at a time; he was losing weight; everyone commented on his frayed and frazzled appearance. He was drowning in the silent turbulence of his altered life.

A second time he returned prematurely from a sales trip, hoping to catch them together. Again the light was on in the bedroom in the middle of the night. Again he stumbled in to find Jennifer flustered but alone. He explained that he was drunk and bewildered. "I think I'm having some sort of a breakdown," he told her, and this time he called in sick and took a week off, though the Christmas holidays were coming and it looked very bad to do that now. Impulsively he went with Jennifer to Bermuda for four days, leaving the children with his parents, and it was like a second honeymoon for them, the pink sandy shore, the palm trees. But the moment they came home his mind was full of Nort again. A few days before Christmas he had to go to Pittsburgh for a meeting, but when still at the airport he was consumed with the awareness that Nort was in his house, joking amiably with Jason and Samantha. Grimly Finch boarded his plane, sat in a cold funk of silence all the way and, in Pittsburgh, bought a ticket on the next flight back to JFK. A light snowfall had begun, and his car, sitting in the vast lot, looked dainty and virginal in its thin white mantle. He reached home at midnight. The bedroom light was on. Finch let himself in and took the stairs two at a time. Jennifer was sitting up in bed, naked at least to the waist, her bare breasts blazing at him like beacons, and next to her, relaxed, comfortable, his hands clasped behind his head, was a slender, naked young man, perhaps thirty at most, with cool green eyes and dense red hair that clung to his head in a curious caplike way.

Finch felt a kind of relief. "You're Nort?"

"Yes. Is time we finally met, I think, Mr. Dale."

"Mr. *Finch*. Or Dale." Nort had some slight accent. Finch said, "I don't know what the protocol is in a thing like this. I suppose I should be furious and smash things and make threats. But I'm hollow inside by now. I've known about this a long time."

"We know," Jennifer said. "Why else would you have kept coming here trying to catch us in the middle of the night?"

"Twice," said Nort. "This be the third. I thought this time I'd stay and talk with you."

"You were here the other two times?"

"Certainly. But Jennifer wanted no face-to-face. So when the Dale-detector went off, I did the vanish. You follow?"

Finch stared wearily at his wife. "Jennifer, who is this man and how did he get into our lives?"

"He's my nephew," she said.

"You have no—"

"—eleven generations removed."

"What?"

"A remote descendant in my sister's line. He comes from A.D. 2215. He's here to do research."

Finch thought of the toys Nort had given Jason. His eyes glazed.

Nort said, "I make the field trip, you follow? I do genealogical research, visit the ancestors, family anecdotes. In my era is very important, knowing the history. I have made many journeys over a long span."

"He has my whole family tree," said Jennifer. "I never knew it, but I'm descended from Millard Fillmore and Johann Sebastian Bach and possibly John of Gaunt."

Finch nodded. "That's fascinating."

Nort said, "We do not interfere, you know. We move around like spies, doing our studies and never interacting with the past-folk, out of fear of consequences, of course. But this was an exception. I was captivated by Jennifer instantly."

"Captivated," said Finch bleakly.

"Captivated, yes. We became lovers. It is a kind of incest, I imagine, but is not very serious, outside the direct maternal line, yes? My studies suffer. Now I come only to this year. Jennifer is a wonderful woman. You know?"

"I know, yes." Finch looked toward Jennifer. "I haul my ass over eight states peddling primitive data-processing devices while you amuse yourself with a lover from the twenty-third century. That absolutely captivates me, Jennifer. I can't tell you how—"

"Dale, please. You know I love you. But—but—"

Nort looked troubled. "You are not accepting of this?"

"I am not accepting, no," Finch said.

"But this is the late twentieth century, a decadent time for the marriage custom, and you are sophisticated, educated, elite persons. It is my understanding that toleration of non-marital sexual interpersonation is widespread in your cohort. You are displeased I love your wife?"

"Very," said Finch in a gray voice. He lowered himself into the chair by the window and said, "You're a hell of a guy for keeping a straight face, Nort. I have to admire that. Throughout this whole routine you've been very convincing. But I'm worn out, and I can't take any futuristic rigmarole any more. Please put your clothes on and go away and don't come back, and leave Jennifer and me to pick up the pieces of our marriage. OK? Because if I catch you here again, I might do something violent, which is against my nature, and I'll probably have to divorce Jennifer, which is the last thing in the world I want to do even now."

"You doubt I am from a future time?"

"I doubt you are from a future time, yes."

Nort climbed out of the bed. Finch noticed a thin plastic band of some constantly oscillating greenish color around his left thigh. He touched it and disappeared, and when he reappeared, a moment later, he was in a different corner of the room, holding out a folded newspaper to Finch. Finch glanced at it: the *New York Times* for April 16, 2037. The main headline was something about Pope Sixtus performing Easter services on the moon. Finch made a little choking sound and started to scan the other stories, but Nort, with an apologetic smile, took the paper from him, vanished again, and reappeared without it, back in the bed. "I have sorrow," he said softly, "but I am forbidden to let you inspect the newspaper in detail. Shall I do other things? What would convince you I am genuine?"

Finch wanted to sob. He shook his head and said, "Don't bother. I don't need to know. You probably are what you say you are. Will you go away now? Go annoy Millard Fillmore."

"I am loving your wife."

"You *have loved* my wife. That's the correct grammar. It's over. Listen, I'm a ruthless late-twentieth-century man, and you're on dangerous ground. I

have weapons. If you're killed while on a field trip, will you stay dead in 2215?"

Jennifer said, "Dale, stop talking that way."

"What do you want me to say? He flashes in here like something out of Buck Rogers, he screws my wife every time I look the other way, he upsets my daughter and alienates my son with his crazy future toys, and now I'm supposed to—"

"You mustn't threaten him, Dale. You're behaving *extremely* prehistorically. Haven't you ever had an affair?"

"Never. Not once."

"Those motels—"

"Not once. I suppose you've had plenty, though."

"Two before this one," she said, reddening a little. "I thought you knew. This isn't 1906, after all. They were both absolutely casual."

Finch thought of that polished perfect sphere that was his metaphor for the flawlessness of his relationship with Jennifer. He thought of the two-bodied male-female entities of Plato's *Symposium*. His face was leaden and his hands shook.

She said, "This is more serious, Dale. I'm terribly fond of Nort. I love you as much as ever, but he's shown me other aspects of life, things I never dreamed of, and I'm not talking about sex. I mean spiritual concepts, human potentialities, the—"

"All right," said Finch. "I won't try to compete. I won't shoot him and I won't punch him and I won't do anything else uncivilized. Why don't the two of you get the hell off to A.D. 2215 and carry on the rest of your affair there, OK? Go have a flying fuck in the century after next and let me alone. OK? OK? The two of you. *Let—me—*"

Nort disappeared. So did Jennifer.

"Alone," Finch finished weakly. "Jennifer? Jennifer? Where are you? Hey, I wasn't serious! Jennifer! Goddamn it, what kind of sadistic stunt is this? Where are you?"

The cruelty of their game astounded him. He waited for them to pop back into the room as Nort had done with the newspaper, but they did not, and as the minutes went by he began to suspect that they were not going to. Numb with disbelief, he prowled the house, searching closets for them. Suddenly horror-struck, he rushed to Jason's room, then to Samantha's, but the children were still there,

Jason asleep, Samantha awake and troubled by the shouting she had heard. He picked her up and held her a long moment, and tears came to him. "It's all right," he murmured. "Go back to sleep." He returned to the bedroom and sat there until dawn, waiting for Jennifer.

In the morning he phoned the office to say that severe family problems had forced him to return from Pittsburgh suddenly and that he needed an indefinite leave of absence, with or without pay. His supervisor was wholly understanding, not at all skeptical, as if Finch's voice communicated precisely how stunned and bewildered he was. He managed to deliver the children to school, and then spent the morning by the telephone, hoping to hear from Jennifer. But no word came from her all day. In late afternoon he called his parents to say that Jennifer had gone off somewhere without warning and could they please come early for their holiday visit, because he wasn't sure he could handle all this domestic stuff alone. They arrived the next day and asked blessedly few questions. In their generation, he thought, it must have been the usual thing for marriages to break up without warning.

Jennifer did not come back. He felt like someone who had been given a single wish and had used it stupidly: now she was off in the inconceivable future with Nort. Was that possible? Was this not all some kind of bizarre dream? Apparently not, for on Christmas Eve a note from Jennifer materialized inexplicably on the living room table, dated 14 Oct 2215 and wishing him happy holidays and assuring him of her love and telling him not to expect her back. "Sometimes you simply have to follow your destiny," she concluded. "I had only a fraction of a second to make my decision and I made it, and maybe I'll regret it, but I did what I had to do. I miss you, darling. And you know how much I miss Samantha and Jason." Next to the note was a little package with a tag marked Merry Christmas from Nort. It contained a tiny crystal ball that when held close to his eye showed him what looked like an Antarctic landscape, gales howling and placid penguins wandering around on an ice floe. He put it down, and when he picked it up a second time it displayed the Pyramids with a long line of tourists milling about. Finch flung it against the wall and

it cracked in half and turned cloudy. He wished he had not done that.

Getting through the holidays was even more of an ordeal than usual, but his parents were an immense help, and his friends, once they discovered that Jennifer was gone, came magnificently to his aid. He was scarcely alone the whole week, and he suspected that it would not have been hard for him to find company for the night, either, but of course that was out of the question. The children were perplexed by Jennifer's disappearance, but after some disorientation they appeared to adapt, which Finch found more than a little chilling. He hired a housekeeper early in January and, feeling like a sleepwalker, went back to work. Because of the change in his family circumstances, the company took him off the outlying routes, so that he would not have to spend nights away from home.

Some time in early spring he started genuinely to believe that Jennifer had skipped away into the future with her lover. Notes from her arrived now and then, always friendly, with regards for the children and reminders about oiling the furnace and taking the cars in for tune-ups. She said she was having a wonderful time but missed him terribly. There was never any mention of coming back. From time to time, also, little gifts appeared—gadgets, toys, knick-knacks of the future. Perhaps they were meant for Jason, but Finch kept them himself, hoarding them in his closet and examining them at night with awe. He had always loved gadgets—computers, remote-control devices, wrist videos, and such—but these seemed more like miracles than gadgets to him, and he ceased to doubt that Nort was what he said he was. Finch hoped another of the crystal balls would turn up, but it never did. He did get something that appeared to tune in the music of the spheres, and another that could be programmed to give him the dreams he wanted, and one that displayed abstract color-fields of a serene unearthly kind.

When summer came, he drifted with surprising ease into a romance with Estelle, the company's PR consultant, and that carried him into late autumn. Gently she extricated herself from the relationship then, but he had learned how to meet and win women once again, and he ran through a lively bachelorhood in the months that followed.

The first anniversary of Jennifer's disappearance passed. The notes from her and the gifts from Nort came less frequently and then not at all. He was quite competent at running a family without a wife by now, but he had never lost that old sense of himself as an innately married man, as half of a couple, and so, admitting that Jennifer was never coming back, he filed for divorce and won an uncontested decree. That was the strangest part thus far, the knowledge that he was no longer married to Jennifer. He looked for a new wife in his diligent, serious-minded way and, within six months, found one. Her name was Sharon and she was warmhearted and lovely and rather like Jennifer, though her interests ran more to drama and poetry than to music and painting. She had had an unhappy marriage just after college and had a boy of four, Joshua, very bright. Joshua got along wonderfully with Jason and Samantha, they accepted Sharon readily as their new mother—Jennifer was only a hazy memory to them now—and everything seemed to have worked out for the best. Sometimes Finch called Sharon "Jennifer" when they made love, but she was very understanding about that. Sometimes, too, he woke up drenched with sweat, wondering where he had misplaced his one true wife, his sundered half; but whenever that happened, Sharon held him until he regained his grasp on reality. He moved up nicely in the firm, which was expanding at a remarkable rate, and stayed trim and agile all through his forties. Samantha and Jason turned out well, too: Jason went to Cal Tech, joined a West Coast company, and invented an information-encapsulating device that made him a stock-option millionaire by the time he was twenty-two. Samantha grew tall and radiant and even more beautiful, pursued her interest in French, and achieved splendid translations of Rabelais and Ronsard and married the French ambassador. Finch saw less and less of his children once they were grown, of course, but they always came home for a family reunion at Christmas. They were with him that afternoon twenty-three years after Jennifer's disappearance when Jennifer reappeared.

Finch did not know who she was, at first. She quite suddenly was *there* in the living room, a handsome, slender, full-breasted young woman of about thirty, with golden hair in tight waves against her scalp, who wore a clinging garment of metallic mesh. She blinked and looked about and gasped as she saw Finch, who was in his mid-fifties and reasonably youthful-looking for his age.

"Dale?" she said doubtfully.

He let his drink clatter to the floor. "No," he said. "It isn't possible. Christ, what are you doing here?"

"I had to come back. Oh, Dale, it's the wrong year, isn't it? I wanted to see the children again!"

"There they are," he said stonily. "Take a look."

"Where—which—"

Jason was there and Samantha, and also Joshua and some of their friends; and obviously Jennifer did not recognize her own. Finch pointed. The stocky broad-shouldered young man with the earnest myopic gaze was Jason. The long-legged, awesomely beautiful woman was Samantha. Jennifer's glossy poise seemed to shatter. She was trembling and close to tears. "I wanted to see the children," she whispered. "They were so small—he was six, she was seven—oh, Dale, I've set the timer wrong! I've made a mess of it, haven't I?"

Samantha, quick as always, was the only other one who understood. She went toward her mother and stared at her as though Jennifer were an intruder from some other planet. Finch had heard that Samantha often used her beauty as a weapon, but he had never before seen it. Jennifer appeared to shrivel before the sleek, dazzling woman she had helped to create. In a low husky voice Samantha said, "You don't belong here now, you know. This is a happy time for us, and we don't need you and we don't want you. Will you go away?"

"Wait," Finch muttered.

Too late. Jennifer, reddening, dismayed, nodded and said to Samantha, "I'm terribly sorry. I'm sorry for everything." She ran from the room. Finch raced after her, out to the hall, but of course she had disappeared. White-faced, Finch returned to the party. He looked toward Sharon, who was both smiling and frowning. He had never told her or anyone else exactly what had become of his first wife.

"Who was that?" Sharon asked amiably. "Some girlfriend of yours, Dale?" There was nothing like jealousy in her voice. She was only mildly curious.

"No—no, nothing like that—"

"I wonder how she got in here. Like coming out of thin air, almost. Strange. Why did she dash away like that?"

"She didn't belong here," Finch said hoarsely. He poured himself another drink. "She was in the wrong time, the wrong place." He glanced at his daughter, who was flushed with triumph. What power she had, what force! All the same, he was starting to regret that Samantha had driven her off so quickly. With a wobbly hand he raised his glass. "Merry Christmas, everybody! Merry, merry, merry Christmas!"

For a few years after that he found himself wondering, as the holiday season approached, whether Jennifer would make another appearance, like some ghost of marriages past coming round again. Had she tired of Nort and Nort's century? Did she yearn for all she had abandoned? Though there was no longer any room in Finch's life for her, he held no grudge after all this time; he was almost eager to go off and talk with her a little, to find out who she had become, this woman who had once been part of him. But she never again returned. Perhaps she spent her holidays with Millard Fillmore now, he thought. Or singing carols by the blazing Yule log at the fireside of great-great-great-grandpa Johann Sebastian Bach.

Copyright © 1982 by Agberg, Ltd

Jody Lynn Nye is the author of forty novels and more than one hundred stories, and has at various times collaborated with Anne McCaffrey and Robert Asprin. Her husband, Bill Fawcett, is a prolific author, editor and packager, and is also active in the gaming field.

BOOK RECOMMENDATIONS

by Jody Lynn Nye and Bill Fawcett

As this column begins let us offer a few words about what we are doing This is a recommendation column. Our goal is to find new books that are a good read and that you might not otherwise come across. It would be far easier to simply add our reviews to the dozens of others for best-selling authors, but you don't need us to tell you Brandon Sanderson's new book, *Legion*, is excellent. It is and we both expect that. What we can do is help you to discover new authors and new books. This is also why we often suggest a classic book or series from decades ago. So, once more, here are some books that will interest, amuse or excite you.

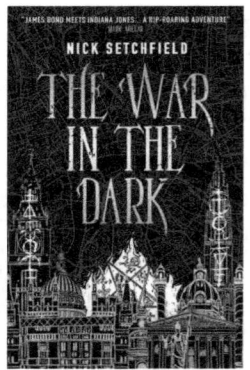

The War in the Dark
by Nick Setchfield
Titan Books
July 2018
ISBN-13: 978-1785657092

The main character of *The War in the Dark* is an operative for British Intelligence, Christopher Winter, and it is set in the early 1960s. He thinks he is an assassin on a routine mission; when things go very strangely and badly wrong, he begins to realize he is

also something else. Impersonating his dead leader, he tries to infiltrate an auction for state secrets. The secret turns out to be anything but normal and Winter finds himself allied to a mysterious woman while trying to save the world from being invaded by a horde of demons.

The action takes the British assassin from London to Moscow and then Cold War Germany. The feel is very solid with, not surprisingly, a strong British tone as the agent uncovers more of the evil conspiracy and finds himself in increasingly bizarre and deadly situations. Bone magic, dark arts, and demonology abound. There is enough darkness and horror for those desiring that alone, but the action and mystery are just as important elements.

The author, Nick Setchfield, is also the features editor for *SFX*, Britain's most popular magazine of genre entertainment for film, TV and books. Like many British authors, Setchfield will use as many words as needed to describe a scene. In this case that is a good thing as more than once you will find yourself noting how well turned some of the phrases are. Saying that, be aware that the action really never stops. It hardly pauses to allow the agent to heal and sleep, much less have tea. Once you settle into its Cold War noir atmosphere, this story becomes a serious page turner. This book is highly recommended for those who enjoy contemporary fantasy, action horror, or if you enjoy things British from Holmes to Bond.

✧

Ball Lightning
by Cixin Liu
Tor Books
August 2018

ISBN-13: 978-0765394071

It would be easy to explain why you should read this book by simply saying Cixin Liu wrote the acclaimed and best-selling The Three-Body Problem trilogy. This is actually one of his earlier novels, originally published in 2005 in China, and just now translated into English. Having said that, be assured that *Ball Lightning* reads so well that at no time will you be aware it was translated from Chinese.

There are two things that recommend *Ball Lightning* to any science-fiction fan. The first is that it is the story of a fictional secret research project that feels much like accounts of the Manhattan Project, complete to political, military, and moral concerns. The second reason is that it pulls you so well into the world of Red China at the start of this century. You find yourself disappointed by ball lightning's failure to destroy an invading fleet centered on a large number of Aircraft Carriers. (Hint: only one nation has that many carriers.)

The story is that of Chen, a scientist whose parents were killed by ball lightning. Ball lightning in the real world is now accepted by most scientists and may actually involve ultra-cold atoms trapping hot plasma. As he first trains himself in mathematics and physics, the scientist begins to learn more about the phenomena. Then Chen is asked to join a team researching ball lightning, later discovering it is to be developed as a weapon. The research, the complications, and his moral dilemmas add to what is a strong character and cultural tale. The characters' problems, from academic competition to patriotism versus humanity, powerfully fill out this portrayal of an obsessed scientist.

Having been written for Chinese readers and during a time when China felt itself under siege, the assumptions and premises in this book are not that of your average American reader. This book can be read and enjoyed by any sci-fi reader. It can also be read simply as contemporary-era novel with sci-fi touches. Those who are interested in world affairs, history, Chinese culture or the US relationship with China may even find in it a few insights.

✧

Mecha Samurai Empire
by Peter Tieryas
Ace SF
September 2018
ISBN-13: 978-0451490995

This is the sequel to *United States of Japan*, but stands alone if you read it first. After reading this you certainly will want more. It is an alternate history where Japan and Germany win WWII and haven't gotten along since. This book is the story of a young man whose ambition is to become one of the Imperial Military's elite, a crewman on the giant mechas. These are a basic technology version of the robot warriors made popular in anime and the game Battletech.

Getting into the Military Academy is hard. San Francisco born Makoto has the disadvantage of not coming from a connected family. Then the young student manages to annoy the testing officer and is rejected. Having no other goal and no real home, he enlists with a commercial mecha company and survives their brutal training only to have most of his team slaughtered by bandit-like American rebels in the pay of the Nazis. To survive that attack he even defeats one of the new Nazi Biomechs which combine mecha skeletons and mutated human tissue into a deadly combination. This heroism gains him entry to the Mecha training course at the Imperial Japanese Army Military Academy (in Berkeley) where even before graduation he finds himself in another battle with the dreaded Nazi biomechs.

The book is well written. You soon care about the character, and eventually almost adjust to the quirky alternate time line. As a personal quest, it reads well. When you include that a good portion of the book is mecha combat that is among the best written of the genre, it becomes a quality action novel as well. While about a teenager, and certainly readable by YA and older both with no problems, this book is a good read for all fans. If you regret William Keith is no longer turning out those excellent Battletech novels, *Mecha Samurai Empire* will give you your mecha heroism fix. It will particularly appeal to those who enjoy alternate history settings and military combat.

✧

Wild Hunger
by Chloe Neill
Berkley
August 2018
ISBN-13: 978-0399587092

Wild Hunger is the newest in the best-selling Chicagoland Vampires series, and the first of a new line of storytelling. The book is narrated by Elisa, daughter of Merit, the point-of-view character of the first thirteen (that began with *Some Girls Bite*), and Ethan Sullivan, Master of Cadogan House, the most prominent of the four Chicago vampire enclaves. Elisa is the first vampire who was ever born instead of made, the result of a magical overload in a previous adventure in which her parents were involved. The book follows her back to Chicago after her university education in Paris and as she is fulfilling a year's service to a French vampire enclave, Dumas House. Based on his success in arranging cooperation among the Chicago houses, Ethan has called for peace talks to try and establish the same entente between the European vampire houses. Elisa has a secret that she has kept even from her parents: she and her mother's sword have a bond that rouses fierce magic in her that she must constantly fight to control. She also comes face-to-face with her childhood nemesis, Connor Keene, son of the shifters' Alpha leader, Gabriel. He has grown up gorgeous, competent and powerful, and she has to deal with ambivalent feelings about him.

When the first meeting is underway, the local army of fairies invade, demanding to be part of the negotiations. Fairies are even more contentious and arrogant than either vampires or shifters, but Ethan agrees to let them stay. During the cocktail party that follows the initial session, one of the vampires is murdered, and suspicion falls on one of the shifters. The police and the Ombudsman that intervenes between the mayor and the supernaturals (or "sups," a term that is used from the start of the book but not explained immediately) step in. Elisa knows the shifter, and believes that he is innocent of the crime. Against the orders of her parents and local custom, she begins her own investigation. It is up to her to discover who killed the vampire, and what they hoped to gain by it. From there, the story unfolds into unexpected dimensions, putting Elisa, her family and House, and her closest friends in danger. Neill's storytelling takes you along for a wonderful ride, full of great characters, effortless description, and imaginative magic. After one book, I'm a fan.

If you like vampire stories, adventure, and a little romance, you'll enjoy *Wild Hunger*.

Frankenstein, or The Modern Prometheus
by Mary Wollstonecraft Shelley
Various Publishers

This month's classic is considered by many to be the first genuine science fiction novel. Shelley was only seventeen when she wrote this book in 1814, as part of a bet between herself, her future husband, the poet Percy Bysshe Shelley, and his fellow poet, Lord Byron, to see who could write the best horror story. Inspired by a visit to the part of Germany near Frankenstein Castle and the scientific research of Luigi Galvani, who experimented with using electrical current to stimulate dead tissues to move with a semblance of life, Mary amused herself by writing a story of a troubled scientist, Victor Frankenstein, who assembles a huge creature out of human body parts and brings it to life with lightning.

Unlike nearly all of the movie representations, the monster is not an unthinking behemoth, but a sensitive, intelligent person. It flees Victor's home and laboratory after the murder of Victor's youngest brother. Victor believes that he is responsible for the murder and pursues him. The monster sees its reflection in a river, and realizes that it is hideous. All humans who see it fear it. The only person he is able to befriend is the blind father of a family upon whom the monster has been eavesdropping to learn to speak. He also learns to read by finding a satchel of books lost in the woods.

He confronts Victor and demands that he should be allowed happiness. The scientist must create for him a female of his own kind so he won't be alone. Victor agrees, then fears it will lead to the two creations engendering a race of monstrous beings. He destroys his work again and again. The monster has been watching him covertly, and vows that if he cannot be happy, Victor will also suffer. He kills Victor's bride, and flees into the north. Victor pursues him. Starving and exhausted, he falls into the care of a ship's captain (who is the narrator of the book). He will not give up his quest to stop his creation, but he is too weak. He dies, and the monster mourns over his body.

It's a marvelous, atmospheric, tragic and moody tale, suitable for being read on the same kind of rainy days on which it was written.

Copyright © 2018 by Jody Lynn Nye and Bill Fawcett

Larry Niven is one of the true giants of science fiction, with classics and bestsellers like Ringworld, Lucifer's Hammer, *and the* Man-Kzin Wars. *A constant bestseller, Larry is the recipient of multiple Hugo and Nebula Awards, is a Nebula Grand Master, and has been a Worldcon Guest of Honor. When we asked him to give us something to replace his frequent collaborator Gregory Benford's column for this issue, he happily offered us the following.*

GOD NEEDS COLLABORATORS

by Larry Niven

I can't remember how long ago I started thinking in these terms. At first the questions were, "Why is there a universe? Why are there minds? Why is there anything?" Jerry Pournelle asked these questions often.

And my tentative answer was, "God wants companionship. Someone to talk to on his own level."

"How's that working out?"

"There are hopeful signs. Wait a little longer."

But then I started to notice how neat ideas always seem to work out. For a while. Then they change.

Genesis. Neat story. But it reads like a conspiracy, and where did Cain's wife come from? Something new was needed.

Noah's flood. Neat story, and if you look, you can actually find fossils where there is no sea. Perhaps Earth was once all water? Continents that drift around was a much wilder idea.

The Earth is round, not flat. Neat idea, and it would answer thorny questions: what are things like at the edge? What if there's no edge? If you look for proof, you find it: shadows that move with the seasons, easily enough to measure if you travel a little north and south. Pendulums.

Newton and gravity. If you look, you can measure how it works. Nobody looked before. Planets circling the sun: not just a neat idea, but a lesson in humility and a sense of perspective.

Greek elements: they fit with every kind of matter you look at. Earth, water, air, fire; solid, liquid, gas, plasma; and two more states of matter, condensed matter and neutronium, that the Greeks never ran

across. Can't include black holes because they're not exactly matter. Maybe we need to include superfluid. And Bose-Einstein condensate.

It looks, from a certain viewpoint, as if God is adapting sufficiently neat ideas. The universe is a work in progress.

Early in the last century notions started coming thick and fast. The size of the universe kept expanding. It might have been infinite for awhile, but perhaps that was too unwieldy. The big bang was an absolutely neat idea if you like explosions, which God apparently does, and when you look in the right place, the sound of the explosion is in the microwave background. Study of the oldest galaxies with better and better telescopes showed an age of twenty billion years, then fifteen (when DC Comics got me involved) and now 13.7 billion.

Special relativity was simple enough, and hey! It meant that various creations couldn't reach each other. Without the lightspeed barrier, primitive ecologies would be constantly replaced by invaders before they could become interesting. This way we get less conquest, more variety across the star lanes. For awhile relativity may have meant that God couldn't act retroactively; but then Carl Sagan asked Kip Thorne to design him a time machine.

Extrasolar planets were always a neat idea. Human astronomers of course went looking for worlds like Earth, when their techniques got good enough. They found planets in the Goldilocks Zones of nearby stars, just as they had hoped.

Earth is near the inner edge of Sol's Goldilocks Zone. Another lesson in humility, and it adds a sense of drama. Humanity has always been under threat from something or other: it keeps us thinking, planning. Is that a part of the pattern? A universe designed for storytelling.

Special relativity, gravity as multidimensional geometry, is irresistibly neat. Quantum theory may be too confusing. There is as yet no resolution between the two. They say string theory resolves it all, but they say there aren't any experiments possible to prove string theory.

They'll come up with something. God is waiting for us to straighten it out.

Copyright © 2018 by Larry Niven

Robert J. Sawyer is the Hugo, Nebula, Campbell Memorial, Heinlein, Hal Clement, Skylark, Galaxy, and Seiun Award-winning author of twenty-three science-fiction novels, including the trilogy of Hominids, Humans, and Hybrids, which won Canada's Aurora Award for the Best of the Decade, and the #1 Locus bestsellers Calculating God, Triggers, and Quantum Night. Rob holds two honorary doctorates and is a Member of the Order of Canada, the highest civilian honor bestowed by the Canadian government. Find him online at sfwriter.com.

DECOHERENCE

by Robert J. Sawyer

THE NOBLE MISSION

I have great sympathy for those who put their feet in their mouths while being interviewed on TV. The lights are hot, the cameras are rolling, and the interviewee is expected to be witty, urbane, and erudite without any do-overs; it's a tightrope walk, and can be nerve-wracking.

Which is why a recent gift touched me so. When I got home from the 2018 World Science Fiction Convention in San Jose, I found a twenty-by-twenty-inch metal plaque waiting for me. It showed a beautiful photograph of the Orion Nebula in all its swirling purples and pinks, with these words superimposed over one corner:

"Science Fiction is a mode of interrogating the future that allows us to prepare positively to take proactive steps to make a better tomorrow for the human race. There is no more valuable or noble mission to be a part of."

The words were attributed to me. Honestly, I had no recollection of having said them, but the plaque had been sent by Matthew Cimone, one of the producers of the documentary film *Chasing Atlantis*—about the space shuttle, not the undersea kingdom—for which I'd been interviewed (and Matthew himself had taken the wonderful nebula photo at Simon Fraser University's Trottier Observatory). Those two sentences must have spontaneously tumbled out

of me during the lengthy interview they'd done in my home and Matthew had been so taken with them that he'd had the plaque made as a gift for me.

Now, if I'd been writing instead of speaking, I'd have been a bit less prolix, dropping the largely unnecessary "to prepare positively," but, like I said, no do-overs on TV. Still, I stand by the sentiment. We science-fiction writers *are* doing something valuable and noble, crucial and important; it's *not* just, or only, or merely, entertainment. It can and should be taken seriously by politicians and policymakers, by scientists and social planners, by voters and activists.

That interview for *Chasing Atlantis*, by the way, was just one of almost 400 TV interviews I've done over the years. That's a lot, yes, by the standards of almost any writer, but a science-fiction writer *isn't* just any writer: he or she is a technological and sociological prophet, an expert prognosticator, an informed and compelling commentator on where we are now and where we might be going.

Other forms of writing may, on average, sell more copies (I'm looking at you, fantasy fiction), but can you seriously imagine *any* fantasist being asked to comment routinely on news stories, or to advise government agencies as many of my colleagues and I routinely do?

I'm old enough to remember my own favorite SF author, Arthur C. Clarke, sitting next to Walter Cronkite during coverage of the *Apollo* missions, and my friend the late SF writer Jerry Pournelle (yes, liberals and conservatives *can* be friends!) was instrumental in developing many of the Reagan administration's space initiatives.

Early in my career, I sat more often on the other side of the table, being the interviewer rather than the interviewee. In 1989, I spoke with SF writer Kim Stanley Robinson for CBC Radio. During that interview, Stan outlined the key to the extrapolative knack: an understanding of history. A good SF writer first asks how we got to where we are now and only after understanding the forces that shaped the present does he or she begin to map out the suite of probable directions those same forces might propel us toward in the future.

And people at the highest levels *are* listening; Hugo winner *The Three-Body Problem* by Cixin Liu was one of President Obama's recent reads.

Yes, sometimes we gussy ourselves up as "futurists" or "foresight consultants," but we earned our chops writing science fiction—by doing research-intensive, skeptically minded, careful and thoughtful extrapolating. (I like to quip that the difference between a science-fiction writer and a futurist is the latter can get away with asking for twenty times more as a speaker's fee.)

But, really, donning those guises is a polite (wait for it) fiction. Whenever one of us is invited to comment to the press, appear on TV, or give a keynote at a science or technology conference, it's because a journalist or event organizer is a fan of our novels, recognizing how insightful they are (whether they're advocating for a positive future or sounding a warning call against a negative one).

As I write this, I'm about to get on a plane for Beijing. My colleague Derek Künsken (an *Analog* mainstay whose first novel, *The Quantum Magician*, I commend to your attention) and I are appearing at the World Conference on Science Literacy, a three-day event sponsored by the China Association for Science and Technology.

Why bring SF writers from half a world away for a conference that isn't even about science fiction? Because the Chinese government has come to recognize what we in the West have known for decades now: getting young people to read science fiction is a sure-fire way to get many of them to go on to careers in the STEM professions of science, technology, engineering, and mathematics.

At Dragon Con in September 2018, I was on a panel about hard science fiction moderated by Les Johnson from NASA's Marshall Spaceflight Center, whose opening remarks were precisely that: not only himself but the *majority* of his colleagues got interested in their career areas *because* of reading science fiction.

China, though, is facing a crisis: overwhelmingly, young people there are choosing to study either business or international relations. Having a million people around with such majors is perhaps useful, but to be the world leader it wants to be, China understands that it needs *hundreds of millions* of scientists and engineers, and that the best way of getting them in the next generation is by inculcating that cardinal science-fictional virtue, the sense of wonder, in the most direct way possible: encouraging the reading of science fiction.

Whether it's in contextualizing science news stories, helping shape policy, or encouraging the best and brightest minds to help make a better future for us all, science fiction *is* important. And, yes, gosh darn it, there is no more valuable or noble mission to be a part of.

Copyright © 2018 by Robert J. Sawyer

Michael Swanwick is a multiple award-winning writer in science fiction and fantasy. Hugo, Nebula, Locus, World Fantasy, he has them all. Yet this genuinely nice man makes those around him comfortable as he relates his experiences. If you haven't read a Swanwick recently then do yourself a favor and pick up one or more of his books or short stories.

Joy Ward is the author of one novel. She has several stories in print, in magazines and in anthologies, and has also conducted interviews, both written and video, for other publications.

THE *GALAXY'S EDGE* INTERVIEW

Joy Ward Interviews Michael Swanwick

Joy Ward: How did you get into writing?

Michael Swanwick: I've got three origin stories. I'll go with the first one. My sister sent home a box of books from college, as she was done with paperbacks, and one of them was the first volume in *Lord of the Rings*.

I finished my homework one night at eleven o'clock and I said, "I'll just read a chapter or two before I go to bed," and I started to read it. I stayed up all night reading that book and I read—I skipped breakfast reading it, I walked to the school reading it. As the homeroom bell rang, I finished the last word. I was then sixteen.

That book just rings me like a bell. I wanted to write a book exactly like that and uh, I changed overnight from wanting to be a scientist to wanting to be a writer.

JW: What, as you said, rang the bell? What is it about writing? What is it about as you're reading that book that really gets to you like that?

MS: Sub-creation, just the idea of making something really, really wonderful and that's really what I want. I'm not after the money, which is a good thing, but I'm not after the awards. I just want to write something I would really love to read. You have to be mad to be a writer and you have to be mad about

fiction and you have to be mad about the proofs. That's my hardest. I can say I'm just a fan of wonderful writing. I want to write as best I can and I want to write better than I can.

JW: What does great writing do?

MS: It creates its own world. It creates a world that you want to live in and that, briefly, you can live in. An alternative to our world and in one way or another, a better alternative to our world. One which…one which makes sense where our world does not. When it reconciles itself to ours it helps us reconcile ourselves to our world. It's one that makes sense of our world. These are all noble aspiration.

It makes me want to write better. I don't think you ever reach the top of that mountain. There's always more to go. There's always further to go and the higher up you get, the further away from where you are you can see. I'm not too modest but I'm really hoping that I can make myself a better writer.

JW: You received a lot of attention fairly early in your career.

MS: And they were both in the same category too, which got me a lot of attention which is a really good thing for a new writer to have. It did something even better which was they both lost. 'Cause I've known a lot of people who won right off the bat, won an award and it kind of soured the process for them to go from unpublishable to, let's say, Nebula award-winning in one story. That puts a lot of pressure on a writer. And then from every year, from that point on, uh, every year they don't win a major award is failing to live up to the original promise. It can be a terrible thing to happen to you as a writer. But I lost, and I kept on losing and losing.

When I finally won an award ten years later I won a Theodore Sturgeon Award. That felt really good. By then I felt I'd lost enough that I deserved to win one, so I've enjoyed the award process and watched it. I love watching it like a horse race, I love rooting for my favorites. I love applauding whoever wins, and I've enjoyed the whole process and resented it all because I didn't win right away.

JW: When you found out that you won the Theodore Sturgeon, what went through your mind?

MS: I was delighted, I was happy, I was surprised, I was amazed. It was all good things and every award that I won since it felt exactly the same way. I won five Hugo Awards in a period of six years and for a period of six years. The last one I was sitting there in the audience. I only had four behind me so you think I was taken for granted. They announced my name and I teleported to the stage. Maryanne, who's sitting next to me, said she knew I wasn't expecting it. This came as a surprise to me because I hadn't kissed her before I went up.

Awards don't really change your life. They're just wonderful, delightful things that happen to you sometimes if you're fortunate.

The first time I was up for a Hugo and the reason I was up for a Hugo was I co-wrote *Dogfight* with William Gibson.

He was very hot at the time and I think *Neuromancer* just come out. So naturally anything with his name on it cut right on to the pound. I remember going up the escalator to the awards and I saw William Gibson come down the escalator fleeing the awards. He saw me seeing him and his look, got this expression, "Oh, God, busted." Then he smiled and said, "I hope you win, Michael."

He continued to flee. I went and I sat there. They didn't put the nominees upfront that year. I'm not sure why but they put a long line of awards on a table. It looked like the teeth of a comb.

I waited through several awards and you don't know how many awards there are until you're up for one. And then, while the MC was talking, the same woman came walking out across the table, picked up a Hugo, walked off stage.

So I count the number of Hugos again five times. There's only one each. To make a long story short, we lost. So the next day I'm sitting and talking in the green room. I'm sitting and talking with George Martin and Michael Bishop, two of my heroes. You know, you think they can do no wrong and they

were all talking about the awards. It turned out that they had noticed that too and they've been doing the same thing.

I realized that at that moment that they had been up for the same award as I had been up for. We're all there doing the same thing, counting the awards as one. I'm sitting here talking with Michael Bishop and George Martin as equals. This is really, that was what it felt, that was my reward.

It just knocked me out. It's as if you could sit and talk with Faulkner and Jane Austen as equals. Really good writers. Other than my family's life, other people who I value the most. That was just a great experience.

JW: How did writing become that kind of a force for you?

MS: Just reading, just from reading and falling in love with what I read. It's that simple.

JW: I'm hearing that other writers have made a major impact on you, not just as the writers but personally.

MS: Some of the writers in science fiction are really good to each other. The impression I get is about the New York City mainstream writers tend to be a cut-throat batch. They're always feuding with each other. The feuds in science fiction are relatively few, relatively far between and not—and the hatred is not there. There have been a lot of writers encouraging young, unpublished writers who could do them no possible good. That's just become the standard. Robert Heinlein helped out Ray Bradbury a lot. One time Theodore Sturgeon wrote to Heinlein saying that he had no ideas. He just ran dry. He didn't know what to do. Heinlein sent him a long letter and gave him a batch of ideas. He kept writing them until he had written them out. By that time, he was writing his own again. Robert Heinlein gave him a story that he could've written in the afternoon and it was a great story. That was astonishingly generous.

I sat and watched Charles Sheffield explaining the business of science fiction to this young female unpublished writer. He just gave generously of his knowledge. No benefit to him whatsoever. This has been the standard in the field. It means a great deal to me to be a part of a group that are very generous, very open-hearted to other writers.

JW: Where do you see your writing going now?

MS: Right now it appears to be going to more interest in fantasy. I started out to write fantasy, high fantasy, serious fantasy and it took me two or three years to read everything that had ever been published in fantasy. There's a lot of fantasy DNA in science fiction and the way that it will, my load is shifted to science fiction because it's just as hard to write the story but you also have to have the science so since it was more difficult, of course. I was young, my loyalties go to whatever is most difficult.

I shifted off into science fiction now around 1990. It was in Ireland '91, '92. I was in Ireland for the first time. Everything we saw there was so different from how we pictured it. The castles were smaller. The ruins looked different. When you went up in a Norman keep, it looked over and looked down in the field right next to it. There's a stone circle. Everything looked different. Amazing how it looks like it was built by a race of conqueror hobbits. It's monumental and cute at the same time. We were photographing an earth fort. There's a bord failte sign that identified it as a fairy ring. We're taking photographs of it and this ten-, twelve-year-old boy comes up and says, "What are you doing?" Maryann said, "Oh, we're photographing the fairy ring."

He said, "Don't tell me you're still believing in fairies," with a disgusted look on his face. I realized that I couldn't write some kind of fantasy. I wanted to write because the people in British Isles grew up with things like ring forts and stone circles, sometimes literally in their backyards, and Americans grew up reading their books.

I feel myself gravitating more toward fantasy these days, partly because I can see better how to do it and keep it honest with my own experiences. Also, I looked back at some great science fiction. You look at *Necromancer* now and parts of it are dated because technology's moved on and there's a lot of really good science fiction that gets forgotten because the technology moves beyond it and that's kind of a trap I'd like to avoid.

JW: What advice do you give young writers? When you're talking with young writers what do you tell them they should be doing?

MS: They should be writing the kind of stuff that they want to read. They should write what they love and they should not be trying to follow the dollar. They should not be trying to latch onto the new cyberpunk or the new weird because by the time that you hear about a movement, it's already over. You can only succeed at the kind of stuff that you want to write and there's no guarantee you will succeed either. It's a hard business. There's not a lot of people make a living from it.

It's just like the value of a Greek painting. Look what somebody can do with oil paints. Look at what somebody can do with words. In the face of the heat death of the universe, it means nothing but as human works go it's a *Moonlight Sonata*. A million years from now that will be forgotten, but in the meantime, doesn't it make you feel good to know that somebody of your species could write that? Wow, that's so beautiful.

What science fiction does is it brings you new ideas. It brings an idea that you simply cannot have without the whole science fiction apparatus. I think that's probably its greatest contribution. Me, I'm in it for the story.

JW: Any other words of wisdom you'd like to pass on?

MS: Put down the iPad, read more novels. Read. It doesn't matter whether it's science fiction or fantasy or mainstream. Read more novels and read lots more short fiction. Short fiction is a gorgeous literary form. Nobody can make a living doing it and therefore, that collection of short fiction by your favorite author, that was a labor of love. Show them the love back. Go ahead and read it. If you happen to have enough money, buy the copy but read in the library if you don't. Nobody is gonna be angry at you. Short fiction can be held in your mind all at once. A short story does one thing absolutely perfectly well:

It breaks your heart or it fills you with wonder or it teaches you something new. Just amazes you. A novel could have lots and lots of amazement but you can't hold it in your mind at one time.

JW: How do you want to be remembered?

MS: I'd love to have the books remembered, I'd love to have the books still read, that's what I really want. I value them because I value them. That's it, that's— I'm just trying to make my contribution to the great ocean of literature and I would like it to be a contribution that was worth making.

Copyright © 2018 by Joy Ward

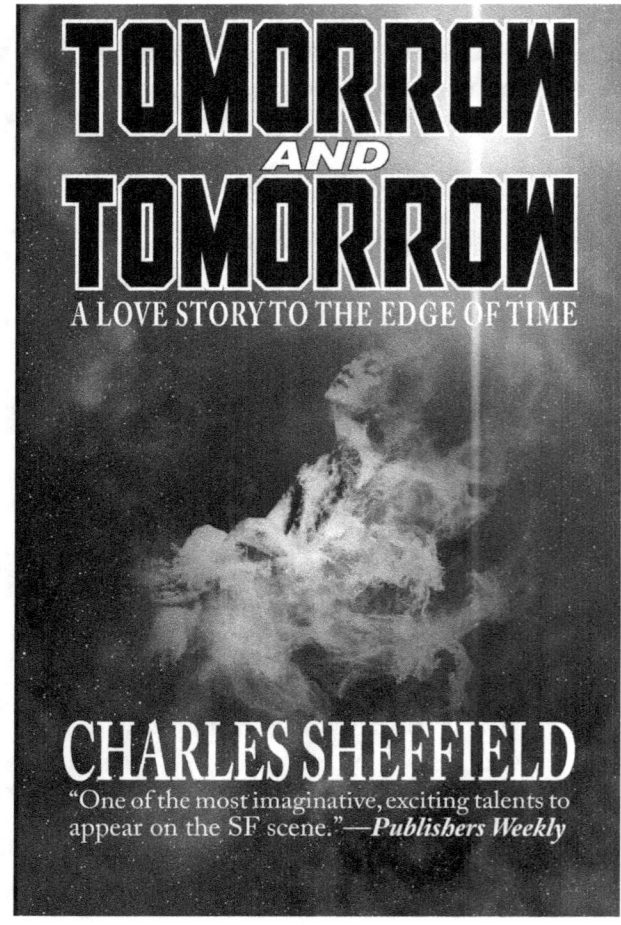

Tomorrow and Tomorrow by Charles Sheffield. Copyright © 1997 by Charles Sheffield. Parts of this novel are drawn from the novella, *At the Eschaton*, by Charles Sheffield, published in the collection *Far Futures* (Tor Books, 1995).

Phoenix Pick Edition April 15, 2017

Charles Sheffield was a Hugo and Nebula winner, as well as a Campbell Memorial Winner. He served as President of the Science Fiction Writers of America, and also put in time as Chief Scientist of the Earth Satellite Corporation.

TOMORROW AND TOMORROW
(part 2)
Charles Sheffield

7

"A Wild Call and a Clear Call That May Not be Denied."

Drake was working. It was late or early, depending on the definition. The improvements to his body included a lessened need for sleep, and he did most of his private thinking and searching long after midnight. Tonight he had lost track of the hour as he strove to understand, for the hundredth time, the complex medical environment of Ana's disease. He could see why an ailment that had been bred out of the human race would attract little attention in the present day; but it seemed to him that treatments for other conditions might apply to this one.

He was toying with the daunting idea of learning Medicine—a multiyear commitment—when his outer portal reported a caller. He glanced up at the clock. Eight in the morning. He had time for a short nap, then he ought to call Par Leon and plan the rest of the day. They worked together flexibly and well, swapping opinions and thoughts and notes whenever either of them felt it useful; but they seldom met in person.

So who could be visiting, so early and uninvited? He lived in a tiny apartment. It was furnished with minimal facilities, and in four years he had never had a visitor.

The portal again reported a request for attention. He approved it, and stood up as the interlocking doors opened.

The caller was a woman. She did not wait for Drake's invitation before she entered. She walked in and swept her gaze over the interior of the apartment. She seemed to take everything in with a single glance from a pair of sapphire-blue eyes.

"You're Drake Merlin," she said firmly. "I'm Melissa Bierly."

She looked right at him, and he experienced for the first time the full force of her. Even long afterward, even when he knew the whole story, he was never able to explain the source of that peculiar power. She was striking looking, certainly, with a round, symmetrical face framed by straight black hair and wide eyes of pure deep blue; but a composer, especially one who had written music for movies, was exposed to many striking women. His first impression was that she was tall. Then she came closer and he realized that he was wrong. Her head scarcely came to his nose.

"Do I know you?" Drake said at last. He was sure that he did not. He had met hundreds of people since his awakening, usually through Par Leon and their mutual researches; but he would not have forgotten Melissa Bierly.

"Apparently not, though it would have been possible—just." She had switched to English. "We were around at the same time, but you were frozen when I was only one-year-old. I went to the cryowombs twenty-four years later, and this is the first resurrection for each of us."

Dead at twenty-five—younger even than Ana. Drake gestured to a chair, and she nodded and sat down. He sat on the low bed, facing her.

The sapphire eyes looked right inside him as she went on, "I was revived two months ago. As soon as I could, I checked how many of us there are. Do you know that number?"

He shook his head, still without speaking. It was a question of no interest. At best it was irrelevant to his needs; at worst it would lead to an interaction with other Resurrects. That could waste time and distract him from his goals.

"There were fewer than fifty thousand placed in the cryowombs," Melissa went on. "Forty-eight thousand eight hundred and ninety-seven, to be exact. Most of them entered the cryowombs within fifty years after me. Apparently the idea went out of fashion when the revival success rate remained at zero for so long. Also, life expectancy had increased. Of the total frozen, only a hundred and thirty-two have been resurrected. How many of those have you met?"

"None."

"That's what I thought. As soon as I arrived, one of my first acts was to contact the other Resurrects. They form a closely knit group."

"I am not surprised to learn it." Drake was speaking in English, too, and he felt the shift in mental gears. It was his first use of the language in almost four years. It brought a surge of longing for the past, as strong and inexplicable as life returning with the spring.

He knew that his answer to Melissa Bierly had not been quite an honest one. He had examined the database of Resurrects. He did not remember how many there were, but he recalled that they lived in a colony of their own and spent all their leisure time together.

"But you are unique," Melissa said. The eyes were boring into Drake. "You alone have had no contact with any of the others."

"Did they tell you to come and see me?" The presence of the woman was producing an effect on Drake, relaxing and unnerving him at the same time. Her gray dress was as concealing as Cass Leemu's scanty outfits were revealing, but with Melissa Bierly there was a crackling undercurrent of tension. He did not know if it was sexual or from some other cause. He had not generated it, and he did not want it. But it was there.

The dark head shook firmly, while the eyes never left his. "The others said nothing to me, except inviting me to join their group. I came to you precisely because of your aloofness. You see, I wish to undertake a project. I wish to see what the world has become, everywhere from pole to pole. I do not want to travel with a group. But I do want a companion."

Even before he replied, Drake felt the insidious lure of her suggestion. A knowledge of the world as it was now could only increase the chances of his own success. The data banks were vast beyond imagining, but surely they did not contain everything. Suppose that, in some far-off corner of the Earth, information existed that would allow Ana to be cured?

"Well?" Melissa had moved to stand in front of him, her hands on her hips.

He shook his head. "I'm afraid it's impossible. I'm busy on a long-term collaborative project."

"If it's long-term, why can't it wait a little while?" She moved closer and reached out to touch his hand. It was their first contact, and Drake felt the irrational spark of attraction.

"We wouldn't need to be gone long," she continued. She was smiling down at him. "Come on, come with me. Just for a few weeks. Surely you must have taken breaks in your work before."

"Never."

"How long have you been working on this project?"

"Four years."

She stared at him incredulously. "Without any time off at all? You *deserve* a vacation, and I'll bet you need one. Why not call your collaborator and see if he will agree to it?"

Drake felt no need of a vacation. He had resisted the idea strongly, the half-dozen times that Par Leon suggested it. He had known Melissa Bierly for less than a quarter of an hour. But, beyond his comprehension, he found himself reaching out to call Par Leon.

Leon was sure to say no. There was no way, given the current status of the project, that he would agree. While the call was going through, Drake told himself to expect a refusal. And once Leon had said no, Drake would have something tangible to counterbalance his own irrational urge to say yes, and go off with Melissa to the ends of the Earth.

Then the screen was alive, Par Leon's open, dignified face was staring out at them, and Drake was making a half-coherent request to delay their work for a while.

And Leon was nodding, even before Drake had finished. "Of course you may go. I have plenty of work that I can manage very well in your absence. The project will not suffer. Go, and enjoy."

Even in Drake's dazed state of mind he felt that there was something wrong. Par Leon had no expression in his voice. It was as if the request had come to him as a follow-up on some earlier conversation. Also, Leon had not asked when Drake wanted to go, or where, or how long he might be away. And Drake had provided none of that information. Indeed, he did not know it himself.

But before he could speak again, Leon was gone; and Melissa had taken both his hands in hers and was lifting him easily to his feet.

"There," she said. "What did I tell you? Now that's done, we can sit down together and make plans and begin to get to know each other. You're very cramped in here. Why don't we go to my place? It's a lot more comfortable."

Drake thought for one moment of Ana. She lay secure in her frigid cryowomb, on far-off Pluto. But it was Melissa, warm and breathing and somehow compelling, who held his hands. It was her sparkling blue eyes, rather than Ana's gray ones, that smiled into his.

Unresisting, he allowed her to lead him to the door and out of his little apartment.

Drake was heading for the open air of Earth for the first time in five hundred years. Since the surface seemed to play no part in his plans after his resurrection, he had ignored its existence during his time working with Par Leon. And if he had been asked what he expected to find as the elevator carried him upward, he would have been hard put to provide a single answer. In any case, the answers he might have given were nothing like what he and Melissa found when the deep elevator finally reached the surface.

In the past few days she had taken charge of their lives. Although she had been thawed for less than seventy days, she seemed to know more than Drake about everything in their new world. After the first twenty-four hours he had surrendered his independence. She was like a force of nature. He did not attempt to argue with her or resist her. She knew where they were going, how they would get there, what they would do when they arrived.

Only occasionally, when they were waiting for something, did he notice a difference. The forceful, all-competent manner changed. The blue eyes became frenzied and crazy, and dark shadows crossed her face like demons.

It was happening now. They were at the surface, and the giant elevator doors were ready to release them to the outside air. Melissa should have been bubbling over with energy and excitement. Instead she was withdrawn, staring at the floor a few feet in front of them as if she saw all the devils of Hell in the pattern of tiles. It was Drake who was wide-eyed and curious, too, absorbed to worry about the change in Melissa. Even the doors themselves aroused his interest. They had not opened, like normal doors, but seemed to dissolve to gray mist and then quietly vanish. Was this what the induced teaching meant, when it referred to "the transforming technology provided by a mastery of molecular bonds"?

He stared through the doors as they silently faded. Half a dozen possibilities filled his mind as to what he might see outside: a world completely paved over, with roads and vehicles everywhere? vast amounts of airborne traffic of strange and unfamiliar design, flying above his head? postnuclear devastation? gigantic buildings, arcologies in which half a million people could live? shimmering heat, as global warming ruled; or sheeted ice and visible breath, the precursors to some new Ice Age held at bay in his own time only by the widespread burning of fossil fuels? Or maybe the ozone layer was lost, and sunlight was now so fierce and strong in ultraviolet radiation that unshielded skin would turn purple black within minutes.

All these, and more, had been confidently predicted.

Drake looked. He saw an endless prairie, dotted in the distance with small clumps of trees. Of humans, and human influence, there was no sign. Melissa came to his side and took his hand. He glanced at her and saw that she was back once more to her usual confident self. She began to lead the way, walking toward that far-off blue-gray skyline.

As they went, Melissa explained. She had returned to her normal manner instantly, as soon as the doors were fully open and the surface beyond was visible.

"I could certainly see the signs in my time," she said, "and I'd be surprised if they weren't already visible in yours. If I was asked to provide a single word for what started the change, I'd give one that I've never seen quoted: glass. Before people had glass, there was a time when they didn't have buildings at all. They lived outside, in the middle of whatever was out there—animals of all sizes, from fleas to elephants. They might not have liked it, but they couldn't do a thing about it. As time went on people learned to make buildings and could live indoors.

But if you wanted to see what you were doing, there had to be holes in the walls to let in light. You could make the holes small, so the elephants and wolves and bears couldn't get in. But there was no way of making the holes big enough to let light in, yet small enough to keep insects and spiders and wood lice and centipedes out. People still expected to live in the middle of bugs of all kinds. So they squashed them, or encouraged them—spiders will keep your house free of flies—or just put up with them.

"But then cheap, good-quality glass became available. You could make windows that let the light in and kept the bugs out. And that's when people started to think that spiders and cockroaches and ants were 'dirty,' and even 'unnatural.' I've known women who would scream if they found a decent-sized spider in their bathroom. And as for doing *this*—"

She reached down to the tall grass at their feet, and stood up again holding a big grasshopper gently in her cupped hands. "I knew people who wouldn't touch a harmless bug like this, not if you paid them. Don't you think it's peculiar, even the word *dirty* changed its meaning. We're walking on dirt. Dirt is everywhere. It's totally natural. The ground is made of dirt. But when you live in a totally artificial environment, shielded from the outside, you never see real earth. 'Dirty' things become completely *unnatural,* and you avoid them. The good news is, when people wanted less and less to go outside, because it was full of beetles and gnats and worms and earwigs and leeches, they were willing to let the surface become more like the way it used to be before humans took over." She bent down, released the grasshopper, and pointed away to their left. "Not just grasshoppers and bees and flies, either. Go twenty to thirty kilometers that way, you'll find gazelles and wildebeest and cheetahs. Maybe lions, too."

"Are we in the tropics? Or has the climate changed?" One other confident prediction of Drake's own time had been that in another generation all the hoofed wildlife and the big predators would be gone.

"We're in what used to be Africa, about ten degrees north of the equator. It's what you would call Ethiopia. There has been some climate change, too. Think of this as just like Serengeti, even though it isn't." Melissa pointed again, this time upward toward the afternoon sun. "One reason it's not too hot, it's midwinter and we're fifteen hundred meters above sea level. Feel it in your lungs?" And, as Drake drew in a deep breath of thin but warm and pollen-laden air, she added, "Come on. You've been stuck inside for four years, or maybe it's five hundred and four. Let's see what sort of job they did when they tuned up your body."

She had given up the usual gray dress in favor of bright pink shorts and a red T-shirt. Her legs were shapely but well muscled. She began to run toward the nearest grove of trees, maybe a mile and a half away. After a moment Drake set out in pursuit. They were each carrying a backpack, which when Drake had put it on seemed to weigh next to nothing. Within the first quarter of a mile he changed his mind. He could feel it bouncing up and down on his back, the straps cutting into his shoulders. How could a meal weigh nothing when it was on the inside of you, and so much when you were carrying it on the outside?

He began to pant harder and felt in his calves and thighs the first pain of fatigue and oxygen starvation. The altitude made a tremendous difference, far more than he would have expected, and he had not taken regular exercise since he was thawed. His new body was supposed to make it unnecessary. He forced himself to run for another couple of minutes, then he had to stop. He had forgotten what it was like to be physically exhausted. He dropped heavily to the ground, and lay there panting on the dry, grassy soil.

All the time that he was running, Melissa had steadily increased her lead. She went all the way to the trees, circled them, and headed back at the same speed. She came to where he lay and stood by him with her legs wide apart and her hands on her hips.

Drake rolled on to his back and stared up at her. "What did they do with *your* body?"

"Not a thing. This is the original me." She squatted at his side. She wasn't even panting. "Now do you agree that it was a good idea to get you away from work for a while?"

"If it doesn't kill me when my heart gives out."

"It won't. Any problems like that would have been taken care of. Come on." She reached down and helped him rise to his feet. "We have to keep going if we want to get to a monitor lodge before darkness."

That sounded to Drake like an excellent idea. Lions might be twenty kilometers away. But how far were they likely to travel when they were hunting?

Melissa didn't seem worried, although fast and fit as she was she could not outspeed a hungry lion. On the other hand, it occurred to Drake that she didn't have to. All she had to do was run faster than him.

Drake's idea of Earth's future transportation system, if he had had one at all, was vague, busy, and grandiose—the chaotic vehicle mix of the late twentieth century, extrapolated to become faster, busier, and more tangled.

If the quiet open prairie had not set him right during the afternoon, Melissa did so that night. "The transportation system is all there," she said, "and according to the reports it's an excellent one. You can get anywhere in the world in just a few hours. We'll see it for ourselves when we use it tomorrow. But it's not heavily used. A few sightseers like us; and that's about it."

They had settled into a comfortable lodge, empty except for service machines, and they were eating dinner. It was Drake's fourth meal with another human being since he had been resurrected. After three years of work together, Par Leon had shyly asked Drake if he would like to have dinner in person every three or four months. Drake took that for what it was, a sincere gesture of approval and friendship.

"So what happened?" he asked Melissa, as their empty plates vanished into the table. "I know that the population is down by a factor of ten from our time, but there still ought to be lots of traffic—people and goods. Why isn't there?"

She sighed, with the tolerance of a person with a full stomach. Although she was smaller than Drake, she had eaten at least twice as much. But there was no fat on her body. He put it down to her high burn rate and her endless energy.

"You really did tune out for four years, didn't you?" she said. "It must take a positive effort *not* to know what's going on in the world."

"I was planning to learn a lot about transportation systems, on this planet and off it. But not yet."

"There's less to learn than you might imagine. We could have guessed this, too, if we'd bothered to think. Why do people need transportation?"

"To carry goods from where they're made to where they're needed. To take people to work, and to let them meet each other."

"What you're describing is nowadays called a primitive industrial society. You and I lived at the end of that, though I don't think we knew it. Automated manufacturing and telework were just about to take off in our time. We are now in a postindustrial, machine-supported society. You don't need to carry goods when they can be made on the spot from simple raw materials. The manufacturing is all done by machines, smart enough so they don't need people to watch over them. People still work, but no one goes to work anymore. They don't need to. You must know that from your own project. You told me you don't actually *see* Par Leon more than once a month, and you could get by very well without that."

"So why is there a transportation system at all?"

"Because a few people want one and use one. Because it doesn't really cost anything to maintain it—the machines do all that, without a single human being involved. Same as this lodge. When we arrived, our meals were cooked and our beds prepared, and we didn't even have to request it. It's an odd thought, but if all the people were to die, the housekeeper here probably wouldn't notice. It would carry on as usual. I doubt if there's another person—I mean on the surface—within a hundred miles."

Drake went to the window and gazed out into the warm African night. It was bright moonlight, and fifty yards away he could see head-high grass swaying as some large invisible animal moved through it.

No other humans within a hundred miles of here. But there was a deeper question. What was *he* doing here?

He could not give an answer that made sense. Somehow, Melissa Bierly's requests carried the weight of absolute commands. He did not know how to refuse. If she told him to go outside and face hungry lions, he was sure that he would do it.

And there was another question. What was *she* doing here? Her desire to see the world made sense only if she was looking for something—or running from something.

He could not imagine what; but later, when they were lying side by side in the lodge's quiet bedroom, he heard her sighs. Melissa was moaning softly in her sleep. And every few minutes, until he finally fell asleep himself, he heard the sound of grinding teeth.

Morning restored Melissa's cheerfulness and drive. She announced that she had changed her mind. She wanted to head upward, to the top of the peak that loomed to the northeast, before they used the transportation system and flew to South America.

"Birhan?" Drake had called up a large-scale map and asked for an optimal route. Now he called up a topographic map. "Are you sure? It's a brute. According to this it rises above thirteen thousand feet. We won't be able to breathe."

"I'll breathe for both of us." Melissa was bursting with energy. "I'll help you, and we won't go all the way to the top. Just enough to get a view. Come on, let's go."

The housekeeper had anticipated their need for packaged food, just as it had provided breakfast and had a car ready. It knew which maps Drake had demanded, and it had decided that Birhan was not within a day's walk for a human.

The hovercar moved smoothly, about three feet above the surface, and made almost no noise. It handled all kinds of terrain with ease, water as well as land. When they drifted across the rocky near-dry course of a broad river, Drake looked up from the display that was tracing out their path.

"This is the Blue Nile. I wonder what happened to it."

"Diverted, four hundred years ago." As usual, Melissa knew everything. "It was once completely dry. It looks as though the old dams are breaking down. No one needs them anymore."

The ground was rising steadily, and the hovercar was following the upward slope effortlessly. So far as Drake was concerned he would have been happy to ride all the way to the snow-capped peak ahead. Melissa had other ideas.

"This will do." She stopped the car. "We're at eight thousand feet. Let's head for that, and eat when we get there. The car will stay here."

She was pointing, not at the mountain but at the display. It showed a small flattened area where the hillside leveled off about two thousand feet above them. It could be approached easily from one side,

but the contour lines suggested that the other edge ended in a sheer thousand-foot drop.

Melissa jumped lightly down from the car. Drake did the same, less lightly. He flexed his shoulders. Already he was aware that his lungs were working harder.

They started up. Melissa seemed to have an instinct for the easiest route, and rather than competing, Drake stayed two paces behind and followed her lead. He was afraid that it would be worse than the day before, but Melissa held to a slow, steady pace that he could live with. They were both wearing heavier clothing. Melissa had on thick blue pants and a padded jacket that exactly matched the color of her eyes. Drake wondered how the lodge housekeeper had made or found the color—how it even *knew* the color.

Today, at this altitude, warm clothes were necessary. Drake felt the tingling in his ears. The breeze at his back was chilly, but it seemed to help by pushing him along.

Helped for a while, at least. He was still relieved when they breasted the final rise and emerged onto the little plateau. Melissa did not stop, but went walking over to the far side of it.

"There," she said. "That's why we're here. That's Africa."

She was pointing out to the west. Drake came to her side, then at once stepped back, appalled. The view was incredible. He could see what seemed like hundreds of miles across hills and plains. But they were standing at the very edge of a sheer cliff. It was so steep, it could not be natural. Someone, sometime, for some inexplicable reason, had sheered the whole mountain side to a rock face that dropped vertically without ledges or breaks to a boulder-strewn chasm a thousand feet below.

"Be careful, Melissa." He backed farther and sat down. There was a gusty wind blowing on the plateau, and to be anywhere near the edge was terrifying.

She turned and grinned at him. "You don't need to worry about me. Watch."

While he stared in horror she closed her eyes and walked along the very edge, so close that at each blind step only a part of her foot met the rock. When he was convinced that she must fall, she turned and sauntered over to him.

"All right, then. Lunch?"

"Lunch, dinner, anything you like—as long as you stay away from that edge."

"You worry too much, Drake." She sat down casually at his side. "Can't you see I could do this sort of thing all day, and never get hurt?"

He believed her, but to his relief she followed his lead and removed her backpack. He looked across to the other side of the plateau, with its easy descent. With any luck Melissa would feel they had done enough climbing for the day.

They began to eat. Even in midwinter, the sunlight at this latitude was intense. It picked out every detail of Melissa's face: the contented smile, the glow of perfect skin, and the dazzling blue eyes. Drake decided that he had never in his life seen a woman who looked healthier.

He was staring right at her when the change came. She had just crunched a crisp piece of celery. As she swallowed, the corners of her mouth turned down. Her face flushed darker, responding to a sudden rush of blood. The splendid eyes stared fixedly at nothing, then glared all around.

"It has to be," she said. "It has to be."

She stood up. While Drake sat frozen she walked back five steps. He was still trying to scramble to his feet when she ran forward and hurled herself over the sheer edge of the cliff.

"Melissa!" He forgot his own fears and ran to the edge.

She was falling, her arms held wide. She did not change her position, and she did not cry out. Drake stared in horror as her blue-clad figure diminished in size. Already she had dropped hundreds of feet. Her pose was a swan dive, perfectly balanced like a high diver in the first phase of descent. But instead of water, beneath her lay nothing but solid rock and sharp-sided boulders.

When nothing in the world could save her, the whole cliff face erupted suddenly from top to bottom. It threw off a cloud of dust atoms like a shaken carpet. Instead of falling or spreading, the particles converged to form a dense gray plume that coalesced further as it swooped after Melissa's plummeting body. When it was in the right position, it spread to form a gray blanket beneath her.

She must have seen it coming. She began to scream and flail, trying to avoid contact with the gray layer by changing the line of her fall. It was no good. The blanket reached her and folded itself about her. Drake saw her arms, protruding from the swaddling cover and beating at it desperately.

The downward plunge had been arrested. While he watched, the gray cylinder of blanket moved rapidly to the right, away from the main body of the mountain. In less than a minute it had vanished from his sight.

Drake stared down. Melissa was gone, but the rocky landscape at the foot of the cliff seemed to crawl and surge below him like an oily sea. His legs were too weak to support him. He cried out, and dropped to the rough surface of rock and gravel. He scrabbled at it with his fingers, trying to pull himself away from the edge.

He was still sitting, staring blindly into the fierce winter sunlight, when a wingless craft drifted down to his side.

"It's all right, Drake." Par Leon was inside the aircar. His voice was apologetic. A stony-faced woman was at his side. "Everything will be all right. We're going to take you home."

8

Incomplete Superwoman

The woman's name was Rozi Tegger. Par Leon made it clear, more from his body language than his comments, that she was not a close friend. Both he and Tegger were handling Drake with great care, responding to his dazed questions as the aircar flew them home.

To Drake, only two questions really mattered: *Is she alive? Is she all right?*

"Melissa Bierly is certainly alive," Tegger replied. Leon yielded to her the first phase of explanation. "However, she is far from all right."

"She's hurt?"

"Not at all. Neither of you was in real danger, though we didn't want you to know it. You were monitored from the moment that you left the lodge."

"The hovercar?"

"That, and more than that. And far smaller. The automated safety service makes its own observing and protection units, and there were many billions of them in use all around you today. The ensemble that saved Melissa, after she threw herself off the cliff, is fairly typical. Each unit masses only a fraction of a gram. Each has sensors, flight capability, and real-time communication that allows all units to act in concert. Melissa tried to steer herself away from them and fall headfirst onto the rocks; but in reality she didn't have a chance."

"I saw, but I don't understand. Melissa had everything to live for. Why would she try to kill herself?"

Par Leon and Rozi Tegger stared at each other. The tension in the car could not be missed.

"You have to tell him, you know," Leon said. "If you don't, I will. If you weren't prepared to do this, you never should have started."

"I never thought it would turn out this way."

"Nor did I; but it did."

"I know, I know." Rozi Tegger sighed. "Very well, I'll do it." She turned to Drake. "How much did you learn from Melissa Bierly of her background?"

"I know that she was born one year before I entered the cryowombs. I know that she lived for twenty-four more years, then died and entered the cryowombs herself."

"And that is all?"

"All I remember."

"Very well." Rozi Tegger, like Par Leon, could have been any age. She had thick, chestnut-brown hair, and now she ran her fingers through it. "Let me begin at the real beginning, fifteen years before Melissa Bierly was born.

"The structure of DNA had been known for fifty years, and the first mapping of the human genome had just been completed. Molecular biologists were riding high. A few people were already worrying about the ethical problems involved in playing with human genetic structure, but none of the rules that we have now had been put in place. In fact, to our eyes your original time is most perplexing. Those who felt comfortable about gene manipulation to *cure* disease were often the same people who were strongly opposed to mandatory genetic selection to *avoid* disease. *Eugenics* was a socially unacceptable word.

"When technology flourishes and suitable laws are not in place to constrain its uses, there will surely be trouble.

"A group of scientists with strong social and political goals decided to employ the emerging technology to benefit the human race. They were well intentioned, we do not dispute that. They were also permitted to operate with a freedom unthinkable today. They saw ways to modify the human genome so as to create persons stronger, more intelligent, more long-lived, and more resistant to disease. That is what they did."

"Superman," Drake murmured. But he did so in English, and Rozi Tegger frowned at him in confusion.

"Superior men," Drake added, this time in Universal. "Supermen."

Tegger nodded. "And superior women. Do I have to say more? We did not change the body of Melissa Bierly upon resurrection, as yours was changed. We did not need to. You saw her, yet you were exposed to little of her full potential. She could run to the top of Birhan, or mountains far higher than that, without breathing equipment and without feeling fatigue. She could spend a winter night naked amid mountaintop snow and ice, and come down unharmed. She could hang from the cliff where we found you by one finger, hour after hour.

"But those are mere physical improvements, and we judge them trivial. Of far greater interest are the *mental* characteristics of Melissa Bierly and others like her. She has outstanding intellect. In two months she has come to understand more of this time, and what is in it, than most of us. She mastered access to the general data banks as though born to them. She became conversant with a dozen languages, from Economics to Astronautics, and made their cross-connections with ease.

"But these accomplishments are no better than those of many machines; although we can admire them, they are not the reason for Melissa's resurrection. My own field of study is…." She paused, then said three syllables in Universal that meant nothing to Drake. "I'm sorry, I know that the subject did not exist in your time. You can think of it as the study of all modes of influence. How does one individual persuade another? It is certainly not by words alone. By sound, yes, but also by body position and touch and pheromonal transfer and many other agents. This has been true through all of history. It may well predate the use of spoken language. What fascinated me about Melissa were the records of incredible persuasive force reported for her and her kin. I could not explain it, and I wanted to see for myself. Could it be real?"

"It's real." Drake saw in his mind the sparkling sapphire eyes. "It's more than what you say. She didn't *persuade* me. She made me *want* to do whatever she liked. If she had asked me to jump off the cliff with her, I think I would have done it. But you haven't explained what happened. *Why* did she jump?"

"She did not jump. She *dived*. The distinction is important." Rozi Tegger looked at Par Leon, who nodded grimly.

"Go on. I know this is especially painful for you, but Merlin has earned our explanation."

"Very well." Tegger turned unhappily to Drake. "You spent days with Melissa. Did you ever see changes of mood in her?"

"You couldn't miss it. Most of the time she was full of bounce and cheerfulness. But now and again she seemed angry or worried or desperate. It could switch in a second."

"But you never questioned her as to the way in which she died, before she entered the cryowombs?"

"We didn't talk about that."

"Or of her siblings and kinfolk?"

"It never came up."

"That is not surprising. There were sixteen children in that 'superior' experimental group, including Melissa herself. So far as I can tell, each of them enjoyed an equal degree of physical and mental advantage. However, it is impossible to prove this. No other was placed with Second Chance. And for good reason. All of them, except Melissa, died in such a way that the brain was destroyed. All of them committed suicide. So did Melissa, but she did it by slashing her throat. She thought that no one would find her body for hours, by which time her brain would be past recovery. But she was wrong. She was discovered by accident, very quickly, and prepared for the cryowomb by the scientists who had made her. They knew that they had created an incomplete superior form, one who for unknown reasons was driven to self-destruction. They left posterity to decide where they had gone wrong."

Rozi Tegger sighed. The aircar had entered a deep shaft and was descending. Their journey was almost over.

"And I," she went on, "I in my hubris believed that I could succeed where my ancestors had failed. I would resurrect the one remaining 'superwoman,' to borrow your word. I would make changes, very minor ones, not to her body but to her mind. And then my experiment could begin. Melissa would be allowed to go her way, and by observing her I would learn the nature of her unnatural power to persuade others.

"But in truth I learned only one thing: that the changes I made to Melissa were useless; that the death wish is as strong in her as ever."

"She didn't know about the safety service," Par Leon added, "any more than you did, Merlin. And she didn't just want to *die*."

"She wanted total self-destruction," Rozi Tegger aaid. "You saw how she dived. She wanted to do what she had failed to do five centuries ago. She wanted her brain so completely pulped that there could be no thought of repair and resurrection."

Drake saw again in his mind that dwindling blue-clad doll figure, dropping forever down the stark cliff face. Melissa knew how to control her body attitude perfectly. She would have held the swan dive to the end. If the gray cloud of tiny rescue machines had not interfered, her head would have smashed and splattered against solid rock.

He felt sick: at the thought of what might have happened to Melissa, and also at the realization of the effortless power she had held over him. She had made him ignore his own vows in order to do her bidding.

"But Melissa is still alive. What will happen to her now?" He was almost afraid to hear the answer. If she were released, and came back to him....

"That decision is not mine to make," Tegger said heavily. The car had come to a halt, and she was climbing down from it with the stiff-limbed action of an old, old woman. "It was decreed in advance, before permission could be given for my experiment. If I failed, Melissa Bierly would once more enter Second Chance. That is happening even as we speak. She will remain in the cryowombs until someone—some person much cleverer than I—can free her of that random and irresistible urge for self-immolation."

"Will you be all right?" Par Leon spoke anxiously, and he was addressing not Drake but Rozi Tegger. "Shouldn't you stay a while with us before you go home?"

"I can safely leave." Rozi Tegger gave Leon a grim smile. "I thank you for your consideration, but despite my depressed mood I do not propose to do away with myself. For I am, as I have proved to you so very clearly, far from being a super woman."

Par Leon tried to pretend that the whole episode was over. Drake had to visit Leon and corner him, in person, the next day before they started work.

"There is something that was never explained to me," he said. "I did not ask you when Rozi Tegger was with us, but I think you owe me an answer now."

Par Leon was not good at dissembling. He craned his neck to one side and would not look at Drake. "Indeed?"

"Indeed. I can see very well why Rozi Tegger resurrected Melissa, because it related to her own field of study. But you never met Melissa, and you were never exposed to her power of persuasion. She could add nothing to the work that you and I have been doing, and she could detract from it by slowing our progress. So why did you allow me to go off with her to the surface? Why didn't you say no?"

Leon did not answer at once, and when he did his question astonished Drake. "Did you, uh," he said, "uh, did you…that is…." He paused. "Forgive me for asking, but did you and Melissa Bierly enter into a sexual relationship?"

It was Drake's turn to hesitate. "Yes," he said at last. "Yes, we did. When we were staying at the lodge."

It was a lie, and a possibly unsafe one. Drake knew that he and Melissa had been monitored from the time that they left the lodge. Wasn't it likely that the same automatic safety service had observed everything inside the lodge? And although sex would presumably not have triggered the rescue process, the records of the night at the lodge might be on file somewhere in the data banks.

But Par Leon was nodding and smiling. "I thought so. And that is why I agreed to your going, although I knew that we would sacrifice a little work time.

"I had been worried about you," he went on, before Drake could express his perplexity. "I like to work hard, but you seemed to work incessantly. You did not—forgive me for my intrusiveness, but I thought it important, so I checked—you did not ever form a relationship with any man or woman, although your body modifications at resurrection permit and actually benefit from sexual activity. You had remained celibate for four years. And there was the matter of the woman in the cryowombs, your former wife. Several times, you alluded to her."

Had he? Drake did not recall doing so, but there was no reason for Leon to lie.

"I wondered," Leon continued. "Your obsession with the woman Anastasia was supposedly cured during resurrection. But was it possible that it had been done incorrectly? I wondered this, long before we learned yesterday of another case where changes made at resurrection were unsuccessful. So I was delighted when you called me, to request time to travel with Melissa Bierly. I knew little about her at the time, except the important thing: she was not Anastasia. I agreed, gladly. And as you see, although Rozi Tegger is disappointed by the outcome, I am not. You proved that you have indeed conquered your old obsession. There is no danger of a new obsession, with Melissa Bierly. My fears have been put to rest, and our work can go forward together with new confidence."

He beamed at Drake, who slowly nodded. "I have only one more question. Why did Melissa choose me, of all the Resurrects?"

"I can only pass along to you the conjecture of Rozi Tegger. You alone possess an independence of mind and spirit. The other Resurrects cluster together and follow each other. You pursue your own agenda, steadfastly. Melissa Bierly liked that. And also, she conceivably thought of it as a challenge to her own powers."

It had not been, not at all. Drake realized that. He was dismayed by his own lack of resolve. From now on, he would keep his goal clearly in focus.

And one more thing, above all others: he must never again, under any circumstances, mention Ana's name to Par Leon.

Par Leon's great project continued, faster than expected. He and Drake worked together as a perfect team. By the middle of the sixth year they were approaching completion. They had also become close friends, or as close as Drake dared to permit; close enough, however, to sense that Par Leon, a good man by any moral compass that Drake would ever be able to comprehend, was beginning to worry about something else.

He said little to Drake, beyond hinting at other possible collaborations. Drake read the deeper concern. What would the future hold when the project ended? It had apparently not occurred to Par Leon six years ago, but a resurrection was not unlike a birth. And now, like a parent, Par Leon felt responsibility for the future of his "offspring."

Drake was soon able to reassure him, and in an unexpected way. While they were still putting the finishing touches to their mammoth study of the "ancient" music of the twentieth and early twenty-first centuries, he started to compose again. He had learned during the project that musical knowledge of the time before his birth had some big gaps in it, and facility in different musical idioms had always come easily to him. He could steal tricks from the giants of the past, dress them in a modern style, and pass it off as innovation.

In less than a year he had a burgeoning reputation, which he knew was undeserved, a group of imitators, largely untalented, and—most important—a growing financial credit.

At last he could delicately explore a long-postponed question. He chose his moment carefully, when Par Leon was euphoric over a particular section on thematic influences that Drake had just completed.

"A couple of days more, and I will be finished." Drake did his best to sound casual. "How about you?"

He knew the answer. They had agreed that Leon would be responsible for the final overall review, to ensure uniformity of style.

"Four weeks, at least, from the time that I have all the pieces." Leon sounded apologetic. "I can't do the final assembly in any less time."

"You shouldn't rush. The last review is the most critical one." Drake stretched and yawned. "I could stay around and help you, you know. On the other hand, if you don't need me while you're working through the material, I thought maybe I would take a vacation."

"Do it. You've earned some time off—more than earned it." Leon sounded relieved. The last thing a successful project needed was two people trying to direct the final pen.

"I was thinking of having a look at some of the rest of the solar system. You know, in my time we'd seen pictures of all the planets, but only a handful of people had been as far as the Moon."

"Which is considerably farther than I have been—or choose to go!" Leon's furry eyebrows went up. "Why would you *want* to travel so far? You are not an astronomer, or a terraform designer, or an astronaut. There's absolutely nothing out in space for a musician."

"I think it might help me in composition. New visual experiences always stimulate my musical imagination."

"You mean, we might get new music from you? Then by all means, go, and enjoy yourself. Visit Venus, tour Titan, meet Mars. Produce something to match this." Par Leon began to rap on the desk in front of him the rhythm of the 'Mars, the Bringer of War' section of Gustav Hoist's 'The Planets.' With their own work so close to its end, he was in high good humor.

"I'd like to go." Drake had to be careful what he said next. "I was just wondering if I'd be able to afford it."

The smile on Leon's face was replaced by a puzzled frown. "*Afford* it?"

"The cost of the fares. Mars is a long way away."

Par Leon frowned, as though he did not understand the relevance of the remark. "The cost? Who are you proposing to take with you?"

"No one. Just me."

"Then cost does not enter into it. The ship will fly itself."

"But who pays for the ship?"

"The question is meaningless. There are ships available, as many as you want. But they are manufactured automatically. Machines make them, and they also fly them. Machine use is free. There is no *human* cost to making and flying a ship. Cost becomes relevant only when you demand that human time be devoted to something. Like now." Par Leon laughed, his good humor restored. "I could charge you for this advice, you know. But I won't. Go on, Drake, take your holiday. You've certainly earned it."

"I will. In a few more days."

"But if you are crazy enough to go to space, don't ask me to go with you!"

Drake laughed, too. He did not mention the subject again to Par Leon, but in the next week he quietly took accelerated courses in astronautics, astronomy, and space systems, subjects that previously had never interested him at all. He was astonished by what he found. Par Leon had understated the situation. Ships were available in abundance, with drives that could take them close to light speed. It made Drake reevaluate all his own plans. He had been thinking that he would have to return to a frozen state. Now there might be other options.

He did not even try to understand the technique of enertia shedding that bypassed what should have been a killing 4000g acceleration as the ship moved to and from the light-speed region. That understanding required a working knowledge of a Science language far beyond his capabilities. Instead, he thought of the changes in the world. If this capability had been around at the end of the twentieth century, it would have been used by millions. Now, few people seemed to care. Although the stars were within easy reach, humanity was not stretching out to enfold them. Civilization seemed stable, static, content to remain within the comfortable limits of the solar system. Was that progress, or was it regress?

After nine days Drake was ready. He had done all that he could. The night before he was scheduled to depart he invited Par Leon out for a ceremonial dinner. By this time it was assumed that they would eat and drink comfortably in each other's presence. Leon had hinted once or twice at a more intimate relationship, but he had not been offended when Drake declined.

They went to Leon's favorite eating place, ate his favorite foods, and drank his favorite wines. It was an unexpected bonus that by coincidence one of Drake's own new compositions was playing in the background.

"There." Par Leon jerked his head toward an invisible speaker. "That is real and deserved fame. Music good enough to eat to."

"But not to listen to." Drake shrugged off the compliment. "Table music is like table wine, usually nothing special. Telemann could compose it as fast as he could write it down."

"True. But do not undervalue yourself, my friend. Mozart's *divertimenti* are often both artful and memorable."

The conversation was on satisfying and familiar ground. Drake felt the glow that comes with good, compatible company. He was going to miss that.

The urge to tell the full truth became very great. Surely, if he confided in Par Leon his commitment and the depth of his feelings, the other man would become a willing accomplice.

"Leon."

"Yes?"

"Oh, nothing. I'm just thinking about my trip."

He stifled the idea before it could develop further. His new plans were shaping up, and they were nothing as simple as controlled freezing and a return to the cryowombs. They might lead to danger and destruction. He would not want Par Leon to bear any guilt by association.

He also would not—could not, dare not—do anything at all that might endanger his chances of success.

9

Escape to Nowhere

Drake had decided to proceed with great caution. For at least the first part of his trip, he must look and sound like a genuine tourist. His resurrection helped. He could tell anyone he met that he had been recently thawed (he would not define *recently*). He would say he was still trying to get the hang of his new era. He would gape at anything he saw, like the original hick. He would be free to ask a million innocent questions.

Drake had delved into solar system geometry long before he left Earth. At first he had been worried. By an accident of timing, Pluto was almost exactly at aphelion, as far away from the Sun as it could get. But then he looked at the performance of the ships. They could accelerate so hard, and achieve huge speeds so quickly, that nowhere in the system was more than a few days away. Travel times became irrelevant.

Mars, first, then, just as he had told Par Leon upon his departure. Drake could imagine his friend and mentor checking the first phase of his travel, but he would lose interest once he was sure that Drake had arrived safely.

Mars was described in the Earthside databases as undergoing a "modest" terraforming effort; nothing, the sources said, compared with the major effort going on at Venus. The Mars project was designed only to increase the available surface water, and it did not interfere with life in the Martian interior.

Drake's ship took him to Mars in a day and a half. He landed; and found hell.

The planet was under ceaseless bombardment. Every twenty minutes a cometary fragment, a couple of hundred meters across, hit the surface. It had been directed in from the Kuiper Belt, nine billion kilometers from the Sun, and it struck Mars tangentially, precisely at dawn on the day-night terminator. Each impact came within twenty degrees of the equator. The Mars atmosphere was too thin to carry sound, but land waves shook the surface around the point of arrival.

Drake donned a suit and stepped out of the ship. He was well away from the impact zone. Even so, he felt the compacted rubble of the regolith tremble and shake beneath his boots.

He looked up. The sky was a dirty gray, streaked and filmed with white haze. Most of the added dust and water vapor in the air came not from comet fragments, but from the ejects of vaporized surface rocks and permafrost, blown high into the Martian stratosphere. That permafrost was the main source of atmospheric water. It returned to the ground as a thin drizzle of ice particles. For the first time in a billion years, snow was falling on Mars.

As Drake watched, another ball of fire flamed across the dull southern sky. It moved from west to east, and vanished. One minute later a flash of crimson light lit the southeastern horizon. It was hard to believe that a rough-edged chunk of water ice, dirtied with smears of ammonia ice, silicate rock, and metallic ore, and no more than two hundred meters in diameter, could produce such violence. But a few million tons of mass, moving at forty kilometers a second, carries formidable amounts of kinetic energy. The energy release for each impact was around a thousand megatons. Each arrival had the force of a big volcanic explosion back on Earth. The thin atmosphere of Mars did little to dissipate it.

Drake watched the tumult for a couple of hours. Finally he decided that the open face of the planet, battered by hailstones bigger than the Great Pyramid, was more likely to stimulate nightmares than musical creation.

He went inside the ship and considered his next move. He had told Par Leon that he would visit the Mars deep caverns. Natural formations, kilometers across, they had been interlocked and fortified over the centuries by tunneling and construction moles. Now they stood second only to Earth as a center for human civilization.

Caution said he should visit the caves, as originally planned. After that, his original itinerary called for visits to Europa and Ganymede, the satellites of Jupiter, and to Neptune's big moon, Triton. But a new knowledge was burning inside him. The trip to Mars had changed his perspective on interplanetary travel. He knew that he was, if he chose, only a few days away from Ana. From Mars to Pluto, even without invoking emergency status and maximum accelerations, was just a thirty-six-hour run.

The temptation was too much. He ordered a message sent to Par Leon, back on Earth, announcing his safe arrival on Mars. Then he gave his command.

The ship rose from the surface and arrowed out, directly away from the Sun's warmth. It would bypass Jupiter and Saturn, bypass Uranus and Neptune. It would not stop until it reached Pluto, out at the frigid limit of the solar system; out where Sol was no more than a bright spark in the sky, and the cryocorpses slept their ancient, dreamless sleep beneath the silent stars.

A little knowledge could be almost too much. In six years of work on Earth, Drake had become used to the idea of robotic servants. They were of varying levels of intelligence, depending on their function, but they all had one thing in common: they accepted every command without question, provided that it was not dangerous and did not exceed their available resources of materials or knowledge.

He assumed that it would be equally true on Pluto, and it began that way. His ship landed without incident on the frozen surface. Machines attended his arrival. There were no humans, and he had expected none. The nearest people resided at the research station on Charon, seventeen thousand kilometers away. Pluto and Charon were more like a pair of little moons than a planet with a satellite—Pluto was smaller than Earth's moon, while Charon was half the size of its primary. The pair were tidally locked, always showing the same face to each other. Drake, standing on the surface of Pluto and looking up, saw Charon hanging pendant in the sky above him, like a giant dull ruby. The research station was not visible. From this distance, there was no evidence to be seen on Charon of any human activities.

Even though Charon was so close, the machines on Pluto were designed to operate without advice or assistance from there or anywhere else. Drake's command to be taken to the cryowombs was obeyed without question.

The surface of Pluto was one of the quietest places in the solar system. However, there would be occasional impacts from meteorites and cometary debris. The wombs, for additional safety, had been placed deep within the interior to protect against disturbance.

It had not occurred to Drake that he himself constituted such a disturbance, until he had been led at least a kilometer along a descending ramp. He and his attendant machine entered a large open chamber, where his suit was placed within another and larger one. The space between the suits was filled with liquid helium.

"Is this necessary?" He could imagine the second suit interfering with his mobility.

"It is necessary. There must be no energy release within the vaults to raise the ambient temperature. I myself cannot proceed beyond this point. I am too warm." The machine raised a spidery articulated arm and pointed at a hovering blue pyramid, half a meter on a side. "This is now your guide."

Ever since they left the surface it had become steadily darker. All light sources now disappeared as Drake followed the drifting blue pyramid out of the chamber and into the next level of the Pluto vault.

According to the first machine, the cryotanks were stored in regular rows within the main cryowomb. Drake strained his eyes into the darkness ahead. He could see nothing but the faint blue light in front of

him. He was at the mercy of his robot guide, who must know the deep vault's geometry and contents through programmed memory.

Encased within his double suit, Drake followed the blue glimmer, on and on. Finally it halted. Drake moved closer, and by its feeble illumination he saw the outline of a cryotank. It was like a great coffin, two meters long and a meter wide and deep. Although the cryowomb was kept at a controlled temperature, for double security each tank also contained its own temperature control and source of refrigeration.

"This is the one?" He crouched low, seeking the identification.

He was not sure that the blue pyramid could hear him, understand him, or talk to him, until he heard the sibilant whisper in his helmet. "It is the one."

"I cannot see any identification. Are you sure it is the cryocorpse of Anastasia Werlich?"

"I am sure."

"Then lift it carefully, and bring it with you. Lead us back to the surface and to my ship."

He could see no way that the blue pyramid could exert force, but after a moment of hesitation the cryotank lifted in the low gravity. Two seconds more, and the blue gleam was moving again through the vault. It led the way steadily upward, to the first-level chamber where Drake's outer suit was removed. Twenty minutes more, and he was supervising the careful placement of Ana's cryotank in the aft storage compartment of his ship.

The machine attendants had gone and he was ready to tell the ship to lift from the surface of Pluto, when the communication panel lit with a busy constellation of red and yellow lights.

"The removal of a cryotank from the Pluto cryowomb, and its placement aboard this ship, is unauthorized," said a quiet voice. *"The cryotank must be returned at once."*

Drake cursed his own stupidity. The actions of the machines must be reported automatically to some central data bank. It was only his good luck that screening for anomalies apparently took a few minutes to perform.

Rather than replying, he locked the outside ports and gave the order for instant departure from the surface.

"*The removal of any cryotank from the Pluto vaults is forbidden, without proper authorization,*" repeated the voice. "*You do not have such authorization. Do not attempt to leave Pluto. It will not be permitted.*"

Drake ignored the warning. He dropped into the pilot's seat. Why hadn't the ship taken off? When he left Earth and Mars, his commands had been executed immediately.

He could guess the answer: the ship's automatic piloting system was being overridden from outside. If he wanted to leave, he would have to assume manual control. He knew how to fly the ship in theory, from his crash courses in astronautics and space systems. In practice, he had never tried anything like it.

He hit the switches to turn off the ship's computer control, cursing the messages that came back to him:

"*The requested action will remove the vessel from automated path guidance. Do you wish to proceed?*"

"Yes."

"*The requested action will inhibit the use of all trajectory planning functions. Do you wish to proceed?*"

"Yes."

"*The requested action will also disconnect this vessel from the solar system protective navigation system. Do you wish to proceed?*"

"Yes, yes, yes!"

He was hitting the manual lift sequence, over and over, convinced that outside the ship more direct methods were being put in place to prevent takeoff.

Finally—at last—he saw that the ship was rising. Pluto's surface of rock and ice receded below them.

He set a simple outward course, directly away from the Sun. He did not care where he went, provided it was *away.*

It should have been easy. The Pluto approach corridor had been completely deserted on his arrival. Now it was buzzing with ships. His control board showed scores of them in the space ahead. Where had they all come from? Was it like the automated service that had caught Melissa, a whole invisible safety net of ships that sprang into action exactly when it was needed?

No time to worry about what or why. The ships ahead were converging, moving to intersect the course that he had set for the solar system perimeter. Somehow they knew his flight plan. It must

be transmitted automatically, even when he was flying manual.

"*DO NOT ATTEMPT TO PROCEED.* "The command was louder and more peremptory. "*RETURN AT ONCE TO PLUTO.*"

Drake set the ship to maximum acceleration and kept going, driving toward the heart of the converging cluster of ships.

"*TURN OFF YOUR DRIVE. YOU ARE MOVING IN EXCESS OF FORTY KILOMETERS PER SECOND, AND ACCELERATING. IMPACT AT SUCH SPEED CAN HAVE FATAL CONSEQUENCES.*"

It was a great understatement. Impact with another ship at forty kilometers a second would leave random bits of melted metal and vaporized plastic.

"*YOU ARE ON A COLLISION COURSE.*"

A grating siren sounded in Drake's ear. The ship's own detection system was blaring its warning. Collision and destruction were no more than a split second away.

And then, at the last moment, the other ships sheered off. The center of the cluster became open. Drake flew on through.

He wondered what had saved him. Did the interceptors have their own prohibition against causing harm to a human? Or against permitting their own destruction?

He angled wide of another group of ships that had appeared far ahead. They moved toward him, but he was racing along too fast. He was soon past them. Still at maximum acceleration, he fled for the edge of the solar system.

As soon as the sky was clear ahead, he set a course for Canopus.

At last he was able to breathe. If he might have been judged a murderer in an earlier generation for what he and Tom Lambert had done to Ana, he was certainly considered a thief or worse in this one.

Who cared? He and Ana were together, that was all that mattered. Although pursuit was still possible, he could see no signs of it. And he would be hard to catch. The ship was still accelerating monstrously. Soon it would crowd light speed, moving just 125 meters per second slower than a traveling wave front.

Even that was not the limit. If need be, he could reach within a meter a second of light speed.

But it should not be necessary. He examined the control board. Unless he saw signs of pursuit, their planned top speed would be just right. Relativistic time dilatation was going to be a powerful factor. Years would pass on Earth for every day of shipboard time. The trip out to Canopus and back would be a few months for him, but almost three hundred years back on Earth.

And for Ana?

She was still trapped outside of time, in her personal fermata, a temporal hiatus without end where duration and interval did not exist.

He felt a great urge to gaze upon her face within the sealed cryotank. Instead he moved forward to peer ahead to the distant star that he had chosen as their destination. Even from a hundred light-years away, by some miracle of the ship's imaging system Canopus was already revealed as a tiny bright disk.

He went to where the ship's computer was housed. Now that they were far beyond pursuit, he had returned to automatic control. He was curious to see what the computer looked like, the multipurpose processor that with equal ease planned trajectories, cooked meals, and maintained all the onboard life-support systems.

He lifted the plastic access panel to the main processor, and peered into a small dark cavity. He saw a lattice of red beads, each one no bigger than a pinhead. Tiny sparkles of violet light passed among them. A soft voice from the ship's address system said in mild rebuke, *Exposure to external light sources is discouraged, since it causes the computer to operate with reduced speed and efficiency.*

Drake went back to the controls and turned his attention to the general functions of the ship. It could support him and his life-system needs, apparently indefinitely. Its speed and maneuverability never ceased to amaze him. And yet it was in many ways less surprising than the civilization that had made it. A civilization that could produce such a miracle of performance and potential—and then allow it to go unused; that was the most incomprehensible mystery of all.

Was it the temporal dislocation produced by time dilatation that was psychologically unacceptable to humans? Drake was depending on it. But did others hate to leave, and upon their return find their friends in the cryowombs, or perhaps dead? But as lifespans increased, that would be less and less a factor. If that were the main reason why the ships were not more widely used, the future should see more travel to the stars.

The ship was approaching its planned maximum speed. Drake noticed that the ship's external mass indicator showed more than 140,000 tons, up from a rest mass of 130 tons. To an outside observer, Drake himself would seem to mass eighty-eight tons, and be foreshortened to a length of less than two millimeters. The shields hid the view ahead of the ship, but he knew that the picture he was seeing on his screen had been subjected to extreme image motion compensation. An unshielded view would reveal the universal three-degree background radiation, Doppler-shifted up to visible wavelengths. Far behind, hard X-ray sources were faded to pale red stars.

The ship was nowhere close to its performance limits. If necessary, he and Ana could fly on forever, to the end of the universe. Except that he was confident that it would not be necessary. He closed his eyes and heard a broad, calm melody, the music of the stars themselves, stirring within his brain. He lay back and allowed music to fill his mind.

For the first time in five centuries, Drake was at peace.

10

"Yet Each Man Kills The Thing He Loves."

In the silence between the stars there were no distractions. Drake started to compose again, convinced that it would be his best work ever. It would distill all his emotions, for all the days since that ominous first morning when he had seen a red car in the drive where no car should have been; on through the darkest days, when nothing seemed possible; on all the way to the glad confident morning of the present.

The ship's flight was fully controlled by its tiny but vastly capable computer. In her cabin aft, Ana lay safe in the cryotank. Drake had all the time that he needed. As the days went by, he allowed the new composition to mature steadily within him. If ever he felt like a break, he would go to Ana's room, sit down by the cryotank, and reveal to her his thoughts and dreams.

He assured her that a few months of shipboard time would be enough. Almost three hundred years would speed away on Earth, before their return, and in those centuries Earth's physicians would surely have found a safe and certain cure. If they had not, he would simply head out again, and repeat the entire cycle.

And what if, after many tries, Earth finally fails us?

He imagined Ana's question in his mind, and he had an answer. They would go elsewhere, on beyond the stars in search of other solutions. The ship was completely self-sustaining. It had ample power and supplies for many subjective lifetimes of travel.

But Drake hoped that one trip would be enough. He told Ana that it was one of his smaller ambitions, on his return, to locate the cryocorpse of his friend Par Leon and return the favor. She would like Par Leon.

He was strangely, sublimely happy, as the ship approached Canopus. His original plan had been for a gravitational swing-by, a maneuver that would take the ship through a tight hyperbolic trajectory close to Canopus and then hurtle away again the way they had come.

But perhaps he had been enjoying himself too much to be in a hurry, or maybe he felt a simple curiosity to see what worlds might circle another sun. For whatever reason, he chose to decelerate during the last couple of weeks and put the ship into a bound orbit about four hundred million kilometers from Canopus.

He turned the ship's imaging devices to scan the stellar system. There were planets, as he had hoped, four gas-giants each the size of Jupiter. Closer in he located a round dozen of smaller worlds. But he had ignored or forgotten the infernal power of Canopus itself. It was a fearsome sight, more than a thousand times as luminous as the Sun and spouting green flares of gas millions of kilometers long. The inner planets were mere blackened cinders, airless and arid, charred by the furnace heat of the star. The outer gas-giants were all atmosphere, except for a small compressed solid core where the pressure was millions of Earth atmospheres. No life in any form that he would recognize could exist there.

But he stayed and looked. In two days of fascinated observation, his eyes turned again and again to the fusion fire of Canopus. He wondered. Had some other human been here, when ships like the one that he was flying were new? Had any *intelligence* been here before, human or nonhuman? Or were his the first sentient eyes to dwell on those dark twisted striations—not sun-spots, but sun *scars*—that gouged the boiling surface of the star?

If others had been here, and they were anything like him, he pitied them. Canopus set up in his mind a resonance of terror beyond reason and beyond explanation.

At last Drake could stand it no longer. Like a lost soul flying from hell's gate he turned and ran. He needed the infinite silence of space, and beyond that the comforting shelter of the solar system. If another trip out were necessary with Ana, it would be to a smaller and less turbulent star.

As the ship began to accelerate he turned the imaging equipment for one last look at Canopus, knowing even as he did it that he was making a mistake. The lost souls were there. Unable to flee like him, they burned in dark torment within the stellar furnace. Smoky demons danced about them, in tongues of flame that gaped and gibbered in triumph. Drake shuddered, cringed, and looked away.

As the star receded to a blazing point of light, he tried to settle back into his shipboard routine. But all harmony, mental and musical, had been banished. What he saw, over and over, was that vision of the Pit. He was circling endlessly, in tight orbit around Canopus. Flaming gas prominences, bright jets of green and white and blue danced a witch's sabbat in his mind. He could not eat, drink, or sleep. The urge to see Ana, to seek peace in her face, grew within him.

Finally Drake went aft and sat by the cryotank. It was guaranteed to soothe all worries.

But not today. His mind churned.

"What's wrong with me, Ana? Am I going crazy?"

The usual imagined reply did not come. He stared at the cryotank. There she was, only a few feet away. If only he could see her, just for a second….

The outside of the cryotank was at room temperature. Inside, the cryocorpse was insulated by two more protective layers. Both of them were transparent. He could open the tank, take one look, and close it before there was a noticeable temperature change.

Slowly, he released the seals and lifted the tight outer cover.

She lay quiet in the tank, pale and peaceful as a Snow Goddess. He took one look at her pearly eyes and skin of milky crystal, afraid to open the cover more than a crack. An icy vapor, colder than innermost hell, breathed from within. While he watched, dew formed and froze on the inner layer. Ana's body faded and blurred, like an image placed behind frosted glass.

Rapidly, he closed and sealed the outer lid. That one moment had been enough. He was able to control himself again and think of other things.

He told himself, for the hundredth time, how fortunate he was. He had never dreamed of light-speed ships and time dilatation, when he had made his plans so long ago. At best he had envisioned a chancy succession of freezings and thawings, farther and farther off in time, until at last Ana could safely be revived and cured. He had imagined and dreaded the uncertainty of multiple awakenings, not sure where he was, not sure where Ana might be, not even sure if she still lay within a cryowomb.

Instead of such a dangerous quest, Ana was here with him. He could safeguard her himself and protect her from all risks.

The rest of the journey home was, if anything, more tranquil than the voyage out. During the final phases he scanned all the ship's communication channels electromagnetic and neutrino, wondering what might await him back in the solar system. He found nothing but silence. The centuries must have changed technology again; he had been away long enough for some totally new communications system to have taken over. Three centuries were also—a frightening prospect—time enough for humanity itself to have changed; even, perhaps, for humans to have destroyed themselves.

He would proceed with great caution, until he knew the nature of the system to which he and Ana were returning. While still far from home he decelerated from their near light-speed race. Moving at a steadily diminishing velocity the ship coasted in toward Sol; past the barren and arid Dry Tortugas, the outermost limits of the Sun's gravitational domain; past the outer borders of the Oort Cloud; into and through the Kuiper Belt. There was no sign of human presence. The scouts who had been busy on the Outer System survey when Drake left were all gone.

By the time that they came to the frozen wastes of Pluto, the ship was drifting inward at only a few hundred kilometers a second. Drake was becoming worried. The imaging system, even at highest resolution, showed no evidence of activity on either Pluto or Charon. The research station had vanished.

Did Melissa Bierly lie in the Pluto cryowombs now? Or had a treatment been found, one that could relieve the torment of a flawed masterpiece of genetic science? Drake realized that he was afraid of Melissa's power over him. Rather than approaching the planetary doublet for a landing, as he had intended, he stepped up the ship's speed and headed for the inner planets. He had started from Earth; he would return there, and make his case to whomever or whatever he found.

The mode of his approach to the inner system was taken out of his hands as the ship passed the Asteroid Belt. As they floated high above the ecliptic, a navigation and guidance beam locked on to them, taking over the ship's internal controls. Drake attempted a manual override. It had succeeded once, but now his command was ignored. Powerless to affect his path, he watched the ship steered steadily in to a landing on the surface of the Moon.

The spaceport was new. Drake was dropping toward a flat plain of gleaming yellow, dotted with massive silver columns set in a regular triangular array. Ships, if they were ships, formed dark, windowless tetrahedra at the center of each triangle. Nothing remotely like Drake's ship was visible. Space flight, and perhaps everything else, had changed in three centuries.

A small wheeled guide met Drake at the ship's lock. Its body comprised a one-foot sphere, with a thin upright cylinder above it, and a whisk-broom of flexible metal fibers above that. The broom head dipped toward Drake in greeting. The machine rolled toward a head-high oval aperture at the base of a silver column. Drake followed, ducking his head, and passed through the opening. There was no sign of an airlock, but his suit monitor suddenly showed breathable air and a comfortable outside temperature. He removed the suit as his wheeled guide instructed and followed it along a short corridor to another interior chamber.

One man was waiting there, a dignified figure with the distant eyes of a prophet. Drake had expected more: a reception committee, perhaps, or maybe even a show of force. The man merely nodded and said quietly in Universal, "Welcome again to Earthspace, Drake Merlin."

Drake had been wrong. He had thought himself prepared for anything. What he had never expected was to be recognized, and *named*.

Even with that thought, he realized that he had no reason to be surprised. The ship would have revealed its identity back in the Asteroid Belt, during its first handshake with the navigation and guidance beam of the inner system. The data banks would have shown the ship's history. Presumably they would also have recorded its sudden disappearance from the solar system.

Drake wondered what else the files might say about the ship's run from Pluto. No matter what they said, he would gain nothing by lying about his actions.

"Since you know my name," he said, while the other man regarded him calmly and without expression, "then perhaps you also know my history. If you do, you will realize that I have returned to seek your help."

Drake found it hard to accept that he had been greeted in a familiar language. Par Leon had been able to speak to him on his resurrection, but only because of long preparation for Drake's arrival, and extensive studies of the right historical period.

Had language become static, totally fixed over the centuries because it had become embedded within the universal data banks? Or was the robed figure in front of him simply giving a formal greeting, a single sentence that he had learned of Universal?

But the man was nodding and speaking again. "My name is Trismon Sorel. I know something of your history as it has come down to us from long ago, although a serious…event, almost a century ago,

led to our records being seriously incomplete and inconsistent. In your case, there are two versions of events. One states that three centuries ago you lost control of your ship, and were carried off unwillingly to the far depths of space. Another version suggests that your removal of a cryocorpse from the Pluto cryowombs and the immediately subsequent departure of your ship were linked events. It proposes that your disappearance at close to light speed, however curious and bewildering, was intentional. I await your elucidation. However, we should first proceed to another environment, where we will find conversation easier."

There were small pauses in his speech, slight hesitations in places where it was not natural to break the pattern of words. As Drake was led out of the room and down a spiral flight of metallic stairs, he decided that Universal must be a learned language for Trismon Sorel, just as Old Anglic had been for Par Leon. But to learn Universal so quickly and so well, in the day since the return of Drake's ship to the inner system, was beyond the powers of the learning inducers. It suggested that Trismon Sorel, in spite of his normal appearance, represented some huge advance in human mental powers.

They had entered a room that could have existed in Drake's own time. Only the light lunar gravity, one-sixth of Earth's, told Drake that he was far from home. Sorel gestured to two comfortable-looking chairs and settled into one of them. As the little wheeled servant moved forward with refreshments, he gazed at Drake with steady, knowing eyes.

"Speak, Drake Merlin. Tell your story."

Drake nodded and sat down opposite Trismon Sorel. He felt a rising tension. In a few minutes he would know if the long quest was finally over, and his life could begin again.

"My departure from the solar system was indeed intentional." It had become difficult to speak, and he had to swallow and pause before he could continue. "It was intentional, and done for a good reason. But I cannot begin there. I must begin long ago, more than eight hundred years ago. At that time, the cryocorpse who now lies safe within the ship that brought me here was my wife. After many happy years together, we learned that she was suffering from an incurable disease…."

As Drake told his story he was forced to relive scenes that he had suppressed for centuries. If Ana was to be helped, Trismon Sorel had to know everything: all Ana's symptoms, the progress of her illness, the manner of her death, the procedure in her freezing.

Sorel listened intently. He raised his hand to interrupt only when Drake spoke of the awful hours with Ana at the Second Chance cryonics facility.

"One moment. You say that the original medical records were stored with the cryocorpse. Are they there now?"

"They should be. Everything should be there, inside the cryotank."

"Then before we proceed further let me summon the necessary experts, in both antique Medicine and Languages. Let me say at once, we are able to cure all known diseases. That includes every past disease of which we have ever heard. However, we will need to examine the records and the cryocorpse itself." He sat, eyes distant, for three or four seconds.

Two waves of emotion swept through Drake. He felt a wild and terrible joy, like an agony of relief: Ana would be cured at last. But he also felt a superstitious awe. Trismon Sorel's advanced mental powers seemed to include telepathy. "You are speaking to other people directly, by transmitting your thoughts?"

Sorel looked puzzled, and again there was a brief pause before he smiled. "Not in the way that you are perhaps thinking. I can do no more than you yourself will be able to accomplish in a few days' time. You will share your thoughts with others. You will have instant access to all information in the data banks. You will calculate faster and better than the computer of the ship that brought you here. Look."

He turned his head and raised the hair above his temple. Drake saw a faint, thin discoloration, normally covered by the hairline.

"That marks where the implant sits," Sorel went on. "It is normally installed in early infancy, and can be changed at any time. It is tiny, smaller and thinner than a pin, and it serves multiple purposes: as a body function monitor, as a slave computer, and as a transmitter and receiver. Commands, requests, data, and programs can be sent or received. I can speak with data banks or with other individuals. I have requested via the Copernicus network that both medical and language experts go directly to your ship. And I am able to speak to you now, in real time, because although your language is new to me, I am employing the language translation modules within the Tycho network."

Some transfer of information was still directly from person to person. Sorel read Drake's misgivings from his facial expression. "Do not worry about this. In your case—as in all cryowomb revivals—the implant will be totally optional. Before you make a decision you will have ample opportunity to observe its use in others. But I can assure you that if you do proceed, you will find it hard within a few weeks to believe that you were ever able to function without such a service. You will possess total recall; you will be a calculator beyond the most powerful computers of your time; and you will have immediate access to every data bank within the solar system—although, naturally, access and transmission time to people and data banks on other planets is considerable. Do you have questions, Drake Merlin?"

"Only one. I want to know if Ana can be cured."

"I have asked the medical team that question. They are already on board your ship, and they are performing their assessment. I will inquire as to their progress. One moment."

The gray eyes widened. Their expression again became remote and preoccupied. This time the wait stretched on, to become one minute and then two.

As the silence continued, Drake felt a knife of tension twisting inside him. If communication was mind-to-mind, what was taking so long? He was afraid that something was going wrong, but what could it possibly be? He comforted himself with Trismon Sorel's assurance: this society was able to cure all diseases of humans, including every known past disease.

But it was taking too long. Finally he could stand to remain silent no longer. "Are you talking to them? What do they say to you?"

Sorel's eyes focused again on Drake. "I am talking now to the medical specialists. It is somewhat... complicated. Give me one moment more."

The gray eyes were changing. They became gentler and more personal. At last Trismon Sorel nodded, as though confirming something that he already feared. He spoke to Drake more slowly, choosing his words with great care.

"They ask me to ask you certain questions. The woman in the cryotank, Anastasia. According to our records she had been constantly maintained in the Pluto cryowombs. Is that correct?"

Drake nodded.

"And when you found her, she was within a cryotank?"

Again, Drake nodded.

"You did not remove her, but you brought the whole cryotank with you on board the ship?"

"That's right." Drake's mind was filled with foreboding. "I had the tank carried from the cryowombs to the ship, exactly as I found it. It was done very carefully. The gravity on Pluto is low, and the machines had no trouble handling it."

Trismon Sorel was frowning. "Then it is difficult to see how there could be any problem. Unless—Drake Merlin, think hard. Did you open the tank, for any reason, after your ship left Pluto?"

Drake saw again before him Ana's peaceful face, her pearly eyes and milky skin. He felt a sickness like death. "I did open it. Just once. The outer case, for a few moments, after we left Canopus. The inner seals were unbroken. I looked for only a second or two. I was careful to seal the cryotank afterward…."

It was pointless to try to explain why he had done it, to say that he had been unable *not* to do it. Trismon Sorel was regarding him sorrowfully, across an eight-hundred-year gulf. Somehow his face was Tom Lambert's, and also Par Leon's. The eyes spoke the same sad message.

"Drake Merlin, a Pluto cryotank is not designed for sealing and resealing. Closing calls for special equipment and special procedures, available only in the cryowombs. When a seal is broken, it is assumed that the person will at once be resurrected, or special resealing methods must be adopted. Do you understand what I am saying? With an imperfect seal, suitable conditions cannot be maintained within a cryotank."

"Then Ana…."

"One moment more. Again I must consult the specialists, and the data banks." The eyes once more became unblinking. The silence dragged on and on, longer than before. When Trismon Sorel at last focused on Drake, his face was beyond doubt.

"I have checked all our references. The medical team, at my request, did the same to provide independent confirmation. We have formed the same conclusion. The problem that faces us is quite different from that of curing a disease. The damage caused to a body, and particularly to a body's brain, when a cryotank is opened and resurrection is not performed at once…that damage is permanent. It cannot be repaired, and there can be no possible revival. Now, or ever.

"I am sorry, Drake Merlin. Anastasia is dead. Forever dead."

Forever dead. Ana is dead. Trismon Sorel's words echoed those of Tom Lambert, so long ago. But this time Drake heard the ring of complete certainty.

Yet each man kills the thing he loves. He, not disease, had killed Ana. Like Orpheus of the old myths, he had pursued his Eurydice through hell. In his case it had been a double hell of cryodeath and Canopus, but like Orpheus in Hades he had found his love and brought her back toward life. Like Orpheus he had looked at her; and in looking he had lost her.

With that thought age-old barriers came down inside his mind. For the first time he noticed a spicy fragrance in the air that he was breathing. He felt a steady dry breeze blowing past him, and far-off along the corridor he heard the faint concert pitch A-natural of vibrating metal. It was as though all his senses were opening, after long centuries of hibernation.

Trismon Sorel was speaking again. "One possibility remains. Anastasia, the woman that you knew, cannot be reanimated. That is quite impossible. However, many whole cells remain intact within her body. She could be cloned without difficulty. Her growth and education would begin anew. But it would, you must understand, be a *new* Anastasia. There is no hope of sufficient memory transfer from undamaged cells for any inkling of her former existence to pass to her new body. Your former relationship would of course be known to *you*, but it would be irrelevant to her. Should we proceed?"

The temptation was enormous. To see Ana once more standing before him, blooming and vibrant as he had once known her.…

That was the selfish answer. There was a better one: Ana had the *right* to a healthy new life in this world, eight hundred years beyond their own time. He could not deny it to her.

She would live again. And yet...

It would not be the Ana that he knew and loved. It would be a quite different person. Could he bear to look on her, a woman who was Ana and yet not Ana, a woman who would not feel for him the overwhelming love that he felt for her?

Except that he had no choice. Ana deserved resurrection, and a new life.

Sorel had been waiting sympathetically. Drake nodded at last. "Proceed. Make a clone of Ana."

Trismon Sorel also nodded, and smiled. Drake saw the relief on his face. Sorel knew, with the authority of eight hundred more years of science and technological progress, that the Ana whom Drake had known was gone forever.

But—

A tiny seed of doubt sprouted deep in Drake's mind. But what would science say in another three hundred years? In a thousand, or ten thousand, or a hundred thousand? Science had come so far. Surely no one, least of all a scientist, would say that it was now at an end and could go no further.

Trismon Sorel was talking to him again, trying to catch his attention. He forced himself to listen.

"Ana cannot be revived and cured," Sorel was saying, "not in the way that you hoped when you took her body from the cryowombs. But we can help *you*."

"Me?"

"Certainly. We can cure you. There is evidence that a cure was attempted three hundred years ago, but it clearly failed. We have superior techniques now. They can end your obsession with Anastasia. It would, of course, be done only with your consent."

"Do I have a choice?"

"You have an infinite number of choices. The right to self-determination—even self-destruction, if you wish it—is basic." Trismon Sorel leaned forward. "Now I would like to speak personally, for myself alone. I hope that you will agree to a cure, and enjoy your own new life. I have vast sympathy for you. I have searched the whole data bank as we have been speaking, and your suffering seems unique. No quest and sacrifice comparable to yours can be found, anywhere."

"I have not suffered." Drake had made up his mind. "I have not sacrificed. And I know what I would like."

"State it."

"I would like a cloned form for a new Ana, just as you offered."

"We have agreed, that will be done. But for yourself?"

"I want to remain here just long enough to be sure that Ana's cloning can proceed without problems. Then I wish to leave."

"Leave?" Trismon Sorel was bewildered. "Go from here? Go where? The universe is open to you, but we can offer you everything that your heart might desire."

"No, that is not true. You cannot offer me the Anastasia that I know and love. And that is what I want—all I want. Put me back into the cryowombs, with Ana's body at my side. Let us travel together to the future."

"But I told you, the real Ana, the Ana that you knew, is not in that body. Too many brain cells have been destroyed. Your Ana is gone."

"She is gone. But gone *where*?"

"Drake Merlin, that is a meaningless question. It is like asking where the wind goes when it is no longer blowing, or where is the odor of a flower after the flower dies."

"It seems a meaningless question today. But it may not always be meaningless. You told me that I have an infinite number of choices. My choice is simple, and I say it again: I want to be placed in the Pluto cryowombs. Do I have that right?"

"You do." Trismon Sorel could not conceal his dismay and disappointment. "We cannot deny it to you. But I beg you to reconsider. You can return to cryosleep for as long as you choose, but when will you be awakened? In a century? In five?"

"I do not know. I want to leave this instruction with my freezing: Awaken me when new evidence comes into the data banks that seems relevant to the recreation of Anastasia's *original* personality. And not until then."

"It can be done. But I must be honest with you. I do not think such new evidence will ever appear. If you hope to sleep until your Ana can return, I believe that you will sleep forever."

You have everything to lose. You're healthy, you're productive, you're at the height of your career. And you are asking me to throw all that away, to help you take the chance that someday, God knows when, you might— just might—be revived. Don't you see, Drake, I can't help you. Across a gulf of eight centuries, Tom Lambert's words reverberated in Drake's mind.

"I've heard that logic before," Drake said, "and it proved wrong. I will take that risk. It is smaller than risks that I have taken in the past. Can we begin…now?"

"If you insist." Trismon Sorel held up his hand. Drake was already rising from his seat. "But there is one thing more. While we have been speaking, a group-mind meeting has been in progress involving every human within easy signal range. A conclusion has been reached. Your request will be granted, but with one condition: You do not go alone. You will have a companion for your travel into the future, just as each of us has a companion, to share our fortunes and to stand by our side through good and bad."

"I desire no woman in the cryowomb with me, other than my own Ana. And no man, either."

"We would condemn neither living man nor living woman to such an uncertain future. Your companion will not reside in the cryowombs. It will be a Servitor, designed for on-demand operation, exactly like my own Servitor." Trismon Sorel gestured to the little wheeled sphere with its metal whisk-broom head, waiting quietly at his side. "So long as you do not call upon its services, it will remain dormant and in communion with the data banks. When you need a companion or an assistant, it will be there to obey your commands."

Sorel stood up. "Come with me now. The preparations are already beginning for the cloning of Ana. While that is proceeding, I will explain to you the endless virtues of the Servitor class. And you can decide on the appearance and name of your own personal model, to travel with you into the undiscovered country of the future."

continued in issue 36…